¡SCANDALOSA!

A HONEY BLONDE CHICA NOVEL

Michele Serros

SIMON PULSE

New York   London   Toronto   Sydney

This book is a work of fiction. Any references to historical events, real people, or real locales are used fictitiously. Other names, characters, places, and incidents are the product of the author's imagination, and any resemblance to actual events or locales or persons, living or dead, is entirely coincidental.

SIMON PULSE
An imprint of Simon & Schuster Children's Publishing Division
1230 Avenue of the Americas, New York, NY 10020

ALLOYENTERTAINMENT   Produced by Alloy Entertainment
Designed by Andrea C. Uva
The text of this book was set in Scala.
Manufactured in the United States of America
First Simon Pulse edition October 2007
2 4 6 8 10 9 7 5 3 1
Library of Congress Cataloging-in-Publication Data
Serros, Michele M.
¡Scandalosa! : a honey blonde chica novel / Michele Serros.— 1st
Simon Pulse ed.
p. cm.
Summary: Continues the teenaged exploits of Dee Dee,
Raquel, and Evie—three upperclass, Mexican American
best friends growing up in Southern California.
ISBN-13: 978-1-4169-1593-5 (alk. paper)
ISBN-10: 1-4169-1593-1 (alk. paper)
1. Best friends—Fiction. 2. Friendship—Fiction. 3. Mexican
Americans—Fiction. 4. California, Southern—Fiction.] I. Title.
PZ7.S4884Sc 2007
[Fic]—dc22
2007026783
ISBN-13: 978-1-4169-1593-5
ISBN-10: 1-4169-1593-1

¡SCANDALOSA!

1

"I DON'T KNOW, EVELINA. . . ." LINDSAY, THE GOMEZ' HOUSEKEEPER, shook her head as she stepped down into the den. "Your mother said you have to be with a driver. A licensed driver."

Evie was just five weeks away from taking her driving test, but she had yet to master the challenge of three-point turns, confront the perils of parallel parking, and how the hell, she wondered, could she check her blind spot if it was *blind*? In short, Evie was desperate. She had a ways to go before the state of California would ever issue her a driver's license and had no choice but to ask—okay *beg*—Lindsay to let her borrow her car. With no Sirius, DVD player, or heated seats, Lindsay's ten-year-old sedan was far from a G-ride, but lowly beggars can't all be big-time players, right?

"Come on, Linds." Evie exhaled impatiently. "I'm just gonna be practicing on the street, in front of the house.

Nothing's gonna happen. It's Saturday—everyone's washing their cars in their driveways, not out driving them in the street. It's, like, the best time for me to practice."

Actually, what really made it the best time for an afternoon practice session was the sole fact that Evie's parents were away on a mission—the never-ending search for the perfect shade of green place mats to match the deck furniture's green cushions. Adults could be *so* controlling, and Evie's parents were no exception. Whenever she practiced driving with them, they spent the entire time pointing out everything that she was doing wrong. Wasn't the whole point of being in the driver's seat to savor the taste of freedom and independent thinking?

"I don't think so. . . ." Lindsay shook her head slowly. The latest installment of *La Cueva Sucia*, her favorite soap opera, was just starting, and she was *not* going to miss it. She clicked on the Gomezes' plasma.

"Lind-*say*." Evie followed her down the two steps that led into the den. As any questioning teen knows, an adult's reluctant "I don't think so" is as good as a semisoft maybe, which could easily progress into a firm yes. "We live on a cul-de-sac. It's not like cars go speeding by all the time. It'll be totally safe. And the more I practice," she continued, "the better I'll be for my test. Then you won't be having to cart me around anymore. Don't you want a break from being a chauffeur?"

She cocked her head forward and to the right, a gesture copied from her best friend, Dee Dee de LaFuente, who probably lifted it from Gwen Stefani in an old No Doubt video. Whenever Dee Dee let the right side of her head tip to the side, she got her way. Sure, Dee Dee had angelic long bleached-blond hair, delicate features, and those hypnotizing blue contact lenses, but couldn't a brunette with medium-length hair and brown eyes get the same outcome?

"Well." Lindsay looked at Evie. "I guess . . . maybe . . . it would be okay."

Yes!

"Get the spare keys," she told Evie as she pushed Meho, Evie's gray tabby, aside and made room for herself on the den's smooth leather sofa. Lindsay had already been lured into her habitual trance by *La Cueva's* tall, dark, and handsome leading man, Ronald Joseph Vega. "And stay in front of the house. Do *not* leave Camino del Rio."

"I promise!" Evie sprinted as fast as her metallic gold flip-flops could carry her toward the kitchen. When she saw the keys hanging from the key rack, she didn't know which were the spare keys Lindsay had been talking about, but no worries. She snatched both rings off the kitchen's metal key holder, grabbed her iPod (with more than 1,100 downloads) and her wallet (containing a freshly issued driver's permit), and skipped out of the house.

But once Evie got out to the driveway, her honest-to-goodness plans of taking Lindsay's sedan immediately fell by the wayside. There, parked to the left of Lindsay's car, was

Evie's mother's brand-new Mercedes. Actually, not *brand* new, but definitely new to her mother, Vicki Gomez. The Mercedes was a good thirty years old, a classic by anyone's standards, and with its high-gloss burgundy paint job and supreme detailing by West Coast Designs, the Benz was stunning beyond words. But the *cali de la cali?* A fuel conversion by LoveCraft's BioFuel in Los Angeles. Yes, the Mercedes had been converted to run on vegetable oil rather than on diesel. Gas was *so* passé, and fuel conversions were *the* thing done to cars in SoCal. The Benz, of course, was the talk of Rio Estates, and Vicki Gomez just loved, *loved* the attention.

Evie looked at the gleaming Mercedes and then at Lindsay's nondescript four-door sedan, which suddenly seemed dull and lifeless. Was there really a question of which ride she should choose for her practice spin?

She opened the driver's-side door of the Mercedes and got in. Evie inhaled the aroma of the vintage white leather and looked at herself in the side mirror. She had clearly made the right choice. She took out her cell from the front pocket of her gray-and-red Señor Lopez pullover and immediately speed-dialed her boyfriend, Alex Perez. How cool would it be to swing by his house and, for once, offer to drive *him* some-where? Evie listened to the phone ring a few times. And then, alas, the dreaded voice mail greeting: *"Duuude . . . Make it brief. Not a bio."*

Evie remembered that Alex had gone to Sea Street with

Mondo that morning, and she felt slightly disappointed. It was almost 1 P.M., and he *still* wasn't back from the beach? At the end of last semester, the Flojos (which had consisted of herself, Alex, Mondo, Raquel, and Raquel's former boy, Jose) had pretty much disbanded. But Alex still surfed at Sea Street, and Mondo still tagged along with him. While they all still wore flojos (flip-flops), Evie didn't so much have the same *flojo* ("lazy") mind-set as she had the semester before. Now she went surfing and was learning how to drive. This semester, she was less Gomezzzzz and more Go-*mas*.

When Alex's brusque-sounding message finished, Evie decided to leave neither a brief message nor her autobiography, thank you. She hung up and speed-dialed her ADA, Raquel Diaz. The literal Spanish translation for ADA was *amiga del alma*, a "friend of the soul," a soul sister, really. ADAs were tighter than mere BFFs, and as everyone who was anyone knew, a *sister* was much more *íntima* than a simple *friend*.

After a few rings, Evie was met with Raquel's infamous Bullwinkle yawn on the other end. "What up?" Raquel answered sleepily.

"Not you, obviously." Evie switched from her mother's favorite old-school station, Hot 92 Jamz, to Dios (Malos). Nothing like brown-boy emo bumping the speakers to calm one's novice nerves. The melodic undertones quickly relaxed Evie.

"Hey, I'm coming to pick you up," she announced to Raquel. "Let's cruise the Shores."

Raquel lived next door to Evie, a mere eight hundred yards away, and really didn't need to be picked up to go anywhere. But still, just saying "I'm coming to pick you up" made Evie feel mature, adultlike. Unlike Raquel and their other ADA, Dee Dee, Evie didn't have her own car and had to shotgun it everywhere. From parties in Spanish Hills to surfing at Sea Street, the high school production of *Driving Miss Evie* was outgrowing its rehearsal space. She needed to showcase her driving talent to a wider audience.

"You ain't picking me up to go anywhere." Raquel's voice was throaty and harsh. "I ain't even awake."

"Well, get up," Evie ordered. "I got my mother's car."

"What do you mean, you got your mother's car?" Raquel asked. "Ol' Vicki Gomez must be out of the country, 'cause you know there's no way you'd risk taking her precious veggie grease–mobile out if she was even near the 805."

"Not quite out of the country," Evie mused. "But the next best thing. She's at the factory outlets with my dad. They'll be gone all day."

"And la Lindsay?" Raquel inquired.

"Oh, she's far away in *novela-vela* land." Evie adjusted the seat so it was closer to the gas pedal and positioned the rearview mirror so she could see all things slow and less important behind her. She turned the key in the ignition. "Come on, the day's almost over."

The day was actually far from being over. It was barely one

o'clock in the afternoon. To a party *puta* like Raquel, the day was practically just starting.

"And," Evie started to explain, "you know I need a licensed driver to really go anywhere."

"Nuh-uh," Raquel said quickly. "*No* friggin' way. Don't you know the leading cause of teen fatality is teaching a newbie to drive? You best find yourself another tutor, Eves. I'm outs."

"Raq, come on," Evie pleaded. "It'll be fun."

"And who says I ain't already having fun?" Raquel let out a low, muffled laugh. Evie heard another voice in the background, a male voice. She suddenly felt the effects of third-party damage.

"Who's that?" she asked.

"I can tell you who it ain't." Raquel laughed softly again. "It's ain't Jose, that's for sure."

Ever since Raquel had caught Jose sneaking around with Alejandra de los Santos last semester, her Buddy List of bad boys was being utilized to the max. It didn't help Raquel's ego that Alejandra de los Santos headed the Sangros, a foursome of *fresas ricas* from Mexico City whose big designer boots and even bigger attitudes clashed with the Flojos' designer flip-flops and laid-back outlook. Of course, Raquel had felt completely humiliated and betrayed when she discovered that her boy had cross-pollinated with one of *them*. Evie and Dee Dee had actually been foolish enough to become sorta friends with Alejandra last semester. But that was when they were just fresh-off-the-boat freshmen and didn't know any better. Not only was Alejandra a *sangrona*, plain and simple, but she also pimped the scarlet letter *S* proudly on her chest.

"O-*kay*, Raquel." Evie struggled to shift from reverse to first gear. "I'll let you go do whatever, with whomever. Just call me later."

"Yeah, yeah," Raquel said before hanging up.

Evie looked at the clock on the dashboard of her mother's Mercedes. *La Cueva Sucia* was a one-hour program, which meant she had only forty-eight minutes to roll. She speed-dialed Dee Dee's number next.

"Hi, Evie!" Dee Dee practically chirped on the other end.

Evie smiled to herself. Dee Dee was the yang to Raquel's yin. Little Miss Sunny Delight to Raquel's Little Miss Understood, Dark and . . . Delight-less. Dee Dee would definitely be up for a drive.

"You're in a good mood," Evie said.

"I just got off the phone with Rocio." Dee Dee's voice got dreamy. "Oh, Evie, I love him *so* much."

Rocio was Dee Dee's long-lost boyfriend she'd had to leave behind in Mexico City when she and her father returned to California. Dee Dee had moved to Mexico from Rio Estates with her father four years earlier, soon after her mother died. Their new home was still in Rio Estates, just a few blocks away from Evie's and Raquel's houses, and included a larger pool, a yoga-and-workout center, and, imported directly from

Mexico, a new stepmother for Dee Dee, Graciela Rodríguez Von Simon, a former soap opera actress.

"Hey, so I've got the Benz," Evie bragged as she slowly entered Camino del Rio and cautiously looked down the street in both directions. "I thought I could come over and pick you up."

"Right *now*?" Dee Dee asked. "I can't. I have a meeting with Eileen Cervantes."

"Eileen? Who's that?"

"She's connected with Las Hermanas," Dee Dee explained. "And I'm meeting with her at four."

"At four?" Evie rechecked the time on the dashboard. "Dee Dee, it's barely one o'clock."

"I know. I'm totally running late. I'm so nervous. I've already smoked three Caribbean Chills this morning."

"No," Evie started. "I mean, why are you getting ready now?"

"Evie, it's for *Las Hermanas*," Dee Dee said, as if Evie were crazy for asking. "I have to make the right impression. Eileen is the first cousin of the former director's wife, and she's going to give me some hints that are going to help me."

"Oh," Evie said sarcastically. "I didn't realize what a *great* contact you had."

"Evie, don't make fun." Dee Dee sulked for a few moments. "This is the final year before I can be nominated so I can be an Hermana by junior year. You know Las Hermanas has been my dream since, like, forever."

It was true. Ever since Dee Dee was a little girl, she had always talked about being a Las Hermanas debutante. Her mother was one, her grandmother was one, so, of course, Dee Dee not only wanted to be one, she *had* to be one. Las Hermanas was the oldest and most respected debutante society in the county. It was started by the wives of the early Southern California landowners, many of them Hispanic and all of them wealthy. Dee Dee's father didn't have such regal connections with early Ventura County, but Dee Dee's mother, the late Margaret de LaFuente, sure did. Her family had owned multiple ranches in the area long ago, when the area was still a part of Mexico. You couldn't get more regally connected than that.

What with Dee Dee's calculated attempts to obtain a key to the city, Raquel jonesing for a key to the nearest minibar, and she herself most desirous of the keys to any available automobile, Evie sometimes wondered how all three girls could each be so unique and remain ADAs. But then again, no matter what kinds of keys they longed for, the three of them had the sort of friendship history that you just don't find on MySpace.

"Of course I know how important Las Hermanas is to you," Evie told Dee Dee as she struggled with the Mercedes' gears. "I just need someone to help me with my driving.

"Por fa," Dee Dee answered. "You don't need anyone to help you drive. You're already good. Really."

"If I'm such a good driver"—Evie was not buying Dee Dee's flattery—"then why don't you ever let me drive Jumile?"

Sailors christened boats, socialites attached pretentious tags on pet Chihuahuas, but in SoCal, it was in proper order to conjure up a cutesy name for one's car. To own a nameless vehicle? Unthinkable. Jumile (V-plates: JUMILE) was the name of Dee Dee's lime green VW Beetle, and she was very protective of him. She never let anyone—including Evie—drive him, not even once.

Dee Dee had gotten her VW's name from the particular tree beetles found in the hills of Taxco, Mexico. Every year, the first Monday after *El Día de los Muertos*, the locals would hike into the hills of Taxco and gather up the little green beetles, otherwise known as jumiles. Later the locals would roast and grind up the bugs, celebrating the new seasonal harvest with *salsa insecto*.

"*'Sta loco, no?*" Dee Dee had smugly stated after she'd bragged about the fact that she had been adventurous enough to partake in the beetle eats, as if to prove that under her pricey Michael Kelley–styled hair and M.A.C.–made-up face, she could be *loca* in her own right.

Raquel's parents had just bought her a Beetle a month ago for Christmas, and naturally Evie wanted a Beetle too. She wanted hers to be red, cherry red with the V-plates of CHRYBMB, as in Cherry Bomb, the name she'd picked for her Beetle. She also wanted a sunroof, Bose speakers, fresh-cut hibiscus flowers in the bud vase, and the quintessential decal that identified Evie to the hilt: an outlined pair of white flip-flops, stuck smack center of her back window. She had already purchased the decal months ago at the Walden Surf Shop, and now all she needed was a brand-new car to attach it to. Simple enough, no?

"Well," Evie started as she headed south, down the eucalyptus-lined street of Calle Bonita toward the main gate of Rio Estates. She was ready to gun the engine and make a run for it. A cruise by the Shores was calling. "I guess I'll just take a drive by myself."

"Why don't you take Alejandro or Raquel?" Dee Dee asked.

"Alex is out at Sea Street," Evie said.

"Surfing again?"

"Uh-huh." Evie turned up Dios (Malos). "I'm gonna hook up with him tomorrow. We might take the boards to Santa Barbara."

"Mmm-hmm. No offense," Dee Dee started slowly as though she was applying mascara. "But don't . . . you . . . ever . . . get tired that . . . all . . . you do with Alex is . . . surf?"

"What do you mean?" Evie asked as she shifted down to bring her mother's Mercedes (V-plates: GO MEZ) to a stop. It stalled. *Sheeyat.* Evie started the Mercedes up again.

"Don't get me . . . wrong. I think it's cool that . . . you . . . two have something major in . . . common, but"—Dee Dee finally put her vocal cords on the right rpm—"it's just, I mean, in Mexico, boys take girls out on dates. You get to dress up and have a nice dinner, go dancing."

"Dee Dee." Evie rolled her eyes to the side. "I'm fine with the stuff we do. Alex is my bud and Sea Street is *our* place."

True, Sea Street had pretty much been deemed Evie and Alex's place, at least by Evie. Last semester, she used to kick it on the promenade wall with Raquel, Jose, and Mondo while watching Alex surf. Now that she was officially Alex's girlfriend and she officially surfed (not quite *Blue Crush*, but *still*), it was safe to say that Sea Street was their place.

"Your *bud*?" Dee Dee asked. "Oh, I thought he was your *boyfriend.*"

Evie just knew that Dee Dee's blond-tinted eyebrows had risen in surprise.

"He is." Evie felt she had to defend his title. "But he's also my buddy, my friend. And that's very important in a relationship."

"*Claro*, of course it's important. I was just asking, that's all." Dee Dee paused. "So, what about Raquel? Did you call her to go driving?"

"I already did, but she's totally out of it."

"Out of it or hungover?" Dee Dee asked.

Evie was reluctant to go into the minuscule dish she had on Raquel. All three girls loved each other unconditionally, of course, and granted, all of them indulged in ad bevs, but Dee Dee tended to judge Raquel's recreational drinking more critically. Not that Evie could blame Dee Dee—ever since her breakup with Jose, Raquel's party patterns had been a bit off the charts.

"So listen, just stay on the line with me," Evie suggested. "You can be, like, my virtual licensed driver. I guess a Mexico City license is better than nothing."

"Mande?" Dee Dee did not find Evie's jab funny. She was very protective of Mexico City, her beloved former home of four years.

"Nothing." Evie tried to backpedal. She knew better than to dis the almighty Mexico. Besides, she was now approaching Calle Agua Caliente and had to focus. The transmission of her mother's Mercedes revved hard as she fumbled into second gear. Damn. Could it be that her father had accidentally filled the fuel tank with vinegar instead of vegetable oil? Evie's efforts made her sound like an amateur barista-in-training, grinding espresso beans to a pulp. She reached the intersection just as a silver sports car pulled up, but she could not remember who was supposed to go first.

"Hey, *maestra*," Evie started. "I'm at a four-way stop and I forgot, who has the right of way?"

"The car on the right," Dee Dee said matter-of-factly.

"Uh—" Evie looked over at the sports car. "—she's not moving."

"Then just go, I guess," Dee Dee said.

A horn behind Evie honked. She looked in her rearview mirror: she'd been completely unaware that there was even a car behind her. She shifted from neutral to first gear and stepped lightly on the gas, but for some reason, her mother's Mercedes screeched backward. *Sheeyat!* She felt a solid thud from the back. Evie had mistakenly put the Mercedes into reverse and smacked . . . right into the car behind her.

"Oh, my God!" Evie screamed as she dropped her cell phone into her lap. She felt her throat plummet to the bottom of her stomach. Her chest grew numb. She did *not* just hit another car.

"Wha—? —pened?" Dee Dee's phone connection cut in and out. "What —ong?"

Evie picked up her cell. "Dee Dee!" she yelled into the mouthpiece, "I just hit a car! Oh my God, what do I do?"

"What? Oh *my* God. Are you okay?"

"Yeah, I think so. I . . ." Evie checked the rearview mirror. The driver swung open his car door, and Evie could see that he was a young guy, short and stocky, with a shaved head. He was wearing a super-size football jersey throwback with the sleeves cut off, and he lifted his thick arms in a thuglike challenging *What the*—? stance as he went over to the front of his car. He was definitely someone you normally didn't see behind the cloistered wrought-iron gates of Rio Estates.

"If you weren't so busy yakking on that damn cell phone," he ranted toward Evie, "maybe you'd know how to drive. Pay attention, you *pinche idiota!*"

"Oh. My. God." Evie sank into the leather upholstery of the Mercedes' seat. She held her head and the "damn cell phone" down, away from his view. "Dee Dee," she whispered, her voice starting to crack, "he's *totally* raging at me."

"*Who?*"

"This guy. The guy whose car I hit." *How* could she have hit a car? And with her mother's prized Mercedes! If this guy didn't kill her, her mother certainly would.

"Dee Dee," Evie pleaded, "you gotta come. *Now!*"

"Oh my God!" Dee Dee was horrified. "Where are you?"

The guy was now on the other side of the driver's door. He tapped on the side of the window with the back of his hand and glared at Evie. "Hang up the damn phone, turn off the friggin' music, and get out here and deal. What, you want me to call the cops?"

The cops? Oh God, the situation was not getting any better.

"Dee Dee." Evie could still feel her throat in the pit of her stomach. "I . . . I have to go."

"Wait! Evie, where are—?"

But it was too late. Evie had already snapped her phone shut. She somehow managed to unplug her iPod, open the Mercedes' heavy door, and step out.

"I am *so* sorry!" She looked over at the guy's car. It was a lowered Honda or Toyota or something like that. "Did I ding it?"

"Uh, *yeah*," the guy remarked hostilely. "You jacked it up, all right."

He walked back to the front of his car, and Evie followed him. He crouched down to show her.

"*Mira,*" he said. "Right there." He pointed to his bumper.

Evie looked. And looked. And looked. She strained to find

something out of the ordinary, something concave or indented, but couldn't detect anything. Then finally she saw it. A small, deep nick, the size of a dime—okay, *maybe* a quarter. "You mean *that*?" She ran her finger over it.

"Yeah, I mean *that*." The guy looked at her as though she were crazy.

Evie looked over his car's bumper and then at her mother's Mercedes. The Benz appeared flawless.

"I'm gonna need your license," the guy said. "And all your insurance info and shit."

"My license?" Evie's heart dropped.

"Yes." He looked at her as though she was some rookie student driver, which, of course, she was. "Your *license*."

"Um . . . right," was all Evie could say. She went back to her mother's car and stretched across the front seat to get her cell phone off the floor. She speed-dialed her home number.

One ring, two rings . . .

Come on, come on! Evie cried in her head. *Come on, Linds! Answer the phone!*

Three rings, four rings.

"Bueno? Gomez residence."

Finally.

"Lindsay!" Evie sobbed into her cell. "I hit a car! I need help!"

"Ay, Dios mío!" Evie could hear the heels of Lindsay's Aerosoles already sprinting across the ceramic tile of the den. "Are you okay? I'm coming out."

"I'm not in front of the house. I'm—"

"*What?*"

"I'm over here," Evie said. "I'm on the corner of Calle Agua Caliente and Calle Soccoro."

"*What?*" Lindsay repeated. "Why are you way over there? I told you—"

"Lindsay, I know, I know. Please, just come now." She looked back at the driver to make sure he couldn't hear her. "And—" She hesitated. "—and I'm in my mother's car."

"*What!*"

"Lindsay, please, just come now. I'll explain later. Just come. Now!"

"Stay *right* there!" Lindsay told Evie.

Evie hung up and slowly got back out of her mother's Mercedes.

"Um," she started to tell the guy, "I forgot my wallet, so my housekeeper's coming to bring it. Right now."

"Like, *right* now?" He pulled out his cell phone and checked the time.

"Yeah, like right now. She should be here in a few minutes." Evie looked down the street. "We live just a few streets down, on Camino del Rio."

Camino del Rio. Why? Why hadn't she just stayed on her street like she was supposed to? Why hadn't she just practiced with Lindsay's car like she said she would?

Evie looked at the guy, who was now leaning against the

front of his car. What if the cops *did* come? She had practically stolen her mother's car, and she didn't have insurance or even a license! Evie glanced over at the driver; his eyes were angry and impatient.

Evie looked up at the street signs of the intersection: Agua Caliente and Socorro. Yes, she was definitely in "hot water" and needed "help." Badly.

2

IT SEEMED LIKE FOREVER BEFORE LINDSAY FINALLY SHOWED UP. WHEN she did, she was out of breath, her dark wispy bangs were stuck to her forehead with perspiration, and she was on foot.

"Lindsay," Evie started, "why didn't you just drive your car?"

"Because," Lindsay huffed between breaths, "you took both set of keys." She grabbed the key ring from Evie's grasp. "I didn't have the keys to my own car!" She took a breath and looked Evie over. "Are you okay? What happened?"

"She slammed right back into me. That's what happened," the guy answered for Evie. "Did you bring her license?"

"Her license?" Lindsay looked at Evie.

"I'm also gonna need insurance info," the guy repeated to Lindsay. He had already gotten a pen from his glove compartment and clicked it. He was ready and waiting.

Of course, Evie had neither a license nor car insurance. But as any California driver knows, it's not about sweating fellow fender benders, but rather making sure that said fellow fender benders had good car insurance or, at the very least, a good connection to repair any damage they were liable for.

Lindsay had car insurance for her own car, but no worries that Evie had just done the damage while driving her mother's Benz. Lindsay could still use her connection to take care of the problem. No one wanted his or her insurance rates to be raised because of some teenager's appetite for adventure.

Lindsay looked over the driver's bumper and squinted, just as Evie had before, but she didn't say anything at first. "My brother-in-law works at Williams Automotive," she informed the guy. "I'll call him tonight. I'd rather not have my insurance billed for this."

That was enough for the other driver. He didn't even care if Evie had a license or not. Everyone in the whole county knew about Williams Automotive. They fixed all kinds of cars, "From Model A's to *Orales*." *Orale* was Spanish for "cool!" or "right!" but at Williams Automotive, and pretty much in the whole 805, *orale* meant "lowrider." As Evie had noticed earlier, the guy's car swept the street, barely an inch from the ground, which definitely put it in the lowrider category.

After an exchange of info, the man and his dime-size dent finally went on their way.

"Oh God." Evie caught her breath as soon as he was gone. "Lindsay, thank you *so* much. I thought he was gonna kill me. God, talk about a rage-aholic."

Lindsay pursed her lips and took a walk around the Mercedes to double-check that there was no damage. Evie followed, and, fortunately, there was nothing. *Nada.* Vicki Gomez's classic grease-mobile had been spared.

Lindsay got into the Benz's driver's seat. Evie opened the passenger door and got in.

"Evelina—" Lindsay started the Mercedes. "—You told me you were taking my car, and you told me that you were going to stay in front of the house and—"

"I know, Lindsay." Evie felt bad. She hated letting Lindsay down. Lindsay was often her only ally, and now she had been purposely dishonest with her. "I'm sorry. I am *so* sorry. I was in front of the house, but then I got on the cell with Dee Dee and—"

"You were *talking*?" Lindsay tapped the brake pedal and glared at Evie. "On the *phone*? While driving your mother's Mercedes?"

Was that steam coming out of Lindsay's nostrils?

"You are lucky you didn't kill yourself!" Lindsay shook her head as she held the leather-encased steering wheel with one hand while making the sign of the cross with the other. "Your parents are going to be *very* unhappy about this. *Muy enojados.*"

"Lindsay, please," Evie said. "You *can't* tell my parents. It was an accident. I *was* in the driveway, just like you told me to be and then . . ." She really didn't have anything else to add to her plea. "Please. They don't need to know, and the dent on that guy's car, I can totally pay for it. I will, all of it. I promise."

"How are you going to pay for his car?" Lindsay shook her head in disbelief. "It could be a lot of money, Evelina. A lot."

"I can use my birthday money," Evie offered quickly.

Lindsay looked over at her again. "You got money for your birthday? Already?"

"Um, no," Evie confessed. "Not yet, really. But you know Grandma Chablis always sends a check, and now that it's gonna be my sixteenth birthday, I'll probably get more money than usual. Sabrina did."

Lindsay didn't say anything, because she knew it was the truth. Evie's grandma Chablis, her father's mother, always sent her grandchildren checks with a substantial amount of zeros for their birthdays. Could it be guilt that she was the absentee *abuela* and rarely attended her own grandkids' birthday parties? That she preferred teaching winemaking at UC Davis or taking last-minute trips to Italy over helping fill some Dora the Explorer–shaped piñata or leading the traditional Mexican birthday chant of *"Las Mañanitas"*? Whatever the case, neither Evie nor her sister, Sabrina, questioned Grandma Chablis' motives or lack of attendance at their birthday parties. They'd been cashing her checks ever since they'd learned what the word *endorsement* meant.

"I don't like keeping secrets from your parents," Lindsay continued.

"Lindsay, please," Evie begged. "It would just stress them out, and they don't need to be more stressed than they already are. You know how bummed out my dad has been, about the fat-free *pan dulce* and everything."

Lindsay didn't say anything as she drove on Camino Pacifico and turned onto Camino del Rio. It was true that Evie's father, who owned four successful *panaderías* in the 805, had invested a lot of money and time in his fat-free sweet bread idea and then lost a lot when it didn't do so well in sales. Since then, money had become a very sore subject in the Gomez household.

Evie looked out the window. She was already on thin ice for breaking her curfew (*again*) with Raquel (*again*) over Christmas vacation, and all she needed was a third strike that could land her in internment (*again*). In California, the "three strikes, you're out" law was harsh, but Vicki Gomez could be just as severe.

When they finally pulled up to the house, Evie was mortified to find her father's Escalade parked in the driveway. What were her parents doing back so early from the shopping the outlets?

"Your parents are home." Lindsay looked at her wristwatch

as though Evie couldn't see for herself that they were indeed home. "And your mother is going to wonder why we took her car." She pulled up into the circular driveway, and Evie thought she seemed just as uneasy about the whole situation.

Evie clenched her jaw. "Hey, Linds . . ."

"*Mande?*" She parked alongside the Escalade and turned off the Mercedes' engine.

"Nothing." Evie slumped her shoulders. She knew it was no use. She would have to face the consequences.

They entered the house, and after being in the bright afternoon sun, Evie needed a few seconds for her eyes to adjust to the darkness inside. Lindsay stepped down into the den, where the closing credits of *La Cueva* were rolling down the TV screen. With annoyance, she clicked both her tongue and the remote's power button. Obviously, in her haste, she had forgotten to TiVo her favorite *telenovela*.

"We were wondering where you two were." Evie's father looked up. He was sitting on a stool, going over the morning mail at the kitchen counter. "The front door was open and the TV was left on."

"Where did you take my car?" Evie's mother asked Lindsay from the dining room table. She was sorting through a pile of place mats, all of them in different shades of green. "Is there something wrong with your car, Linds?"

"We were just . . . ," Evie started, not sure how she was going to finish.

"Yes, something is wrong," Lindsay quickly interrupted as she entered the dining area. "I don't know what, but we thought that Molesto had gotten out and when my car wouldn't start, I hope you don't mind, we used yours and started driving up and down the street, looking for him." She clicked her tongue again and ran her fingers through her hair in pseudo-exasperation. "But the whole time I guess he was just next door, chasing the Milnes' cats or something. He must have got back into the yard under the fence, where he's been digging."

Evie looked over at her, in surprise.

"Oh, no." Evie's mother feigned concern. "We'll have to get that hole fixed. We wouldn't want dear ol' Molesto getting out."

Vicki Gomez actually despised Molesto, the black Labrador that had once been Sabrina's. It would be her ultimate dream come true to have him run away and never return to the Gomez residence. Last summer, Sabrina had been working for El Misión, and Molesto (then properly named Ernesto) was training to become a Seeing Eye guide dog. Molesto flunked not just a few, but all of his obedience classes, and Sabrina, feeling sympathy and concern over what would happen to dear old Ernesto, begged her parents to let her take him. Of course, they conceded, and at the time he was a cute blind-school-flunkie pup, but now Sabrina was back at Stanford, and Molesto was displaying the true colors of his Spanish nickname—he was *quite* bothersome.

Evie looked up at Lindsay and caught her eye. *Thank you,* she mouthed when her mother wasn't looking. She owed Lindsay big-time.

"Linds, if there is an emergency and you can't use your car, you can absolutely take mine, but I don't ever want Molesto in my car," Evie's mother said. "He'll scratch up the leather and leave his hair all over."

"*Sí, sí, claro,*" Lindsay agreed.

"And I'll take a look at your car in a bit, Linds." Evie's father continued peruse the mail. "I hope it isn't anything too serious." He shook his head. "The last thing anyone needs is more bills."

"Oh, no, no," Lindsay said awkwardly. "I don't think it is." She gathered old newspapers off the counter and took them to the recycling container outside. She was smart to make an early exit before Generals Vicki and Ruben Gomez got too inquisitive.

Along with the relief, Evie felt another wave of guilt. She didn't want Lindsay to get in trouble with her parents on account of her own deliberate delinquency. Lindsay was like family, but then again, no other family member was on the payroll as she was. Her father *was* pretty stressed about money lately—who knew what desperate action he might take?

"Well, once Sabrina comes home—" Evie's mother held up two separate, but obviously similar, place mats to compare them. "—Molesto won't be bothering the neighbor's cats so much."

Evie had forgotten that her sister was due home the following week. Sabrina had decided to take a short break from her
studies at Stanford University. Evie didn't know the whole
story, but she knew that her sister was really bummed about
breaking up with her boyfriend, Robert, and just needed some
time off. Evie was really apprehensive about Sabrina's return.
In a way, she liked being the only child in the household. She
got a lot of attention. Okay, sometimes maybe too much. But
as soon as Suprema, as Evie often called her, was in the picture, all attention went to her. Suprema was nineteen years
old—three and three-quarters years older than Evie—and, like
the whole rest of the Gomez family, she was an overachiever.
Now that Suprema was going to be back home for a while, the
differences between the two girls were going to become
painfully apparent again.

"When is Sabrina getting here?" Evie pulled up a stool next
to her father. She helped herself to some nuts from the
ceramic bowl on the kitchen counter.

"Sometime late next week," her mother said. "She's flying
down."

"Flying down?" Evie kept the cashews but put the dreadful
Brazil nuts back in the bowl. "What happened to her Mini?"
(V-plates: 4 BRINA)

"Nothing," her mother said. "One of her girlfriends will
drive it down later."

It all seemed very odd to Evie. What was the urgency to

have Sabrina home so soon? Was the whole drama of having her car driven down really necessary? Stanford University was only five hours north of Rio Estates, and the whole family (including Sabrina) relished the scenic drive along the California Gold Coast between their home and the university. Why wouldn't her sister just drive home, as she usually did?

"I could drive her car down," Evie volunteered. Sabrina's Mini Cooper was brand new, silver, with two black stripes down the hood. It was polished, petite, and it *purred*. What chica wouldn't want to cruise a Mini?

"No. You. Can't." Her father emphasized each word with a slow nod of his head. "It'll be a while before you can go making trips like that." He opened another business envelope and started to read the contents. "Evie—" His casual tone suddenly dropped to serious. "—what's going on here?"

"What's going on where?" Evie grabbed more nuts and looked over toward the paperwork he was reading.

"Your quality check," he said.

Sheeyat! How could Evie have been *so* careless? QCs came out every three weeks, more or less. This was her first quality check of the new semester. If only she had checked the mail instead of rushing to go out driving, she could have retrieved the incriminating evidence addressed to "The Parents or Guardian of Evelina Maria Gomez." This would have bought her some time to think of . . . something.

"Evie"—her mother pulled back her blond hair and looked

at the paperwork over her husband's shoulder—"you're getting two C's, one in English." She pointed to the two letters,
as if Evie needed help seeing them. "How can that be?"

"I have no idea," Evie said. Civics and English were not her
favorite classes, but she hadn't known she was doing *that* badly.

"Well, you better get an idea. An idea of how to change these
grades. We don't have you going to Villanueva for nothing. Do
you know how much it costs us to send you there?"

Evie didn't say anything, and neither did her mother.

"And you're already a sophomore," her father added.
"These grades count. You have to maintain a high GPA if you
want to get into a good college. How do you think Sabrina got
into Stanford? And you know our agreement," her father said.
"No birthday party at Duke's if you can't keep your GPA up."

Evie had sorta forgotten that particular clause of her birthday agreement. This semester, she had become so wrapped up
in having Alex as a new boyfriend and in learning how to drive
that she had forgotten about the fine print. But Evie could tell
her father was really serious just from his tone.

In just under two months, on February 29, to be exact, Evie
was going to turn sixteen, and this particular birthday was
special for two reasons. One was that there was actually going
to be a February 29 on the year's calendar. Being a leap year
baby, Evie had no choice but to celebrate her birthday either
on the twenty-eighth of February or the first of March. Not to
be all *sentida* about it, but it sorta sucked not to have your

birthday party on your actual birthdate. The second reason that this birthday was going to be extra cool was because Evie's parents were going to throw her a "sixteeñera"—more Sweet Sixteen, way less *quinceañera*. And of course, that meant only one thing—a Mexican-style luau at Duke's in Malibu. Duke's was a super cool restaurant that overlooked the Pacific Ocean and was named after the OG Hawaiian surfer himself, Duke Kahanamoku. All of Evie's favorite *Laguna Beach* and *O.C.* stars lunched and "canoodled" at Duke's, and her sixteeñera party had become the talk of Villanueva Prep. How could it not? After all, her father had already secured DJ Chancla to spin nothing but classic surf and power pop, plus there would be Polynesian dancers and a full buffet featuring Hawaiian-style *lechón*, with the suckling pig's head and everything. Evie's mother had also planned to make gift bags filled with Mr. Zog Sex Wax, flip-flops, a fifty-dollar gift certificate for Walden Surf Shop, as well as customized sun visors with the words EVENING WITH EVIE stitched in hot pink on the front. But the main attraction at Evie's Sweet Sixteeñera? Raquel's connection. Raquel knew this guy, Dario Regalado, who had a cousin, Petey. When Petey wasn't getting all goo-goo eyed whenever he was in the presence of Raquel, he was bartendering at Duke's. When he'd heard about Raquel's ADA having her Sweet Sixteeñera at his workplace, he'd instantly raised his hand and offered to fire up the Lava Flows and Tropical Itches for all Evie's guests. He told Raquel that all she had to do was supply the booze, which was no problem because, of course, Raquel had *another* hookup at the Liquor Warehouse. Friggin' Raquel—was she the bestest ADA or what? There were to be no frat-boy red plastic cups full of watered-down keg beer at Evie's party. Her ad bevs were going to be classy, lethal, and free. Could a party be *mas* epic?

"I can do it. I can bring the grades up," Evie said, trying to convince her parents and herself. There was *no* way she could not have her sixteeñera. "It's only Civics and English. No problemo."

"Oh, it shouldn't have even *been* a problemo." Her father tossed the mail back onto the kitchen counter. "But you should be concerned."

"And I'm afraid we are going to need to know that you are improving, *in advance* of your party," her mother said. "We still need to send out the Evites *and* the formal paper invites. You're the one who wanted the specialty invitations with hibiscus petals."

"What do you mean by 'in advance'?" Evie asked. She put the nuts she'd been holding back in the bowl. Suddenly she was no longer hungry.

"Evie, don't do that." Her mother frowned. "Either eat them or throw them away." She went on. "What I mean is, your next quality check is in three and a half weeks, the first week of February, and your birthday is on the last day of February. So we'll have to see how your next QC is."

"*What?*" Evie balked. "You want me to have straight A's in three weeks?"

"Of course not," her father said. "You just need to show us that you are serious about improving. Like your mother said, 'in advance.'"

Like your mother said. Evie really resented when her parents formed a faux united front.

"But I just started the semester," Evie protested. "How am I going to tell you *beforehand* what my final GPA will be?"

"So, should we go on this?" Her father retrieved the quality check and held it up. "Are you telling us that these are your final grades?"

"No." Evie slumped in her seat.

Her mother took the piece of paper, rolled it in her hands, and tapped Evie under her chin with it. She softened her voice. "Don't worry, Evie. I know how important this party is to you. You can do it." She reached for some nuts and then stopped herself. Nuts were not on her new SoCal diet.

"Of course you can," her father said. "I remember one time when Sabrina got her quality check and was so upset when a B brought her whole average down."

Again with Suprema.

"She was very determined to improve, and she did," Evie's father continued as he looked over the rest of the mail. "That kind of focus is in the Gomez blood." He smiled proudly, as if the family's ambitious bloodline originated from him and only him.

Just then Molesto came prancing up. Evie's mother's Bluetooth receiver was sticking out of his mouth, completely covered in dog slop.

"Molesto!" her mother cried out. "Ruben! Call him! He's got my phone!"

Evie's father got up from his stool. "I got it, I got it. Mo-*les-to*, here . . . ," he called in a singsongy voice. He pretended to hold something in his clenched hand, high above Molesto's head. "Doggie treat. *Mira*."

Molesto's big dark eyes followed Ruben Gomez's fist. His tail wagged and his two front legs bowed downward. He promptly dropped the earpiece and barked in anticipation.

Of course, Evie's father had nothing moist and meaty in his hand. He quickly grabbed the Bluetooth away from Molesto and gave it to his wife. "Ah, sorry, young guy." He offered condolences as he rubbed Molesto's head.

Evie's mother held the saliva-saturated Bluetooth delicately with two fingers and went to get a paper towel to wipe off the slobber. She shook her head at Molesto. "God, he is *such* a dumb dog!"

Evie stared at her quality check, back on the counter, where the two glaring C's taunted her. She placed her elbows on either side of it and her chin in the palms of her hands. She glanced at Molesto, who looked so utterly befuddled that Evie's father had no treat in his hand. She sighed. *The Gomez blood.* Could it be possible she was somehow related only to Molesto?

3

AS SOON AS SHE COULD PULL AWAY FROM HER PARENTS, EVIE RAN UP
to her room and texted Dee Dee and Raquel the "Rio Estates
Emergency" distress signal:

> **ER/RE!**

Dee Dee texted back right away:

> **Cn u cme here?**

As did Raquel:

> **Same plce?**

Raquel's quick response surprised Evie. Fun time with
Rebound Boy must have ended.

The ER/RE! distress signal announced that one of the three
best friends had to discuss something of dire importance and
that they *had* to get together immediately. Even as little kids,
before they were introduced to the technical world of text messages and IMs, Evie, Dee Dee, and Raquel would always meet

up by the secluded area at the far end of the Rio Estates golf course. It was private and safe—well, unless a runaway golf ball came whizzing by at ninety miles per hour, which actually happened pretty often.

Because Dee Dee was still fussing over her *"muy impor- tante"* Hermanas meeting, the girls decided to meet at Dee Dee's house instead of the usual "same plce." Raquel picked Evie up in her Beetle for their ER/RE! meeting.

Raquel's Beetle was black, lowered, and named B.J., as in Beetle Juice, not the *other* thing, and had the vanity plates to prove it: BTLEJCE. B.J.'s bud vase was a receptacle for cigarette butts and gum wrappers, and stuck across the top of B.J.'s front window was *SoCal* in white Old English script. When Evie got into B.J., she could instantly smell the residue of pot, evidence that Raquel must have been hotboxing the night before with the nameless boy.

As soon as they got to Dee Dee's, Evie and Raquel were loaded up with the requisite Snapple and pita chips, courtesy of the de LaFuentes' housekeeper, Marcela, and made their way up to Dee Dee's bedroom upstairs.

"Oh my God," Dee Dee said as soon as she opened her bedroom door. "You're in one piece!" She reached out and hugged Evie. "What happened with that guy? You just hung up on me, and I kept calling and calling you. I had no idea what to think."

"You won't even believe today." Evie shook her head. "Oh.

My. God. The Fear Factor was cranked to high. I mean, this dude was so right in my face, with his jersey and shaved head—you just know he was some gangbanger ready to cap my ass or something."

"*Please.*" Raquel grabbed a handful of pita chips from the bag and smirked at Evie. "A *gang* banger? In Rio Estates? And if he *was* a gangbanger, what kind of jersey did he front?"

Evie looked at Raquel. It was *so* like her to try to act like she held all knowledge of street sense and sensibility. Ever since Raquel had broken up with Jose, it was like she was on a quest to prove she was still just as scandalous as when she dated him—if not more so. Whereas any cool girl at Villanueva (Raquel claimed there were only three—her, Evie, and, of course, *la otra* ADA, Dee Dee) would gain cred to inspire jealousy in an ex (with, say, a hottie short-boarder with major-label sponsorship or with a member of a local neo-Nardcore band), Raquel was was dating down, *way* down.

"Raquel, you were *not* even there," Evie insisted. "You didn't even see this guy. He was all in my face and just ready to throw down."

Okay, maybe a slight exaggeration, but Evie felt the need to color up her story, at least for the sake of her suburban pride.

"*Ay,* well, I'm just glad it's all over with." Dee Dee checked the heat of the hot rollers on her head. "When I got your text, I didn't know what to do. What happened to the veggie Benz? Anything?"

"Nothing," Evie said. "But I dinged the other guy's car. Luckily, Lindsay's got this brother-in-law or something at Williams Automotive, so it shouldn't cost too much."

"What, you're gonna have to pay for it?" Raquel asked.

"What, you think I'm gonna ask my mother to have her insurance take care of it?" Evie asked. "Yeah, right."

Evie got up from the edge of Dee Dee's bed and paced on the wide-loop shag carpet. "But that's not the worst part. I got my quality check today, and my parents are totally freaking out. They told me that I couldn't have my party unless I bring my average up by the time I get my next quality check. That's in about three and a half weeks. There is *no* way I can bring my average up in time."

"How bad was your QC?" Dee Dee held up two different blouses in front of her vanity mirror. She tilted her head back and forth in indecision.

Evie couldn't help but feel slightly annoyed that Dee Dee was choosing between necklines and fabric while they were discussing her crisis. That was the problem when the girls didn't have their ER/RE! meeting at the golf course: multitasking led to multithinking.

"It was okay." Evie took a sip of her Kiwi Strawberry. Dee Dee was the brain of the three of them, without even trying. Sometimes it made Evie feel inferior that no matter how much she studied, it was always Dee Dee who got better grades, and so effortlessly. "I mean, I got two C's." Evie looked down at her Snapple. "One in English and the other in Civics."

"How could you be getting a C in English?" Raquel flipped through Dee Dee's *Teen Vogue*. Far from her personal flavor, but it wasn't like she was about to waste her time with any of the *moda estylo* zines that Dee Dee got direct from Mexico. "Harrison is total kickback. Even I'm doing good in her class."

Great. Even Raquel was "doing good" in English. Could Evie feel even *mas* inferior?

"Well, I'm not doing so hot," Evie said as confidently as she could. "I hate English. All Harrison does is make us write. 'Write your feelings, write your thoughts, write what you know.' Sheesh, I'm barely sixteen; what am I supposed to know?"

"Uh, maybe how to properly shift a gear into drive?" Raquel teased.

Evie threw her another look.

"Ugh. I *hate* writing," Evie lamented again.

"I don't. I love writing," Dee Dee said. She hung up the reject blouse after settling on the boring beige one with the conservative neckline.

"Since when?" Evie asked suspiciously. Dee Dee hadn't *loved* to write so much when they were younger.

"*Since* I lived in Mexico," Dee Dee claimed. "That was the best thing about going to school there." She suddenly got dreamy eyed. "I got to write and read in Spanish, *the* Romance language, all the stuff by Neruda and Sor Juana Inés de la Cruz, and, of course, love letters from Rocio."

Raquel threw Evie an exasperated *Here we go again* look. Evie and Raquel had both grown weary of the Rocio Valentine eternally pinned on Dee Dee's heart. If she wasn't texting him *larga distancia*, she was gabbing with him in that show-offy big-city *español* of hers on her cell. It was one thing to say a boy was the love of your life, Evie thought, but another thing to friggin' talk about him *venticuatro/siete*.

"So why don't you just do some community service crap or something for extra credit in Civics?" Raquel grabbed some more pita chips from the bag and turned her attention back to Evie. "Vasquez-Reyes Alarcón loves that kind of stuff."

"Oh yeah?" Evie took another sip of her Snapple.

"Uh, *yes*," Raquel answered. "How do you think Jose skated through Nueva when he used to go there? Picking up roadside trash off Vineyard Avenue wasn't *always* a court-appointed assignment."

Evie laughed. "*Serio?*" Jose had always bragged of his little run-ins with the law, but he never bragged about the consequences that followed.

"Seriously." Raquel smirked with evil pleasure. "*What* a loser."

"And," Dee Dee added, "I'm sure you could volunteer for something like the Surfrider Foundation and Adopt the Beach. Something totally Evie Gomez."

"Yeah," Raquel agreed. "That would be way cooler than being stuck after school every day with some boring-ass tutor in SSIT."

"*No,*" Evie said. "There is *no* way I'm gonna get tutored in SSIT."

Sabrina used to be a tutor for Star Students in Training, and Evie remembered her coming home from school complaining about all the "slow" students who didn't "get it" as quickly as they "should." To Evie, SSIT was more like *SHIT*, and its real acronym said it all. Evie didn't wanna "sit" around Villanueva after school any longer than she had to.

She tipped her head in thought. Maybe Raquel was right. It might be fun to work at local beach events with other ocean-minded people like herself. She could definitely get Alex to help her. Then they could go on romantic beach walks together after spending sunny afternoons serving lemonade at, say, a surf contest or beach cleanup.

"Yeah." Evie felt encouraged. "That might be cool."

"Look," Raquel continued. "You could do some community service for Civics and then write a paper about your experiences for English. Make it a paper full of hardship and woe. You know how Harrison loves all that 'struggling brown people' stuff."

"More writing?" Evie gawked. "*No* thank you."

"I can write the paper for you," Dee Dee offered. "You can just basically tell me what to say, and I'll write it. A-plus quality."

"In English or the *Romance language?*" Evie smirked, and Raquel's laugh came out as a snort.

"I could do it in *français* if you want." Dee Dee smiled back smugly.

"Okay, Frenchie." Evie finished the rest of her Snapple. "Just make sure you do a good job. If I don't get my average up, the sixteeñera is off."

"And we don't want that." Raquel helped herself to more pita chips. "It's been a friggin' dry spell around here."

"You're telling me." Dee Dee unrolled her hot curlers.

Raquel looked over at her. "Since when have *you* been Miss Party Thang?"

"Since I ate green beetles in Mexico," Dee Dee said. "You know, you *don't* down them with *milk*, Raquel."

* * *

By the time Evie and Raquel left Dee Dee's house, Evie was feeling much more hopeful. Her cell vibrated on the drive home—a text from Alex. She hadn't talked to him yet that day. Wait until he heard what kind of day she'd had! But when she opened her cell, she couldn't believe what she read.

SW Swell @ C st.

Cnt make 2morw. Srry!

As Dee Dee would ask, Mande? There was a southwest swell at the Sea Street break, and so now he was canceling their plans to go to Santa Barbara? Just so he could go surfing? Again? Argh!

"What's wrong?" Raquel glanced over at Evie's phone. She knew the side effects of text wounds.

Evie reread his text message again and felt the pit of her stomach quiver. He hadn't even invited her to go along! She and Alex had been going out only a little over two months. Could it be that he was already losing interest?

"Alex is totally flaking on me." Evie glared at her cell phone screen. "We had plans to go to Santa Barbara tomorrow, but now he wants to go surfing, again."

"That's what happens when you date a man whose first love is following his stoke," Raquel joked.

But Evie didn't laugh.

4

"I'M TOTALLY SORRY ABOUT YESTERDAY," ALEX SAID, APOLOGIZING FOR the millionth time. The first 999,999 sorrys had come that morning in the car as he drove them both to Villanueva Prep. "I promise we'll go to Santa Barbara. Soon."

Evie was putting her books away in her locker for lunchtime. "Don't make promises you can't keep." She knew she was acting like a baby, but she was getting a little tired of Alex's flakiness. This seemed to be happening a lot lately: There was the time they'd had plans to go to the skate park on Rose Avenue, and then he'd flaked because the head gasket on Mondo's Marauder (V-plates: SRF PNK) had blown and he needed a ride to Oakview. Then there was the time when they were supposed to go up to the Cross to watch the sunrise together and then, at the last minute, Alex wanted to predawn curb-camp so he could be the first in line for a "totally epic" board sale at Anacapa Surf Shop. Evie sighed. Maybe Raquel was right. Could a girlfriend compete with the search for stoke that so many surfer boyfriends were born with?

"No, but really," Alex said again as Evie rearranged her books and folders so everything would fit in her locker. "I am *so* sorry."

One million and one.

Alex looked over her *O.C.* magazine cutouts taped to the inside of her door. They were primarily of Seth. *Seth.* Sigh. "You *like* this guy?"

"What's wrong with him?" Evie asked.

"Nothing," Alex said. "If you like dorks."

"He is *not* a dork." Evie slugged Alex on the arm. "He's sensitive and sweet."

"I can be sensitive and sweet." Alex put his arm around her shoulders. "Come on, you know that I'll totally do whatever I can to help you with this volunteer thing. I don't like seeing you so bummed out."

"Hey!" Dee Dee came up behind them. "*Qué pasa,* lovebirds?"

Raquel was behind Dee Dee with her iPod cranked to high.

"Nothing, *now.*" Alex smirked as he pulled away from Evie.

"Hey, you guys!" Raquel yelled at Evie and Alex.

"Raq"—Alex motioned to her ears—"*calm* the wheel!"

"Oops, sorry." Raquel removed her iPod plugs.

"When are you gonna get a decent headpiece?" Alex

frowned at her white plastic earphones. "Those suck. No wonder you have to crank it up."

"Sor-*ry*," Raquel said. "Not *everyone* has a boyfriend who buys her four-hundred-dollar Bose headphones." She glanced into Evie's locker, where such headphones, a Christmas gift from Alex, were carefully tucked in their black pouch on top of her books and notepads. "You two are such *i-Snobs*."

"And proud of it." Evie loved that she and Alex shared another thing in common other than their love for the ocean: their arrogant attitude toward music and tech equipment.

"Hey." Alex rubbed his stomach under his T-shirt. "Let's bail for lunch. I'm jonesing for a guac dog."

"*Yo también.*" Dee Dee smacked her lips.

"*No.*" Evie felt irritated. "Remember? I gotta go to the counseling office and get some numbers for volunteering. You guys said you would help."

"Oh yeah. That's right." Dee Dee frowned. "I completely spaced."

Evie's mood turned back to sour as she shut her locker door. How could her own boyfriend and best friend not remember the major dilemma she was still facing? She hadn't thought of anything else the entire weekend.

"Aah, Gomez, come on." Alex clicked his tongue and put his arm around her. "You know we're here for you. Always."

When they got to the volunteer board in the counseling center, they discovered, as Evie had guessed, that there were few volunteer options left.

"See!" she huffed. "I knew this was gonna happen. I told my parents that there was no way I could get my average up in time. If I don't get rid of those two C's, my dad's totally gonna cancel the party."

"I'm still not buying that your parents might pull the plug on the party," Raquel said. "Vicki G. is all about being the hostess making the most mess. She never gives up an opportunity to showcase swank."

"No," Evie said. "She is *very* serious. Both of them are."

Alex read the listings from the volunteer board out loud. "Here's some help needed: 'Working with the elderly, three days a week.'"

"Eww." Raquel curled her upper lip. "Working with molder folk? Evie, you do *not* want to do that."

"Yeah, I'd have to agree." Alex nodded. He pointed out another listing. "Check out this one: 'Tutoring youth at risk.'" He suddenly smirked. "What youth isn't 'at risk'? I mean, aren't we all 'at risk'?"

"Yeah." Evie laughed. "You're at risk every time you paddle out on that twelve-hundred-dollar Aviso board of yours."

"Or when you buy some of Mondo's home blend," Raquel complained. "Which, by the way, that dude owes me." She pulled out her cell phone, ready to text a customer complaint to him. "I gave him three C-notes on Friday, and I don't smell the scent of freshly cut lawn."

Evie felt a little uncomfortable hearing about Raquel's latest transaction with Mondo. Raquel had upgraded from last semester's dime bags to this semester's oz's.

"No cell phones," Miss Peterson, the office secretary sang as she walked by the four of them to her desk.

"I'm only texting," Raquel explained, not bothering to look up.

"You know the rules." Miss Peterson pointed to the doorway. "Take it outside or it will be confiscated."

Raquel rolled her eyes at Evie as if it wasn't her own fault she was being shooed away. "I'm just gonna find out what's up with Mondo. I'll be right back to help you."

"Yeah, yeah." Evie knew better than to really count on Raquel. Once party supplies entered the picture, she became suddenly unavailable to honor any duties she might have committed to earlier. "Just go."

"I'll be right back," Raquel said. "Promise."

As soon as Raquel was out of earshot, Dee Dee leaned in closer to Alex and Evie. "So, what's up with Raquel?" she asked.

"What do you mean?" Evie asked.

"She's been going a little off the deep end, don't you think?" Dee Dee glanced toward the hallway where Raquel was standing. "Do you know who she has been going out with? Did she tell you?"

"Nuh-uh," Evie answered. She didn't like to admit she didn't know something so personal about Raquel. During the four years that Dee Dee had been away in Mexico City, she and Raquel had become very tight. And now, here was Dee Dee knowing something about Raquel that Evie didn't? It didn't seem right.

"Davey *Mitchell*." Dee Dee lowered her voice and looked over to where Raquel was now making a call in the hallway.

"Davey Mitchell?" Evie repeated the name. "Who's that?"

"Ronnie Mitchell's older brother," Alex answered.

Evie knew of Ronnie Mitchell. He was one of the Bard Boys and had been kicked out of nearly every public school for causing all kinds of chaos. However, she didn't know too much about his older brother, Davey.

"He's practically twenty-two years old," Dee Dee said. "And he did time at the CYA."

"Really?" The California Youth Authority housed inmates ages thirteen to twenty-four. It wasn't just a probation agency or juvie. Kids housed at the CYA had done some pretty *questionable* things.

"*Yes.*" Dee Dee knowingly raised her eyebrows. "Raquel was actually bragging about it. I'm a little worried about her. She's becoming such a *leva*."

"Okay, *tías*." Alex put his hand on both Evie's and Dee Dee's shoulders. "'Nough gossiping by the clothesline. Come on, Raquel is your friend."

"We're *not* gossiping." Dee Dee shook her head. "Raquel *is* our friend, and we're just concerned. You should talk to her, Evie. She'll listen to you."

"Listen to me? Say what?" Evie asked.

"Anything," Dee Dee said. "Just say something."

Evie looked over toward the quad where Raquel had now found Mondo and was talking to him in person. She wondered if Dee Dee was making a bigger deal about Raquel than was actually called for.

"You know," Alex started, as if he were reading Evie's thoughts, "we all go through phases. Maybe that's what Raquel is doing. Just give her time. She's a smart girl. She'll figure it out."

"I sure hope so." Evie took a deep breath.

Just then, the door to one of the counselors' offices opened. None of them could help but hear the *voice*, the thick Spanish-accented whine of Alejandra de los Santos. It took over the whole hallway. She was just concluding her session with her counselor, A through H.

There were only three counselors for the entire student population at Villanueva, and each one was assigned to students based on the first letter of their last names. There were Counselor A through H, Counselor I through Q, and Counselor R through Z. Because their last names started with *G* and *D*, Evie, Dee Dee, and Raquel had Counselor A through H. Alejandra de los Santos had him as well.

"No," Alejandra informed A through H, "I don't plan on living on campus during my internship. I have to live on campus *here*, and if I'm going to be donating so much of my time at Yale, I want to be able to be completely free when I'm done putting in my hours."

"Alejandra"—A through H already sounded annoyed and slightly tired—"I hope you think more of your internship than just putting in hours. Thousands of other high school juniors across the country would die for the opportunity to intern at Yale. Don't take it so lightly." A through H was the oldest of all the counselors, and Evie wondered if his noontime impatience had something to do with needing a noontime nap. Or maybe he was just exhausted by Alejandra's all-the-time arrogance?

"I know," Alejandra said quickly, as if she didn't want some know-it-all high school counselor telling *her* how to think. "*Pues*, thank you for your time."

As she left his office, Alejandra couldn't help but come face to face with Evie, Dee Dee, and Alex in the counseling office's narrow hallway. How lucky was Alejandra that Raquel had just left? Raquel *hated* Alejandra. Soon after Raquel found out that she had been seeing Jose secretly behind her back, things started to *happen* to Alejandra. Her silver Audi (V-plates: DFDIVA) had been keyed, derogatory Spanglish had been scrawled on her locker door, and accidental "domino" slams in the hall had occasionally led to Alejandra falling flat on her ass. Were all these *incidentes* initiated by Raquel? Hmm . . . perhaps.

Alejandra's almond-shaped eyes scanned the three of them, and, perhaps to appear unfazed and possibly to exclude Alex and Evie, she shot off Spanish in rapid-fire to Dee Dee.

Dee Dee, however, answered in English, slowly and calmly. "Oh, my father loves his new position," she said. "But I *really* don't think *your* father got him his job, Ally. I mean, my father has his own credentials. But it was very nice of your dad to mention the position to him."

Evie couldn't believe what she was hearing. Had Alejandra been insinuating that her dad had gotten Dee Dee's father his new position as chancellor at Cal State University Channel Islands? She couldn't believe that Alejandra would be so bold, especially when she was alone against the three of them. Her sidekick Sangros, the *ah*-migas—Natalia, Xiomara, and Fabiola—were nowhere around.

"So," Alex asked Alejandra earnestly, "you're doing an internship at Yale?"

Evie pressed her foot into the side of his flojo. *Alex, who freaking cares?*

"*Claro.*" Alejandra smiled, staring deeply into Alex's eyes. "This summer. But I still don't know," she sighed heavily as she tugged on the blond strand underneath her prominent mane of dark hair. Last year, the Sangros' trademark had been their vivid blond highlights. But this semester they all had returned from Mexico City after Christmas break with a new look. Except for a thin solid strand of blond, the Sangros had dyed their hair black. Not brown or dark brown, but black, practically *bruja* black. Which was actually a fitting choice, since they all were *brujas*, and then some.

"I might just go back to Mexico and intern at UNAM," Alejandra continued. "I really miss the sophistication of city life." She glanced at the volunteer list in front of them. "Are you doing an internship *también*?" she asked Alex. "*Oye*, maybe we could both do one at UNAM together. That would be fun." She glanced over at Evie.

"Uh, no," Alex said. "I'm not looking for an internship, but Evie is. Actually, she just needs some volunteer credit, or else she can't have her party."

Evie's face burned. Could Alex be more *tonto*?

Of course, Alejandra knew about Evie's Sweet Sixteeñera. Everyone at Nueva was talking about it, and that included Alejandra and her fellow Sangros.

Alejandra looked at Evie and then at the volunteer board. "Well, good luck, Evelin-*a*. You know, maybe my father can help. He has lots of contacts and is very charitable to those in need." She glanced back at Dee Dee.

"Oh, I don't need help," Evie answered quickly. Know-it-all high school juniors were just as bad as know-it-all high school counselors. "I'm just gonna volunteer a few hours a week."

"I wasn't talking about volunteer work." Alejandra smiled slowly. "I'm talking about your little party. What made you decide to have it at Duke's?"

"What wrong with Duke's?" As soon as the words came out of her mouth, Evie regretted asking. What did she care what Alejandra thought? She wasn't even anywhere near the guest list.

"Well, for one thing . . ." Alejandra took another deep breath, as though she had an extensive list of problems to read off, but then her eyes gazed over Evie's shoulder. "*Ay*, never mind." She patted Evie's shoulder. "If that's what you want for your little party. *Naco.*" Then she clicked away in her high leather boots . . . *just* as Raquel reappeared. *Coincidence?*

"Okay, it's *on!*" Raquel held up her hand to high-five Alex. She had no idea that her nemesis had been so close by. Couldn't she smell the residue of "sulfur de Sangro" still wafting in the air? Raquel patted the zippered outside pocket of her backpack. "So, I got the goods from Mondo. Four-twenty in the 805—you wanna go out to the Tree?" she asked Alex.

Alex looked at Evie. "Uh . . ."

"Are you serious?" Evie couldn't believe that he was actually thinking of bailing on her. Again.

"Gomez—" Alex tilted his head to the side. "—don't be like that. . . ."

"Be like what?" she asked. He was so *not* fronting a Dee Dee pose with that little head tilt of his. "Upset that you are flaking on me, again? You said you were gonna help me find work."

"Evie," Raquel said, "don't be all uptight. Besides, how many pairs of eyes do you really need? Dee Dee can get you started, and we'll be back before you know it. I got Rodriquez-White after lunch, and there is no way I can deal with her without being lit."

"Just go." Evie waved them both away. She was now certifiably annoyed.

"Are you sure?" Alex asked. "I mean, if you really, really want me to stay . . ."

"No . . . just go already."

"Cool!" Alex gave Evie a peck on the cheek and took off with Raquel.

"Don't worry, Evie." Dee Dee squeezed her shoulder after Alex and Raquel were gone. "We'll find something, something *muy bueno* for you."

"Yeah." Evie looked after Alex and Raquel as they headed toward Juniper's Tree, the big oak at the far end of the quad, for their little smoke-out session. "I could use something, or someone, *muy bueno* in my life right about now."

5

"AND WHY DO YOU WANT TO WORK AT A HORSE RESERVE?" A THROUGH H
asked Evie as she took a seat in his cluttered office.

Dee Dee had picked what seemed like an ideal volunteer
position for Evie: caring for horses at the Southern California
Horse Reserve.

"You'll get to be outside and it's close to school," Dee Dee
had pointed out. "And horses are *so* sweet. Everyone likes
horses, no?"

"Uh, no," Evie had said. "I mean, yes." She was always
unsure how to answer questions that ended in *no*. Were you
to say no as in "I agree with you," or "Yes, I agree to your no"?

"Everyone does like them."

Simple enough, Evie thought. But now A through H needed
to know exactly why she wanted to work at the SCHR. How
should she answer him? That the SCHR was the only option

available on the volunteer list that didn't involve old people or thugs-in-training? That if she didn't get some volunteer credit under her belt, like, *soon*, she was gonna be celebrating her sixteenth birthday at the banquet room of the Sizzler? Of course, she had to give him the kind of answer that all high school counselors want to hear.

"I really want to give back to my community," Evie stated simply. She looked into his eyes with as much sincerity as she hoped she could possibly project.

"Your community?" A through H breathed heavily as he looked over Evie's file. A through H had always been a big man, but he had returned from Christmas break even heftier. *Too many tamales?* Evie wondered. "I thought you lived in Rio Estates," he said.

"I do," Evie answered. Rio Estates was a high-end gated community with no suitable space to board a horse, but of course, he knew that. "I just want to give back to my equeen community."

"Do you mean *equine*?" He looked up from Evie's file and smiled.

"Yes," Evie answered. Wasn't that what she had just said? "I was reading on their flyer that they needed help caring for horses. I want to do that."

"Well, you do know that it's already three weeks into the semester." A through H adjusted his wire-framed glasses and looked over the dates on the calendar hanging to the left of him.

The calendar was a Villanueva school calendar, twelve months with twelve full-color pictures that depicted the "best of" at Nueva. Two years ago, Sabrina had been featured for April in her tennis outfit. When the calendar had come out, Evie's father had purchased almost five thousand copies and handed them out at the country club and at his *panadería*. Normally, Mexican bakeries gave away religious calendars, and only during the Christmas holidays. But the year that Sabrina was featured on the Villanueva calendar, Evie's father had skipped La Virgin de Guadalupe and had his employees hand out La Suprema, Our Lady of Eternal Achievement.

"And you know you're supposed to clear any interest in volunteer work with your instructors from the very beginning," A through H continued. "The reserve may not even have an opening."

"But they have a listing on the volunteer board," Evie told him.

"Oh, those listings are so outdated." A through H opened his desk drawer and shuffled around in it. "We have an intern who is supposed to keep on top of them, but he's always talking on the office phone or texting on that cell phone of his." He sighed again.

"Do you need someone to work in the office?" Evie's words practically sprang out of her mouth. An office job would be *so* cool. She would have full access to hallway passes, student files (wouldn't Raquel *love* to get ahold of Alejandra de los

Santos's folder!), and the Internet (though most likely with limited viewing blocks). Plus, she'd get to work during class hours, and *all* for course credit. *Qué* cake. "Because I could do that too."

"I thought you wanted to work with horses?" A through H smiled and then frowned as he pulled a cloth from the drawer and started to clean his glasses. "At the reserve."

"Oh, I do," Evie answered. "I was just asking. I mean, if Villanueva needs help, I totally wanna help."

Nice save?

"It's refreshing to hear such school spirit." A through H continued to clean his glasses, wiping the lenses meticulously. "Well, if we can't get you at the reserve this semester, there's always their summer program."

"*Summer* program?" Evie was appalled at the thought. "No, I have, I mean, I'd *like* to work this semester."

"And the urgency is because of your love of horses and has nothing to do with the two C's on your last quality check?" He held up his glasses to the sunlight to inspect them.

"Well . . ." Evie felt her neck flush. "Maybe," she answered sheepishly. "Just a little."

"Don't worry, Evie. I'll see what I can do." A through H smiled again, this time a calm, somewhat reassuring smile. He put his glasses back on. "I'll give the reserve a call and see if they have any more openings. I think I can pull some strings. But you still have to get the okay from your instructors."

"I will," Evie answered.

"By the way, how is your party coming along?"

"My party?" Evie asked.

"Yes," A through H answered. "I hear from many of the instructors that it's been quite the talk on campus, and quite the distraction in the classroom."

"Oh." Evie cringed. "I didn't know that. I'm sorry." Should she offer him an invite?

"No worries." A through H took off his glasses again and looked over the thick lenses. "Just try to focus on matters at hand, Evie. Your grades need improving. You know, I was your sister's counselor when she was a student here. How is she doing at Stanford?"

"Great," Evie answered. When was Suprema not doing great?

"That's no surprise," he answered. "That girl is one focused individual. A real go-getter."

Evie stared glumly at the school's calendar.

"Uh-huh," was all she could think of to say.

❀ ❀ ❀

As Evie soon found out, A through H was good on his word. He pulled enough strings to yank out a last-minute internship for her at the Southern California Horse Reserve. Then he sent an e-mail to both Vasquez-Reyes Alarcón and Harrison and encouraged them to allow Evie to do the extra credit even though the semester had started. Counselor A through H held true to his administrative title, A–H, as in *Aaah*. . . . Evie could relax, if only just a little.

But her moment of serenity was short-lived. Encouraging e-mail from a counselor or not, A through H reminded her that she still had to get final approval from both Vasquez-Reyes Alarcón and Harrison. Since Raquel had said that Harrison was a pushover, Evie decided to ask her first.

"Oh, this sounds wonderful," Mrs. Harrison said as Evie eagerly held out the official paperwork for her to sign. "I like that you want to learn more about ranchero life. You should use as much Spanish as possible in your essay."

"No problemo," Evie told her with confidence. And it wouldn't be a problemo, considering that it would be Dee Dee writing the whole thing.

"It's actually *no hay problema*," Harrison corrected her.

"Huh?" Evie asked. Had Harrison started teaching Spanish and no one had informed her?

"The proper translation is *no hay problema*," Mrs. Harrison said.

"Oh, sorry," Evie apologized.

"No prob," Mrs. Harrison answered. "So, when you write the paper, give me the mood." She wove her hands dramatically in the air, a gesture that Evie guessed she wanted her to capture on paper. "Let me feel the complexity that is *charro* life."

"I don't know how many cowboys I am going to run into at the reserve," Evie confessed. "But I'll try. So, when I write my essay, what kind of credit will I receive?"

"Depending on the length and quality, and if you do well on your other class assignments," Mrs. Harrison said as she initialed the paper, "you can bring your grade up half a point. By the end of the semester, you could very well have an A."

"Wow." Evie wasn't expecting a full leap to an A. "And that will be reflected on my next quality check? In three and a half weeks?"

"It very well could be," Mrs. Harrison confirmed. "Not the actual A, but the progress you are making. You might get a B on your QC."

"Then I'm really going to do a very good job," Evie assured her.

Yeah, a very good job getting on Dee Dee's ass to write a damn good paper.

"Oh, I know you will." Mrs. Harrison patted Evie on the back as she led her to the classroom door. "I know you have been faced with many obstacles in your life, Evie, being a girl, a young girl of color, and I want to do as much as I can to support you. I want to support my *mujeres!*" She rolled out the *r* in *mujeres* longer than necessary. "I know that if you put your mind to it, you can get anything you want, Evie."

❇ ❇ ❇

Vasquez-Reyes Alarcón, on the other hand, was harder to convince that Evie was an oppressed, upper-middle-class teen struggling for the Malibu birthday party of her dreams.

"I normally don't allow this type of extra credit after the semester has already started," he stated dryly as he erased the chalkboard. He kept his back toward Evie the whole time. "It's standard procedure to request volunteer work at the commencement of a new semester. You know that. If you want to improve your grades, why don't you join SSIT?

"I could get a tutor." Evie tried to remain calm and diplomatic. There was no way she could lose this opportunity. "But I'd really like the experience working at a horse reserve, and Mrs. Harrison and my counselor have already okayed it."

"I'm not swayed by other people's decisions." Mr. Vasquez-Reyes Alarcón kept wiping the board. "That's the problem with a lot of people nowadays in this country. They just go for the popular vote, whatever is fashionable. A lot of people don't think for themselves."

"Oh, I totally agree," Evie said. *Dude, please, just* sign *the paper.* "I mean, all my friends were telling me I should work at a hospice, or with Adopt the Beach, but I felt I could be more useful volunteering at an animal reserve. It's pretty tragic how horses are so neglected in this country. I mean, they were once the symbol of our frontier, right? Now, not enough citizens bother to care about them."

Citizens. Country. Frontier. Words that were music, *patriotic* music, to a Civics instructor's ears.

Mr. Vasquez-Reyes Alarcón turned around to face Evie. The bottom of his nose had been accidentally dusted with powder from the white chalk. *Party hearty, Mr. V!*

He squinted his eyes and nodded slowly. "Good for you, Evie," he said. "It's good to see that you are thinking for yourself. I remember last semester, when you dyed your hair blond and started hanging out with a different crowd, Alejandra de los Santos and all her friends, I became a little concerned about you. You're a bright girl, and now here you are, wanting to do your own thing. Good for you."

Yes, good for me. Evie felt her spirits float higher as Vazquez-Reyes Alarcón signed her sheet. She *was* a bright girl. So bright that no one and nothing was going to dim the wattage of her shine. Who knew? Maybe someday she would be featured for the month of February in Villanueva's "best of" calendar.

6

TO BE PERFECTLY FRANK, EVIE DIDN'T KNOW MUCH ABOUT HORSES.
Most of what she had related to Vasquez-Reyes Alarcón had
been paraphrased from the Southern California Horse
Reserve's flyer. She had, however, loved it when Dee Dee's
mom, Margaret, had taken her, Dee Dee, and Raquel horseback riding in Oakview, and she did fancy herself a lover of
animals. Wasn't she the only one who made sure Meho's litter
box remained semi-clumpless, and wasn't *she* the only one
who rewarded Molesto with bona fide doggie treats after her
father had so cruelly faked him out with his air nothings?

Evie was scheduled for her first day of volunteer work the following Wednesday. Alex offered to drop her off at the reserve
after school, before heading out to Sea Street. As Evie walked
out to the student parking lot to meet him at his truck (V-plates:
SO SURF), she heard someone call out her name.

"Hey, E-*vie*."

She turned around and saw two boys, seniors, walking up behind her.

"Oh, hey," Evie said back.

She recognized the boys from their photos in the school paper's sports page. Normally, Evie wouldn't think much of jocks in their numbered jerseys and with their obnoxiously lifted four-by-fours, but these jocks—*hola*—were on the *water polo* team. She had never bothered to read the accompanying text to remember their names, but Raquel had pointed out the differences among team members, which helped Evie differentiate the two boys who were now walking next to her.

"So"—Fine-Ass Speedo came up to the left of her—"you be the talk of the town, Miss Eves. How's the party planning?"

"Yeah"—Big-Bulge Speedo came up to her right—"you gonna supply customized party hats for all your guests?"

"Party hats?" Evie asked. How did he know she was going to have visors with customized stitching?

"Yeah," Fine Ass said. "You gots to have party hats, like with your name and birthdate and shit like that printed all over them. Especially with all the booze that's gonna be at your party, shit could get out of hand. It's best to play it safe."

Play it safe?

"Actually, I am having hats," she told them.

"*Coo'.*" Fine Ass approved. "My cuz from SB said your party's all over MySpace."

"MySpace?" Evie asked. "Are you serious?"

"Yeah," Big Bulge said. "Your party's gonna knock 805 on its ass!"

"*Mar*-co . . ."

Fine Ass and Evie turned around. It was Alejandra de los Santos and her *ah*-miga, Fabiola, walking by. In their super-spiky stiletto boots, they practically cast shadows over Evie and the two Speedos. Last year, the Sangros wore super-chunky platform boots, but this semester their heels had been trimmed down to sharpened points. Also last year, they seemed to rule the runway of the hallways, but now, as Raquel—or "someone"—was putting Alejandra in her place, they were more simply *sangro*, than super *sangrona*.

"Uh, hey." Fine Ass looked over at Alejandra and Fabiola.

"We're gonna go swimming," Fabiola said, "at the Aquatic Center."

"The Aquatic Center?" Big Bulge asked. "It ain't open now. It's closed between two and five."

"Not for me." Alejandra looked at him alluringly. "I've got connections. My cousin Gabby's ex-girlfriend's roommate is a lifeguard there. *Quieres ir conmigo?*" She didn't look at Evie, and it was clear that the invitation did not extend to her. Evie immediately opened her cell phone and checked for messages that she knew were not there. *Look busy, popular.*

The Aquatic Center was at the far east end of the county, but worth the drive, with its palm tree–lined Olympic-size swimming pool. Besides, the Sangros were known for their topless sunbathing and, at times, bikini-bottom-less swimming. If they were going to the Aquatic Center during closed hours, who knew what could happen? How could two boys, water polo boys, turn down such an enticing offer?

"Uh, no can do," Fine Ass answered, to Evie's major surprise. "I'm talking party talk with Eves, here."

Evie could *not* believe what she was hearing. Had she died and gone to Flojo heaven?

"Yeah," Evie said smugly as she looked directly at Alejandr-*a*. She couldn't help but feel a bit more confident. "Party talk, about my *little* party. At *Duke's*."

Alejandra shrugged her shoulders. "*Pues*, your decision," she said before walking off.

Evie and the Speedos continued walking through the parking lot till they reached Alex's truck. Alex had just taken his short board out of Mondo's Marauder and was putting it into his flatbed. When he wanted to surf after school, he'd keep his board locked up in Mondo's car and then transfer it to his truck after classes.

"Hey, Mark." Alex raised his chin at Fine Ass.

"Dude." Fine Ass looked over Alex's short board. "You gonna rip Sea Street?"

"Nah." Alex curled his upper lip. "Wetsand says flat and glassy. I'm gonna try Rincon."

"You're going to Rincon?" Evie opened the passenger door and tossed her Roxy tote behind the seat. "You didn't tell me that."

She instantly felt left out. As long as she'd been dating Alex, and as long as she'd been surfing, basically the same amount of time, she had never been to Rincon, which was only two freeway exits north of Sea Street. The waves at Rincon were supposedly as fierce as the local territorialism, and Alex pretty much kept Evie away from both. She felt annoyed that Alex babied her when it came to surf conditions (in terms of weather and subculture).

"You didn't ask where I was going," Alex teased. "'Sides, you gotta get from tadpole stage before you can swim with the sharks."

Evie felt a twinge of embarrassment and glanced over at Fine Ass and Big Bulge. How could Alex say such a thing in front of *them*, the two top swimmers of the water polo team? Okay, maybe he didn't treat her like a baby, but a friggin' tadpole, for sure.

"You can't swim?" Fine Ass asked Evie.

"Of course I can swim." Evie wrinkled her brow and shook her head. "He's just being stupid."

"'Cause I was gonna say," Fine Ass started, "if you need help, I could totally help you."

"*You?*" Big Bulge smirked. "After your lousy numbers at the last meet? Look, Evie—" He put his arm around her shoulders.

"—if you ever wanna enhance your techniques—" He patted his chest. "—let *me* know."

Evie could not believe that Fine Ass and Big Bulge, *water polo* boys and *seniors*, were fighting over her. She couldn't help but glance over at Alex, who appeared to be totally consumed with making sure his board was secured in the back of his truck.

"Wow, that's so totally nice of you." Evie smiled. "I gotta admit, I still get a little tense when I gotta turtle turn, you know, under the waves."

"Oh, you don't wanna be tense when you should be having fun. I can totally help you with that." Fine Ass nodded. "Just let me know."

"So, Mark, we gotta get going," Alex said abruptly as he came around to the other side of his truck. "Evie's got an internship over at the SCHR."

"Oh yeah?" Fine Ass looked at Evie and smiled in approval. "Cool, helping the horsies. Very cool. 'Kay, catch you guys later."

"Yeah, Alex." Big Bulge held up his hand to high-five him. "Lates."

"What was *that* all about?" Alex asked as he started up his truck and pulled out of the parking space.

"What was what?" Evie asked.

"Flirting like that in front of me?" Alex said. "So not cool."

"I wasn't flirting." Evie tried to deny it. Had she *really* been

flirting? Or just being friendly? She had read about the differences in one of Dee Dee's Mexican magazines. *"Amante o
Amiga? Combinación Mortal!"*

"Of course you were. *Oh, I get so scared when I go under the
waves!"* Alex said in a high, girly voice. *"Help me, help me!"*

"I did *not* say that." Evie pinched his side.

"Not in so many words you did."

"Aw, you're just jealous." Evie couldn't help but feel a bit
flattered. It was unlike Alex to show his *sentido* side.

"Not even." Alex tried to shrug it off. "I just know that you
wouldn't like it if I did that in front of you."

"You're right," Evie admitted. "But God, it's not like Fine—
I mean, Mark—talks to me every day. He's like Mr. Big Man
of the water polo team."

Alex shook his head in disbelief. "God, Evie. You're so
impressionable. He's not *that* great."

"Right." Evie looked over at Alex. "And you're *so* not jealous."

Alex waited his turn in the student parking lot to make a
left on Ventura Avenue. There was no stoplight, and the long
line of cars, blasting everything from reggaetón to speed
metal, was practically fifteen deep.

"So," Evie started as she pulled down the truck's visor and
checked her face. She was happy to see that she was still tan
just from being at the beach last weekend. Color, any color,
kept her Flojo surfer-chick image up. "Mark said that my party
was all over MySpace."

"Oh, yeah," Alex said. "I meant to tell you that."

"*What?*" Evie asked. "Are you serious?"

"Yeah, I've already gotten two bulletins about it." Alex tapped his horn at the black SUV in front of him that completely dwarfed his own midsize truck. "*Go* already!" he muttered under his breath.

"Oh, man." Evie sank into her seat. "Now I totally gotta make sure that I have a kick-ass party, let alone *a* party. Mark was even saying that I should get customized party hats, can you believe it? It's like he already knew about the visors I'm putting in the swag bags."

"I don't think he was talking about your visors," Alex said. "You do know that party hats are rubbers, right?"

"What? Are you serious?" Evie held her hand over her mouth and laughed. "Oh my God, I am *such* the dork!"

"Maybe you should get some." Alex then lowered his voice to sound like some PSA on MTV. "Remember, you can't share the love without the glove."

"What if I don't *want* that kind of love?" Evie teased.

"Not even for your birthday?" Alex softened his voice and looked at Evie with exaggerated pleading puppy dog eyes. "I mean, you *will* be turning sixteen."

Evie smiled out of embarrassment. "Alex, you're gonna crash if you don't watch the road."

"I'd rather watch you." He continued to look at her.

Evie didn't say anything, but she could feel Alex's eyes

burning right through her. She loved when he got flirty and cute, but sometimes, she had to admit, she just didn't know how to respond.

"Okay, okay . . . ," Alex said. "I don't wanna get the silent treatment." He turned to face the brake lights in front of his truck.

Evie looked out the window at the towering, leafy eucalyptus and aged oak trees lining Ventura Avenue. This wasn't the first time Alex had joked about them indulging in more than carpet time. That's what Evie called their extended play, *carpet time*. If they dared advance onto a couch or bed, it might get *too* comfortable for the both of them, and who knew what else they would or could do. If they stayed on the carpet of either's den or living room, at least the discomfort of the floor or the consequences of rug burns would keep them in check.

Besides, Evie didn't even know if she was quite ready to make the upgrade from carpet time to the big dealio. When Alex had made his first move on her, that move alone had given her the crazy tingles. Could she possibly be ready for more?

It happened at Sea Street, of course, right after a twilight surf session. Alex had come up behind her, and Evie had thought that he was just going to help her unzip her wet suit, as he sometimes did. But when he had gotten her zipper a quarter of the way down, he placed his hands on her shoulders and kissed the back of her neck, a soft, gentle peck. Evie had nearly *died*. She was *so* not expecting it. When she had turned around to face Alex, suddenly his lips were on her lips. Then the mad crazy tingles that had erupted in her belly took over her whole body.

"You're salty," she had teased nervously between breaths.

"Mmmm," Alex had muttered. His lips were cold but soft. "And you're so not. . . ."

The sensation of having Alex's lips on hers was a million times more thrilling than anything she had ever experienced in her life, a sense of weightlessness that made her feel as if she were going to die from excitement. When was the last time she had ever felt such a sensation? At age six, when she had finally found the nerve to kick away from the curb to pedal her Mongoose Chill BMX bike *solita*? Or the first time she caught a buzz from Veuve Clicquot with Raquel? But even those moments couldn't compare to the feeling of sweet, blissful Alex-stasy.

"*Damn!*" This time Alex held his hand on his horn. "What's this dude's problem? Friggin' student driver!"

Evie was instantly yanked from daydream to daytime reality. "Hey," she reminded Alex, "I'm a student driver."

"I'm sure you don't suck this hard." Alex finally pulled his fist off the horn. "He's had three chances to go. *No* balls."

"Hey, Alex . . ." Evie's thoughts were still in Alex-stasy.

"Uh-huh?" he answered absentmindedly.

"When do you think we can go to Santa Barbara?" she asked. "Maybe this Sunday?"

"Uh, yeah. Why not?" Alex revved his engine and ripped a left onto Ventura Avenue. "Hey, you know Gorby?" he asked. "That guy who transferred from Buena High?"

"Yeah, sorta," Evie said. "I mean, I know who he is."

"Yeah, so he was talking about going down to Baja. I was thinking we could all go. Cool, right?"

"Instead of Santa Barbara?" Evie asked. Baja was just across the Mexican border and it was a lot less couple-cute than SB, that was for sure. Still, a lot of kids went to Baja for simple day trips or for the weekend to surf. Evie really had her hopes pinned on going to SB with Alex, but suddenly the thought of going to another country with him, even if it was just south of San Diego, excited her. Carpet time in another country? *Qué romantico.*

"We can still go to Santa Barbara," Alex said quickly. "And maybe he'd wanna come out to SB, too."

"Who?" Evie's mind was still south of the border—the border south of the U.S., that is.

"Gorby," Alex said.

"Can't just you and I go?" Evie asked.

"Uh, yeah," Alex said slowly. "I just thought that because he was new and he surfed and didn't know too many people that it might be cool to take him around. You don't mind, do you? He's good people."

"Oh yeah. Of course." Evie smirked. "I don't mind." She regretted asking if she could have Sunday alone with Alex.

She remembered reading an article, in another one of Dee Dee's magazines, about obnoxious girlfriend types. *"Posesiva o No? Decide Tú."*

"Yeah, I'll have to make sure he gets an invite to my party," Evie said.

"Totally."

"So," Evie started to ask Alex, "what do you think you're gonna wear?"

"Wear for what?"

"Alex." Evie looked at him. "For my party."

"Oh, I have no idea," he confessed. "I don't plan that far in advance."

"Maybe we could go shopping together," Evie suggested.

"Shopping?" Alex looked over at her and winced.

"I mean, we could just go looking at some stuff," Evie tried to clarify. "There's this balcony at Duke's, and it overlooks the ocean and the view is so cool. I was thinking we could have our picture taken on it, with the sunset or something in the background. If we had on outfits that matched, it would be so cool."

"You want to wear *matching* outfits?" Alex covered his mouth and laughed. "Oh, *sheeyat.*"

"No." Evie felt embarrassed. "I'm just saying we could have outfits that, at least, look good together, like coordinated. I want to wear something really fancy, glamorous."

"Glamorous?" Alex asked. "I thought this was a Mexican

luau thing. Won't everyone be in, like, Hawaiian dresses or, like, guayaberas or something?"

"Maybe," Evie said. "But it's an evening party and it's at Duke's. I'm sure people are gonna dress up. I know I am."

"Uh-huh," Alex said. "Well, okay. Whatever you want."

But he didn't sound very enthused to Evie, and it bummed her out. She looked out the truck's window. How could Alex not understand how important her sixteeñera was to her? Sabrina never had such a party, and neither did Dee Dee or Raquel. Her sixteeñera would really set her apart—from everyone. Years later, when people looked at her picture in the yearbook, she wouldn't be remembered as a chillin' Flojo girl or as the chica who had honey-blond highlights one semester. She might not even be remembered as Alex Perez's girlfriend. She was going to be remembered as Evie Gomez, the girl who had the supercoolest Sweet Sixteeñera that, like Big Bulge said, knocked the 805 right on its ass. How could Alex not understand that?

7

EVIE'S RAINBOW FLIP-FLOPS KICKED UP DUST AS SHE FOLLOWED THE
handwritten signs directing her to the SCHR's horse stable.
The signs also made very clear, in large block letters, that NO
SMOKING OR CELL PHONES were allowed on the reserve. But Evie
had to worry about the latter only. She turned off her cell and
stuck it in the back pocket of her cotton walking shorts. *There.*
She already felt proud that she was turning over a new charitable leaf. To donate a whole afternoon without text messages
would once have been inconceivable for Evie Gomez.

But as soon as she saw the other volunteers, seated in fold-
up chairs formed in a semicircle, Evie's stomach slowly
turned with first-day jitters. She remembered that she was at
the reserve *to work*. Well, duh. She would be following orders
and would have to do tasks that she didn't necessarily want to
do. At fifteen and three quarters, Evie had never really had a

job. Sure, as kids, she, Dee Dee, and Raquel had a cute little lemonade stand like all kids had in the summer, and she had often helped her father out at one of his *panaderías*, but both "jobs" were just for fun. Now, cuteness wouldn't cut it. Her stomach turned again.

She looked around the group. The majority of volunteers were not high school sophomores, like herself, but rather seniors. Not *high school* seniors, but seniors, as in senior *citizens*. Old people. There were eight of them, small, slouching, and fragile-looking in baggy, high-waisted jeans and nylon Windbreakers. A few of the men even sported small war veteran pins (World War *I*?) on the lapels of their polo shirts.

To Evie's relief, there was one other volunteer, a girl, who looked about her age. She was slim and extremely pale, with black shoulder-length hair and thick, heavy bangs. The girl looked like Emily Strange, the scowling antiheroine with the crossed-arm attitude she had gotten to know via Raquel's tight baby tees. Evie took a seat in the empty folding chair next to her.

A woman in a denim sun hat walked over and stood in front of the volunteers. Evie shaded her eyes from the late afternoon sun and listened to the woman introduce herself as Lynn, the owner of the reserve, and talk a little bit about its history. *Yawn.* Evie looked around. She'd *better* get credit for this humdrum part of the orientation. She was just about to pull out her cell phone and text Alex, but then she remembered that cell phone usage was a no-no.

"I'm not here that often," Lynn explained to all the volunteers, "so you will be trained by Arturo. He has been with the reserve for over a year, and I really trust him. He's a real *buena persona*. And with that—" She looked over at a guy sitting in the front row that Evie hadn't noticed before. "—I'll let Arturo take over."

Arturo got up from his chair and was greeted with overly enthusiastic applause.

Evie heard the Emily Strange girl mutter under her breath when she saw Arturo, *"Nice."*

Evie looked at Arturo. Yeah, he was nice looking, if you liked that country, rural kind of look, which she didn't. He was tall, like Alex, but not so wiry. He had brown hair like Alex's, but his was a lot shorter. His eyes were light, almost green, and he was very tan, which Evie did like, but he wore cowboy boots, which Evie definitely didn't like. *Qué* fugly.

"My name's Arturo," he introduced himself again. "You can call me Turo if you like, but just don't call me last-minute to cancel your hours."

The whole group, minus Emily Strange Girl, laughed out loud.

Evie looked over the group. Arturo's comment was *so* not LOL-worthy. But she had come to learn, again through Raquel, that sympathy chuckles (sometimes called kiss-ass giggles) could go a long way when directed toward those in charge. ("I *swear* I passed Social Studies," Raquel had claimed, "only because I was the only one in the whole friggin' class who laughed at Mercer's stupid little one-liners.")

"No, but seriously," Arturo continued as he clapped his hands together, "the horses here have already gone through a lot, so if you aren't truly committed to being here, then you need to think of another option for volunteer work. We, actually, *they* really need responsible individuals to help take care of them."

Arturo went on to explain that he was a senior at Thatcher High School and was also an officer with the FFA, the Future Farmers of America.

That just about killed Evie. The FFA? What, he was a sheep-herder, too?

"A lot of people think the FFA is just an organization that focuses solely on raising livestock, but the FFA is much more than that," he was explaining, sounding almost smug. "We learn leadership and management skills. I'm the head director for Ventura County, a position that I'm *very* proud of. Now I'm running for state director, which is a position I feel pretty confident I'll win."

Evie looked around at the group again. Was this guy for real? The Emily Strange girl was working on a blemish under her chin, but everyone else, especially Lynn, seemed very taken by Arturo and his credentials with the Future Farmers of America. FFA? *BFD.*

Arturo went on. "We also have horses that are boarded here." He pointed to five stables toward the far back of the reserve. "They're basically our bread and butter. Their owners' rent pays for our feed, our supplies, and part of our own rent." He rubbed his palms together and paused. Evie took the gesture to mean that the orientation was nearly over. She sat up anxiously in her seat and waited for those three magical words: *So, in conclusion.*

"So, in keeping with that," Arturo said, "who's ready to meet our clients?"

No. There's more? Evie slumped back down in her metal chair. All the older volunteers chuckled again at Arturo's reference to the horses being clients, and they raised their hands in anticipation. As everyone got up to follow him to the stables, Lynn excused herself from the group.

"Have fun and be sure to listen to Arturo," she said before adjusting her denim sun hat and heading toward her pickup truck. "I need to get a new delivery of feed, but I'll be back before you leave."

As Arturo took the group to see the horses, Evie fell into step with the Emily Strange girl, who glanced over at her.

"I like your necklace," she said.

"Oh." Evie fingered the chips of abalone shells dangling from the cord. "Thanks. My boyfriend made it for me."

"Oh." Emily made a face like she just had caught a kitten midyawn. "That is *too* sweet."

Okay, maybe the girl emulated Emily, but she obviously had a *sentida* side.

"What school do you go to?" she asked Evie.

"Villanueva," Evie answered.

The girl threw Evie a knowing glance. "Fan-*cee*. You must have money."

"I don't," Evie answered awkwardly. "But my parents do. Or at least my dad does, but he works. A lot."

"And your mother doesn't?" she asked.

"No, not really."

"Oh," the girl said. "So you *do* have money."

Evie always felt a bit uncomfortable when other cool kids questioned her family's financial position. Money usually represented *novela* vanilla—that is *boring*—and Evie was so not *that*.

"Where do you go?" she asked Emily Strange.

"I don't, really," Emily Strange answered. "I mean, I do independent study at New Path."

New Path was a continuation school at the north end of the county. Unlike Nueva, in all its majestic Spanish architectural splendor, New Path was just a bunch of whitewashed Quonset huts and nondescript bungalows. Evie knew only one other person who went to New Path—Jose, Raquel's ex-boyfriend.

"Do you know a guy named Jose?" Evie asked. She couldn't help but feel a little bit Emily Strange herself, hoping to hear that Jose was doing badly. But he *had* been quite the dick to her and, of course, to Raquel, last semester.

"Jose . . ." Emily Strange Girl squinted her eyes in thought. "Is he a Mexican guy with wild hair, like a 'fro?"

"Yeah." Evie nodded.

"Oh yeah." Emily Girl smiled slyly. "*Everyone* knows *that* Jose."

"I'm sure they do." Evie smirked. "He used to go to my school and—"

"Excuse me, are we interrupting you?"

Evie looked up and realized that Arturo was staring right at her. Suddenly, ten pairs of eyes were on Evie.

"Uh, no." Evie's face felt hot. "I'm sorry. What did you say?"

"Please." Arturo looked upward in annoyance. "I really don't want to go over this again."

"I know." Evie felt the need to stand up straight. "I'm paying attention."

Arturo glanced down at Evie's feet. "And you can't be wearing flip-flops around the stables. We won't be taking these horses down for any stroll on the beach, at least not anytime soon."

All the volunteers, even Emily Strange, chuckled.

"I just came from school," Evie explained. "I didn't know." Her feet suddenly felt naked. She placed one flip-flop over the other.

"You wear flip-flops *and* shorts to school?" Arturo directed his question less to Evie and more to his newly acquired audience that was now at the mercy of his desperate jokes. "And did you used to wear a bathing suit to catechism?"

More tittering from the geriatric gallery.

Where was this guy *from*? Evie wondered. Everyone knew of the lax dress code at Villanueva. And *hello*, that was just a *little* presumptuous of him to assume that she was Catholic and had even attended catechism—which she was and did, *thank* you.

"What is your name?" Arturo looked over his clipboard.

"Evie, Evie Gomez."

"Ah yes," Arturo said. "You were just added, right?"

"Uh, yeah."

The magnifying glass was definitely being held steady and stern over Evie.

"Let me tell you something, Evie," Arturo said. "I know this is a volunteer position, but you need to take your work here seriously. I'm not going to hand out credit just because you show up. You're going to have to work hard."

"I know," Evie said. Jeez, Mr. "Friend of the Animals" was really coming down hard on the two-footed upright mammal that stood before him.

"So, anyway," Arturo continued, still annoyed, "back to the real reason why we're all here: the care and rehabilitation of our horses."

Arturo then led everyone to each stall and introduced each horse by name. Evie noticed that just about everyone took notes, and many went so far as to draw out a diagram of the reserve. She glanced over and saw that even Emily Strange was writing something in her black fur–covered notebook. Evie immediately felt inadequate and didn't know what to do with her empty hands. Usually she would fiddle with her cell phone, but now that wasn't an option.

"Let's go give old Chamuco a visit," Arturo announced after the group had been introduced to the last of at least twenty horses. "Chamuco is one of our oldest residents. He was seized from a ranch in Santa Ynez. When he first came here, he was starving and dehydrated, but he has come a long way."

The whole group followed Arturo to a stall far away from the other horses. A chestnut-colored stallion came over to the group, lazily chewing on strands of hay. He had a dark mane and white stockings on both hind legs; his eyes, however, were oddly clouded, almost pure white. It was clear that Chamuco was blind. The whole group let out a collective sympathetic *"Aaaw."*

"Even though his name means devil in Spanish—" Arturo got into the stall with him. "—Chamuco is one of our sweetest horses." He pulled a carrot out of his side pocket and fed it to Chamuco while he started talking baby talk. "Aw, ar-unt choo, Cha-muuco? You've had a toof time. Poor *bouy.*"

Evie glanced over at one of the volunteers, a woman about four feet tall with gray hair tucked under a silk scarf, who kept scribbling fiercely on her notepad. Evie looked over at the pad. "Chamuco/devil, has come a long way, pick up PoliGrip on the way home."

"Who'd like to meet Chamuco?" Arturo asked, more as a challenge than a question, as if no one would dare enter the stable with him.

No one said anything.

Arturo looked over the group. "What about you, Evie?" he asked. "Why don't you come in and say hi to ol' Chamuco?"

"Me?" Evie pointed to herself. The whole group parted like the Red Sea, as though they were allowing Evie to pass and complete a very important mission.

"Sure." Arturo motioned her to step the inside the stable. "Come on in."

Evie stepped away from the group and slid between the fence's slants. Her suede Rainbow flip-flops sank into the muddy earth, and all the horseflies that had been pestering Chamuco buzzed around her face and hair. She tried to swat them away.

"You have to be careful with horses like Chamuco," Arturo warned her, as well as everyone else. "They can easily get startled and give you a good, swift kick. Which reminds me—" He looked at the group again with a playful smirk on his face. "—did everyone fill out the liability forms?"

Everyone laughed except Evie. She crept cautiously around Chamuco, allowing him adequate space so he couldn't possibly feel threatened, but just as she was making her way to the right of him, her cell started ringing. The wailing cry of Moz blared from the back pocket of her walking shorts. It startled

Evie, but not nearly so much as it startled Chamuco. His entire gigantic body jerked sideways, and his neck arched like a two-ton cobra ready to strike.

"Whoa, whoa, whoa!" Arturo tried to grab Chamuco by his harness. "Easy does it, boy."

Chamuco swayed his head from left to right. He stamped his two front hooves ferociously on the ground, kicking up mud and dirt as Evie cowered at the side of the stable and fumbled to turn off her phone.

"Get *out* of the stable!" Arturo yelled at Evie as Chamuco picked up his pace around the corral. His ears were pulled back, and he was starting to knock his body against the wooden slats of the fence.

The volunteers watched in horror.

"Turo, should we go get help?" one of them called out.

"No, no," Arturo insisted. "I got him, I got him."

After what seemed a good long while, Chamuco finally calmed down. Arturo stroked his mane, offered him another carrot from his back pocket, and talked softly in annoying baby talk. Chamuco, it seemed, was finally *relajado*. Arturo, on the other hand, was *enojado*. Big-time.

"You *cannot* have your cell phone here!" Arturo spat at Evie from the stable. "Didn't you see the signs before you came in?"

"Yeah." Evie tried her best to defend herself. "I mean, yes, I did." She felt horrible that she was to blame for what had just happened. The last thing she wanted was to traumatize some poor, blind, defenseless animal that had already been through so much. "I thought I had turned it off."

"Why would you even *need* your phone?" Arturo snapped. He then addressed all the volunteers. "Do *not* bring your cells near the stables. At *all*. Keep cell phones in your car or in the supply shed."

One elderly man with thick white hair and wearing a light blue baseball cap raised his hand. "Uh, Turdo, I have a question." He looked around at the rest of the group in confusion.

"It's *Turo*." Arturo shook his head in exhausted frustration.

"Oh, um, sorry," the elderly man started cautiously. "Um, none of us have mobile phones. Is that going to be a problem?"

"*No.*" Arturo answered, exasperated. "Don't worry about it."

Emily Strange Girl looked over at Evie. "Boy," she whispered, "it looks like you sure made a friend."

8

"HOW WAS YOUR FIRST DAY, MI'JA?" EVIE'S MOTHER ASKED FROM THE kitchen. She was eating half an avocado sprinkled with chili powder as Evie came into the house with Lindsay. "Did you make any new friends?"

Evie had spent only a little over three hours at the SCHR, but her body ached as though she had busted her butt driving cattle for three years. She saw that Alex had called her four times, but she was so tired, she didn't call him back. She'd nearly fallen asleep in Lindsay's car on the way home from the reserve, which, to Evie, was a good thing. The less time she had to discuss her fender bender with Lindsay, the better.

"Ugh." All Evie could do was groan in resonse to her mother's questions. She went to the fridge and poured herself some Kern's watery *horchata*. Would Lindsay ever find the time to make thick, creamy horchata from scratch, like she used to?

"Alex called and—" Her mother suddenly sneezed as she always did when she got overindulgent with chili powder. "—he said he had been trying you all day on your cell phone but you never answered. He was getting worried."

"We can't use our phones at the reserve," Evie said. "It spooks the horses."

She decided to leave out the incident with Chamuco the Devil. She still couldn't get the look of pure fright in his eyes out of her head, pure fright *she* had caused.

"You have to tell us all about it." Her mother was now scraping the worn sides of the avocado hull with a spoon for any possible remaining flesh. "Your father's gonna be home soon. You want something to eat until then?"

"Nuh-uh." Evie moaned as she took her glass of horchata upstairs with her. "I just wanna take a long bath."

"Evie, wait," her mother called after her. "I want to talk to you."

"What?"

"You know your father is really serious about canceling this party," her mother said.

"I know," Evie replied glumly. Hadn't she just worked her ass off all afternoon to make sure it didn't get canceled? Of course she knew.

"I really need you to know how serious he is. If you don't

bring your GPA up, you will not only lose the party, but *we* will also lose a lot of money. I already ordered the invitations, and there are the three nonrefundable deposits we made for Duke's, for the food, and for DJ Chancla."

"I know," Evie repeated. Jeez, could she feel any more pressured?

"And your father and I have already asked a lot of our friends from the country club and a lot of family to hold the date for the party," her mother continued. "So I just hope you keep that in mind and that you *are* serious about improving your grades."

"Mom, I am," Evie told her. "Can't you tell? Look at me: I'm covered in sweat and shit, and I've been slaving away all afternoon."

"Evie—" Her mother's eyes narrowed in on her. "—do *not* use that language with me."

"Okay, okay, I'm sorry." Evie said, "Can I go now?"

"Yes." Her mother looked at her sternly. "Go on."

Evie continued up the stairs. God, the *nerve* of her mother. It was like her concern about the party was just for her own sake, just to save face and money. If she wanted the party so friggin' bad, why didn't she just clock in under Evie's name and muck horse poop herself?

Evie slowly made her way into the bathroom of her parents' master bedroom and turned the dial of their oversizeddd Jacuzzi to high. After she lit two vanilla-scented candles and mixed her favorite lavender oil into the whirling jet streams, she stripped off her stinky clothes and slid into the hot water. She called Alex from her cell phone.

"So, how was it?" he asked. "I kept calling you and you never answered. I was worried you got dragged off by a horse or something."

"I feel like I was. I am *so* tired." Evie yawned. "And this was just the orientation. The guy in charge totally had it out for me. He's like, this total kiss-ass FFA dork. He made me get in a stall with the most freaked-out horse at the reserve and totally went out of his way to make me look like an idiot in front of everyone."

"What an asshole," Alex said. "Maybe you should just suck it up and find a tutor and forget all this horse crap."

"No way." Evie rubbed a pumice stone across the bottom of her foot. "There is no way in hell I'm gonna join SSIT."

"Well, maybe this guy's just coming on strong at first," Alex guessed. "You know how teachers do that, play the tough guy first and then soften up later."

"We'll see." Evie yawned again. "But either way, he was a jerk, and speaking of horse crap, he put me and this other girl on doodie patrol."

"What do you mean?"

"I mean I have to clean up after the horses," Evie said. "All of them."

"Are you serious?" Alex laughed. "How many horses do they have?"

"Twenty *too* many. Thank God I just have to go a few times after school."

"I hope it's just a few times," Alex said. "You really missed some good surf today."

"Thanks," Evie answered sarcastically. She could hear Alex's TV. "What are you watching?"

"Surf porn," Alex said. "You know, big waves, big music."

"Big boobs," Evie teased.

"Hmmm, I didn't notice . . ." Alex tried to sound convincing. "Oh, Gorby's over too."

"Oh yeah?" Evie asked.

"Yeah, we met up today, and I was telling him about all of us going down to Baja sometime."

So Alex *did* want to make their Baja trip into a surf-dude weekend.

"Well, just make sure it's on a weekend that I can go," Evie said.

"Yeah, yeah," Alex said. "Of course."

Just then Evie's call-waiting double-beeped, and she saw that it was Dee Dee on the other line.

"Hey, it's Dee Dee," she told Alex. "You mind if I take her call? I haven't talked to her since school."

"Nah," Alex said. "I'll try you later tonight."

Evie clicked over to Dee Dee.

"Hola, charra!" Dee Dee said. "So, how did it go?"

"Don't even ask." Evie was set to uncork her whine all over again. "It sucked. Big-time."

"But it's all going to be so worth it," Dee Dee insisted. "As soon as you get your GPA up, you can have your party, and your life will be so set."

"I hope so." Evie wasn't feeling as confident as she had a few days earlier. She ran the pumice stone under the bottom of her other foot. "You should have heard my mother tonight. She was all guilt-tripping me about the party and everything. It's like she's throwing the party for herself or something."

"*Serio?*" Dee Dee asked. "Well, at least she's on your side."

"Well, she could be on my side another way. Like she could grab a shovel and help me at the reserve."

Dee Dee laughed. "So, *oye*, I haven't told you the most exciting news."

"What?" Evie asked.

"I talked to Rocio today . . . ," Dee Dee said, then paused. Evie figured she was trying to create an air of anticipation, but no such air was created. Dee Dee talked to Rocio every day. Their conversations were far from being "the most exciting news."

"And?" Evie asked.

"So guess what?" Dee Dee said.

"*What* already!"

"He's thinking of going to college out here," Dee Dee announced. Evie could sense that she just wanted to explode on the other end of the line.

"Wow, really?" Evie asked. "You mean, here in the U.S. or in Cali?"

"Here," Dee Dee said. "In California."

"NorCal or SoCal?"

"Evie," Dee Dee said. "South Cal, of course. *Qué chido,* no?"

"Uh, no," Evie answered. "I mean, right, it's cool," she corrected. "Is he coming out here because of you?"

"Evie, *claro,* of course." Dee Dee seemed to sound frustrated. Didn't Evie know the depth of his devotion to her? "He hasn't ever had any desire to ever leave La Condesa. That is, until he met me."

"That is so sweet," Evie said. She wondered if Alex would ever do anything like that for her. Making an abalone shell necklace was one thing, but moving to an entirely different country was another. He had, however, suggested they go to Baja sometime soon, and that was another country, sorta.

"So anyway," Dee Dee continued, "Rocio's coming out to research some schools, and I asked him if he could stay a little longer to make it to your sixteeñera."

"Really?" Evie asked. "He's coming that soon?"

"Uh-huh," Dee Dee said. "He knows all about you. He can't wait for your party."

"Wow." Evie felt flattered. She was getting used to the idea that people she had never even met, from Rocio to all her MySpace friends (up to 220!), knew all about Evie, aka RioChica805. At least about her party, anyway.

"God, Evie, your party is going to be *tan chido.*" Dee Dee

continued to make Evie's head swell. "I already know what I'm wearing *and* what I'm going to buy you."

"Really? What are you getting me?"

"I'm not telling you, *tonta*, but you are going to love them."

"*Them?* So it's a plural present?" This would be the first birthday in four years that Evie would get to share with Dee Dee. As a kid, Dee Dee, or at least her mother, was known for doing it up with over-the-top, perfectly selected gifts. Not that presents were what a birthday celebration was all about, but *still*.

"Oh—" Dee Dee's voice broke up over another call-waiting beep. "That's Rocio."

"Of course," Evie said.

"*Ándale, pues,*" Dee Dee remarked.

"Lates." Evie clicked off.

After Evie hung up with Dee Dee, she realized that the pressure was on. She *had* to bring her GPA up so she could have her sixteeñera. She *had* to. She set the Jacuzzi jets back to high. The hot water blasted again, soothing her muscles. She stank like a sweaty horse blanket, her arms ached, and she was still scheduled to practice driving with her father later that evening. And she had yet to check in with Raquel, but when she finally got out of the bath, she was so tired that she fell asleep shortly before dinner and didn't wake up until early the next morning.

9

THE REST OF THE WEEK AT THE SCHR WAS RIDICULOUSLY STRESSFUL
for Evie. Thursday and Friday Alex drove her to the reserve
directly after school to work a four-hour shift, followed by an
evening of homework, phone calls, approval of new MySpace
friend requests, IMs, and *Laguna Beach* before, finally, the
final good-night texting with Alex before going to bed.

Alex:

Nite QT. TTYL

Evie:

Nite :)

By the beginning of her second week of work, Evie noticed
that the palms of her hands felt rough. Now that she was in a
relationship with Alex, she had become a card-carrying hand-
holder. Rough, callused hands would so not do.

"Hey, didn't *Turdo* say they kept gloves around here?"

Evie asked the Emily Strange girl, whose real name was Tori.

"Yeah." Tori looked up from watering down the dirt with a hose. "They have some in one of the bins in the shed."

Evie rolled the muck bucket toward the supply shed to get a pair of work gloves, but when she entered the structure, she was overpowered by the strong smell of peppermint. She noticed a girl in the shed, reclining casually on the top of three stacked plastic bins. Her legs were crossed at the ankles, as if the supply shed were her very own parlor. Evie often escaped the sharp rays of the winter sun by taking short breaks in the cool shade of the supply shed, so the girl's presence wasn't that alarming. Evie glanced over at the girl. She was wearing tight, high-waisted beige riding pants with black leather riding boots that looked so polished, they must have just come right out of the box. The girl also wore a black satin camisole, styled like a corset and fastened with seemingly hundreds of miniature black satin–covered buttons. A single thick gold chain with an amber-colored pendant hung around her long brown neck and rested right in her ample cleavage. And Arturo thought that *she* had dressed inappropriately on her first day!

"Hey," Evie said as she started to pass her.

The girl offered a slight smile but nothing else. Her cigarette, positioned between her thin, delicate fingers, was causing the peppermint smell. Evie knew that Turdo would *flip* if he caught this girl smoking on the grounds, especially in the supply shed. She didn't necessarily like playing horse reserve monitor, but she figured she'd clue in a clueless volunteer.

"Oh, hey," Evie started. "You're not supposed to smoke, especially in here. The guy in charge is a complete control freak and will totally get on your case about it."

The girl looked right into Evie's eyes and took another slow drag from her scented cigarette. "The guy in charge?"

"Yeah." Evie pulled out a small plastic bucket from under a pile of wool blankets. She found a pair of suede work gloves and tried them on. Size Sasquatch compared to her small hands, but they would have to do. "Turdo." She smiled. "That's the little name we gave him."

The girl looked at Evie with a blank expression on her face.

Evie laughed to herself. "You haven't met him?"

"Me?" The girl took an even slower pull from her cigarette and smirked. "Oh, yes, I've met him."

Just then, Arturdo entered the shed.

"Josephina," he said as he took the cigarette from out of the girl's fingers and held it above her head, "you know better than that. *No* smoking." He then put his arm around the girl's waist, making sure to keep the cigarette high, away from both of them, as he leaned in to kiss her.

No *way*. This girl had obviously met Arturdo and knew him well—*quite* well. *Sheeyat.*

"I know." The girl looked toward Evie. "I was just repri-manded? By this helper?"

Reprimanded? This *helper?*

The girl ended her sentences as if each were a question, typical San Fernando Valley speak that had somehow made it down the Conejo Grade and into Rio Estates. This Josephina person had obviously been infected with the inflection.

Arturdo looked over toward Evie. He hadn't noticed that she was crouched down beside the extra saddles and blankets, trying on work gloves.

"What do you need, Evie?" he demanded. He loosened his embrace around Josephina, and she took back her cigarette.

"Just some gloves." Evie held them up to prove that she wasn't goofing off from work or, worse, trying to snoop in his personal affairs. "I was just on my way to dump the daily load."

The girl's body stiffened as she slithered out of Arturdo's arms. "Turo—" Her tone sounded whiny. "*Cuidado.* You're gonna wrinkle my cami?"

Arturo pulled back. The girl looked at Evie blankly, prompting him to introduce her.

"This is Evie," he told the girl. "She's one of the volunteers from Villanueva."

"Villanueva?" Josephina asked.

"Yeah," Evie said.

The girl studied Evie. "I just met a girl? Who goes to Villanueva?"

"Oh, really?" Evie asked. "Who?" Villanueva had about

three hundred students, including the resident students, and everyone knew just about everyone else, or at least their secondhand *chisme*. "You probably don't know her?" Josephina guessed. "Dela? Dela de LaFuente?"

"Dela?" Evie said. "You mean Dee Dee? She's, like, my best friend. How do you know her?"

"You're *Dela's* best friend?" The girl's dark eyes widened. "I would have never imagined that."

"Uh, yeah," Evie said. "We've been best friends since we were little kids. Even when she lived in Mexico City, we were tight."

Not quite the truth, but Evie felt as though she had to prove to this girl, whom she now deemed snooty, that Dee Dee was, indeed, a very, very dear friend, her ADA.

"I just met Dela," she said as she held out her hand. "I'm Josephina? From Las Hermanas Senior Committee?"

Dee Dee had mentioned the Las Hermanas Senior Committee to both Evie and Raquel. The committee was made up of high school seniors who had a small say as to who would be selected as a new Hermana for the incoming year. Dee Dee had the best résumé possible, but it always helped to have a good connection. Could Josephina possibly be one for Dee Dee?

"Oh, right." Evie nodded and shook Josephina's hand. She had forgotten to remove the oversized work gloves and felt like a big clumsy bear mauling a delicate fawn. She wasn't used to an introduction followed with a handshake, unless it was with an adult she was trying to impress. Had she committed a major faux pas by leaving the gloves on? Oh, she hoped it didn't lose points for Dee Dee.

"Are you a volunteer too?" Evie asked.

"Hardly?" Josephina frowned. "I keep my horse here?" She lifted her chin in the direction of one of the back stables. "Princesa? She's mine."

"Oh." Evie looked over in the same direction. "I know Princesa, or at least what comes *out* of her." Evie laughed, but Josephina's face didn't crack a crease.

"No, but really, Princesa is sweet." Evie felt stupid saying such a thing. Was commenting on a pet's poop just as bad as telling a parent that his or her child was ugly?

Just then, Tori poked her head in the supply shed. *"Evie,"* she huffed in annoyance. "The wheelbarrow is still out here. You haven't dumped it yet?"

"I was just about to." Evie slid past Arturdo and Josephina and walked toward the wheelbarrow.

"Tori," Arturdo interrupted, "why don't both you and Evie do it so we can all get out of here quicker?"

"But Evie was gonna do it," Tori protested.

"Just help her," Arturdo said. "It's getting late, and I promised to take Josephina to the pier before the sun sets."

Tori took a hold of the wheelbarrow. "Come on, *Evie.*"

Evie and Tori headed toward the manure pile.

"Who *was* that?" Tori asked.

"I guess Arturo's girlfriend."

"Oh, I thought it was one of your fancy-ass friends from your fancy-ass school."

"*None* of my friends look, act, or dress like that," Evie insisted.

"She looks like she was about to go hunting with the hounds . . . but forgot to change out of her Victoria's Secret nightie." Tori laughed. "What's her name?"

"Josephina," Evie said. "Josephin-*a*."

Evie thought of the Sangros—Alejandr*a*, Xiomar*a*, Fabiol*a*, and Natali*a*. Did all things flashy and bitchy have first names that ended in *a*? Wait a minute, Evie's given name was Evelina, and Tori was actually Victoria, and, of course, Dee Dee was Dela. Oh, *never* mind.

10

WHEN EVIE WOKE UP ON THAT FIRST SATURDAY IN FEBRUARY, HER inner Flojo just wanted an afternoon devoted to complete chill. She had worked a full three weeks at the SCHR, and she still had to go to a fund-raiser for the reserve later that night. Yes, chill was in order. She lay in her bed, blissfully devoid of duties or obligation. Nothing would get her out of bed— nothing, except maybe the call of Sea Street. And sure enough, Alex's text beckoned her.

    C st?

To which she texted back,

    Rdy in 20.

It had been too long since she and Alex had gone surfing, and there was no way she was going to miss out on some choice waves this Saturday. She slowly got out of bed, slipped on her Sanuk Fur-Real flip-flops, and looked for her bathing suit. No doubt she'd also have to wear her full-length winter wet suit, but once she got out of the water, she liked to peel her suit down to her waist so she could brown her shoulders and belly. No matter what time of the year, it was mandatory she stay tan. How could you be a surfer girl and not look like one?

"Lindsay," she called out as she dug to the bottom of her wicker hamper, "have you seen my bikini top? The light blue Roxy?"

"I can't hear you when you yell like that!" Lindsay yelled from the kitchen.

"My bathing suit?" Evie called out from her bedroom's doorway. "The blue one. Have you seen it?"

"No, Evelina," Lindsay answered. "Are you going for a swim? Because maybe you should wait. The pool man was here this morning, and it's still filtering."

"No, I'm gonna go surfing with Alex!" Evie yelled out again. "He's gonna pick me up in a bit."

"Evelina, you can't go to the beach." Lindsay was now coming up the stairs, drying her hands with a kitchen towel. "Sabrina is coming home today."

"I know." Evie went back into her room. She gave up on her hamper and looked around her bathroom floor. Where there once were bikini tops and towels covered with sand, now there were jeans and tennis shoes embedded with mud, straw, and bits of hay. "But not until later today, right?"

"*Sí,*" Lindsay said, "but your mother wanted you to stick around, just in case."

"Just in case of what?" Evie didn't want to waste time looking for her blue suit. Alex was on his way. She grabbed her lime green one from the top drawer of her dresser.

"I don't know, Evelina," Lindsay said. "You should ask her."

"Are you serious?" Evie looked at Lindsay in disbelief. "She wants me to stay home *all day?*"

"I think so," Lindsay said. "But you should really ask her."

Evie marched downstairs and found her mother out on the deck with her father.

"Mom," Evie said, "Lindsay just told me that I have to stick around home today. Is that true?"

Her mother looked up from the deck chair to which she was tying a new green seat cushion. The new green place mats that she had finally chosen just didn't go with the less-new cushions. "What was all that yelling going on inside the house?" she asked.

"Nothing," Evie said. *Don't try to change the subject.* "So, do I have to stay home today?"

"Yes," her mother answered. "I'm going to pick your sister up at the airport, and I need you to be here when we get back. Your father is barbecuing."

"Right." Evie still didn't see the need to stay home *all* day. "So, I'm gonna leave with Alex right now, and I can make sure I'm home by . . . three? Is that a good time?"

"Evie, no." Her mother started to tie a cushion to another chair. "I need you to be here. Besides, you won't be here tonight, right? You have that fund-raiser."

"Yeah, but that's not until later, like at seven," Evie pointed out. "I could be here a whole four hours, just for Sabrina." She looked at her cell phone. T minus ten minutes until Alex arrived.

"Evie, stop it," her mother said sternly. "Sabrina isn't feeling well, and I don't want her coming home to an empty house. You are her sister. You need to be here."

Was it just Evie, or was her whole family getting a little too *sentida* over Sabrina's breakup with what's-his-name?

"Mom," Evie whined, "I've had to work for the last three weeks, and I have to go to the work thing tonight. This is my only day off, and I haven't gone to the beach in, like, forever."

"Evie." Her father threw her a serious look. "You are not going anywhere today, and you shouldn't even be making plans without asking me or your mother. You need to consult us if you are planning a whole day at the beach."

Consult? When did her father start talking like that? Obviously, he had been spending way too much time with her mother.

"So, you're basically saying I can't go with Alex," Evie said, "even though he's already on his way over here?"

Evie's mother threw her a deep, hard look that clearly didn't need a vocalized answer.

"Well," Evie grumbled as she flipped open her cell phone "I *guess* I better text him. Hopefully he hasn't left yet."

"I have a better idea," her mother suggested. "Why don't you call him? Have you ever tried *that*?"

Evie:

> **Cnt go. Mom OTR**
> **Cll me l8r?**

Alex:

> **Bmr. Ttyl.**

Evie stomped up to her room, tossed her cell phone onto a pile of dirty horse reserve clothes, and fell onto her bed. *Grrr!* Sabrina was a family member, not some VIP who deserved a UN welcoming committee. She sat up, grabbed her remote from the nightstand, and pointed it at her CD player. She put on her headphones and cranked up Moz. But by the time she was on the second song, she yanked them off her ears and called Raquel.

"*Ee*-yes?" Raquel answered.

"I hate my mother," Evie announced.

"Are you calling me for sympathy or to plot her demise? Because if it's the latter, you best take a number. I still gotta take care of my own mom."

"Don't tempt me," Evie said. "My mom is totally on my case."

"When is she not?"

"I have to stay home all day," Evie complained. "This is,

like, my one free day in, like, forever, and now I have to stick around just to wait for Sabrina. I totally wanted to go surfing with Alex."

"If you wanted to go surfing so badly, maybe you should've gotten up earlier," Raquel teased. "Isn't that what real surfers do? What is it called? Yawn patrol?"

"Dawn patrol," Evie corrected. "And you are *so* not advising me." She yanked the headphones from her CD player and clicked off Moz, who was depressing her even more. She switched to Go Betty Go. "If I wasn't working at the reserve all week, it wouldn't be such a big deal."

"Why are you working at that horse place so much?" Raquel asked.

"Vasquez-Reyes Alarcón," Evie sighed, referring to her Civics teacher. "He wants me to put in at least fifteen hours a week.

"That's ricockulous!" howled Raquel.

"What's ricockulous?" Evie asked.

"It's like *ridiculous*, but more hard-core."

Evie laughed. "But seriously, I don't know why everyone is making it so difficult for me to do better. And speaking of ricockulous, that guy, Turdo, the one I was telling you about? He's still treating me like such a doormat at the reserve. He makes fun of me in front of all the other volunteers and has me do all the dirty work."

"Sounds like sexual tension to me," Raquel mused.

"*Please*, the thought of Turdo in any intimate setting is just too repulsive." Evie realized that she was not in the mood for any music and clicked off her CD player. "So, do you wanna stop by and say hi to Suprema later?"

"Nah," Raquel said. "I mean I'd like to, but Davey's gonna pick me up."

"Weren't you just with him last night?" Evie asked.

"*Sí, tía.*" Raquel said. "But Los Olvidados are playing the street fair."

"The street fair?" Evie asked. "At Sea Street? I thought that was next weekend."

"Nuh-uh," Raquel said. "It's today. Didn't Alex tell you?"

"No, he didn't tell me. Not yet." Evie instantly felt left out. How could her own boyfriend not tell her that one of her favorite bands was playing a local street fair, a street fair near Sea Street, *their* place?

"Well, when was he gonna tell you?" Raquel asked. "It starts in a couple of hours. In fact, I better get going. Davey's gonna be here any minute, and I've gotta shower and shampoo. She yawned. "Angelina's still gotta give me a bikini wax."

"You have your *housekeeper* wax you?" Evie exclaimed. "That is *so* not right."

Raquel laughed. "Ha, I'm just fucking with you." She yawned again. "Oh, man, Davey and I got so lit last night. You know, I think I'm getting my tolerance up. I was able to pound a six-pack away last night."

"And that's something to be proud of?" Evie asked.

"Uh, *yeah*," Raquel said as if Evie should know better. "So, how long is Suprema gonna visit?"

"You know, I have no idea," Evie said. "Everyone keeps saying 'for a while,' and I have no idea what 'a while' means."

"Well, I hope she's still here by the time you have your party," Raquel said. "Wait until she finds out about all the free ad bevs I hooked up for your party."

"God, Raquel, you have such a one-track mind lately." Evie frowned. "My party isn't until the end of this month, and she'll be back at school by then. Besides, Sabrina's not a party *puta*. You know that."

"Are you kidding me?" Raquel asked. "All those sorority girls play it off like they're all these good little schoolgirls, but not even. One time, I was with Jose, and we went to some frat party over at UC Santa Barbara, and there were all these sorority girls there. They all had fake IDs and—oh my God— they were like the total slutty boozers of the whole party."

"Are you saying my sister is a boozing slut?"

"No," Raquel said. "I said she *might* be a slutty *boozer*. Big difference."

"E-ve-*liiina* . . ."

It was Lindsay calling down the hall from Sabrina's bedroom.

"Hold on." Evie put her bedroom landline to her chest. "*Qué quieres*, Lindsay?"

"Can you help me?" Lindsay called out. "Your mother and sister are coming back soon, and I'm trying to get Sabrina's room ready."

"My mother already left?" Evie asked.

"Yes, to the airport, to get Sabrina."

"Then she won't be back for a few hours," Evie called back. LAX, the Los Angeles International Airport, was a good three-hour round-trip journey from Rio Estates.

"No," Lindsay said. "She's picking her up at the Santa Barbara airport."

"Santa Barbara?" It was unusual that Sabrina would fly into Santa Barbara, a small commuter airport used primarily by jet-setting UC Santa Barbara students, businessmen, or maybe Oprah, who evidently had a house in nearby Montecito. Santa Barbara Airport was only twenty-five minutes from their home. Her mother would be back soon. "Why is she picking her up there?"

"Hel-*looo*?" Evie could hear Raquel on the other end of the landline.

Evie brought the receiver back to her ear. "Oops, sorry."

"Did you call to talk to me or to Lindsay?" Raquel asked.

"Hey, I better call you later," Evie told Raquel. "I gotta go."

"Uh, I figured that," Raquel said before clicking off.

Evie got up from her bed to help Lindsay.

"So, how long is Sabrina gonna visit?" she asked as she walked into Sabrina's bedroom. Lindsay was smoothing out the cream-colored comforter that lay on top of Sabrina's queen-size bed.

"I don't know how long," Lindsay said. "You should probably ask your parents."

Evie looked around her sister's bedroom. Sabrina kept everything in impeccable order. Her room was so tidy and in tip-top tight shape that you could practically bounce a quarter off the whole space—whereas Evie's bedroom was constantly under construction. She did, however, pride herself on the orderly fashion she maintained with her sandals. Three rows of flip-flops (seventeen pairs in all) were lined up on her closet floor. The first row contained the flip-flops with the heftiest price tag, the second row (the shortest row) was all about comfort, and the third row contained ones with jewels glittering from the straps. *Qué* Kimora, no?

Lindsay leaned up from the bed and glanced over at the photos of Sabrina and her now former boyfriend, Robert. They were tacked onto Sabrina's gingham cloth bulletin board. "Maybe we should take those down," she suggested.

"Are you serious?" Evie looked over at the photos. She had just opened Sabrina's vinyl CD carrier case, a relic from before iPod nation took over, and winced at her sister's taste in music. From classical piano to world music, Sabrina listened to ugh-dult music. How could she and Evie possibly be related?

"I think so." Lindsay started to pull out a white plastic

thumbtack from the corner of one of the pictures. "Your mother said she was *muy triste*. We don't want to make her more upset."

"I think she'd be way more upset that we're moving things around in her room." Evie closed the CD case. "She doesn't like her things messed with."

"Maybe you're right," Lindsay sighed. "But my job is to keep things in order, and besides, *I* don't want to be blamed if she gets sad."

"Hey, Linds," Evie ventured.

"*Sí?*" Lindsay tacked the photo of Sabrina and Robert back up on the board.

"I just wanna say I am really sorry about the car accident. I mean, the fender bender. I know you went out of your way to protect me and everything, and I hope I didn't get you in too much trouble. . . ."

"No, no," Lindsay said. "Your mother didn't have any idea what happened, and she's said nothing to me since that day. But what you did was very wrong, and I am very disappointed in you."

Evie's heart sank.

"You shouldn't lie to me or to anyone, Evelina. I hope these are not habits that you are picking up and thinking of keeping."

"No, no," Evie said. "I was just being stupid. It won't happen again." Evie's stomach twisted with guilt—she felt bad about the fender bender and that she was gonna have to dole out some b-day dough to pay for it, but she felt even worse that she had let down Lindsay. She had lied to her, and that was just plain shameful.

"Okay, I want to believe you." Lindsay looked at her. "*Pues*, I also got an estimate for the bill."

"The bill?" Evie's stomach twisted just a slight bit more. "So . . . how much is it?"

"It's twelve hundred."

"Twelve hundred *dollars*?" Evie asked.

"No, pesos." Lindsay smirked.

"Okay," Evie said weakly. That could not be. It was such a small dent! "I can get it. No problemo. Don't even worry."

"Okay, Evelina, I won't."

Lindsay put her hands on her ample hips and looked over Sabrina's room one more time. The carpet was vacuumed, and her stuffed chenille teddy bear hand-sewn by Grandma Cuca was propped against the overstuffed pillows. The TV remote and Sabrina's silk eye mask were poised politely on the night table—familiar *cositas* ready to welcome her when she returned home.

"Well, I think we're done here," Lindsay concluded. "Let's go see if your father needs any help."

Evie followed her outside to the deck, where her father should have been in the midst of barbecuing tri-tip on his new Viking Range grill.

But when they got to the outside deck, Ruben Gomez had

yet to even fire up his new Ultra-Premium. He did, however, look the part of an experienced Grill Master. He wore a stiff red-and-white-striped apron and a Q-tip-white chef's hat that perked practically two feet in height.

"You are *so* not wearing that." Evie looked her father over disapprovingly as Molesto came trotting up toward her.

"Why not?" Her father frowned and positioned his hat to peak higher.

Was it even possible to explain *presentation* to a middle-aged parent?

"Never mind." Evie leaned over to scratch under Molesto's collar.

Her father looked down at Molesto. "I think he knows Sabrina is coming back today. He's had this energy, excitement, all morning."

Was Evie the only one who *wasn't* excited for Suprema's homecoming?

She watched her father take a wire scrub brush to the encrusted grill of his old One-Touch Weber. The rickety legs of the Weber were rusty, and the grill was tar black, charcoal ghosts of BBQs past.

"Why aren't you using your new grill, the Grill Grandioso 3000?" she asked as she took a seat on a deck chair and helped herself to some white corn tortilla chips.

"The *Ultra-Premium*," her father corrected her. "I wanted to use it, but we don't have enough propane, and the extension cord doesn't reach out to the deck. It's all just a mess."

"I can go get some propane," Lindsay offered.

"Nah, it won't be necessary." Evie's father continued to scrub the Weber's grill rack. "It's been a while since I've used this. It should be fun, like old times." He looked over at Evie. "Like when we used to go camping, remember?"

"Camping?" Evie squinted her eyes at her father. It was now nearly one in the afternoon, and the sun was blazing.

"*Yes,*" her father said. "We used this grill when we used to go camping at Leo Cabrillo. How can you not remember?"

"Easily," Evie joked as she crammed more chips into her mouth. Leo Carillo was a state beach between Malibu and Rio Estates, right off the Pacific Coast Highway. The highway divided the hiking trails of the canyon and the sandy coastline of the beach. Depending on what side of the highway you were on, Leo Carillo truly offered the best of both worlds. Evie realized it had been years since she had thought of Leo Carrillo.

"Those were some good times," her father continued. "Remember you and Sabrina would take the boogie boards out and would be in the ocean all day? We couldn't get you out of the water for nothing. You girls were so waterlogged that you looked like those California Raisins when you finally came out."

"Dad." Evie pressed her lips together. "We slept in the Vacationeer, and half the time Mom would get so annoyed with all the loud campers and the mosquitoes that she'd drive me and Brina back home so we could all sleep in our own beds for the night. I wouldn't exactly call that camping."

"But you still came back in the morning." Her father refused to let his positive memories be swept away under Evie's moodiness. "We'd spend the whole day at the beach together. It was so fun. You and your sister were inseparable."

Evie looked at her father struggling with the Weber grill. It was not getting any cleaner.

"So, how long is Sabrina gonna stay?" Evie asked him. Molesto had now rolled over. He wanted his belly rubbed, and she obliged.

"I'm not quite sure. You might want to ask your mother." Her father added more lighter fluid to the coals and then reread the charcoal bag. "You know, we might be eating a little later than planned. I hope Sabrina isn't too hungry when she gets here."

Molesto's ears suddenly pricked up, and as if on cue, the purr of Vicki Gomez's Mercedes followed. He rolled over onto his feet and took off toward the driveway.

"They got back quick." Lindsay looked at her watch.

Evie got up from her chair, wiped the tortilla chip crumbs off her shorts, and went toward the front yard.

"Tell 'em I'll be right there," Evie's father called out as the flames from the grill roared higher. "I don't think I can leave this . . . right now."

Evie came around the house and got to the driveway just as her sister was getting out of her mother's Mercedes. She was immediately taken aback by her sister's appearance. Sabrina looked different—*very* different. For one thing, Sabrina worshipped sunshine like Evie. She pooh-poohed any suntan oil that contained the socially deadly SPF. But now Sabrina was pale, almost a pasty-white pale. The dark roots of her blond hair were practically an inch deep and exposed a form of laziness that Evie had never known existed within her sister. The Sabrina that Evie knew would never walk out the front door of her sorority house, let alone take a trip, looking the way she did now. She was one of those fashion femmes who *had* to make sure that her sunglasses matched her toe polish before even *thinking* of a midnight run to the 7-Eleven.

"Hey, Sabrina . . . ," Evie started to say as she walked toward her sister. She suddenly felt guilty about her earlier resentment. Sabrina looked frail and lonely.

"Hey, Eves," Sabrina said. She clung to the strap of her shoulder bag as if it were a life preserver. Molesto was eagerly wagging his tail at her feet, but she didn't even acknowledge him.

"Where's all your stuff?" Evie asked. She noticed that their mother didn't pop open the trunk to unload a suitcase and that there was no luggage in the backseat of the Mercedes.

"I only have my carry-on." Sabrina tugged at her large shoulder bag. "I didn't pack a lot."

"Why not?" Evie asked. "How long are you staying?"

"Evie." Her mother came around her Mercedes. "Enough with the questions."

"Señorita Sabrina!" Lindsay had come from the backyard soon after Evie. She extended her tanned, wrinkled arms to Sabrina. "Oh, look at you!" She gave Sabrina a long, hard hug. *"Ay, qué flaquita!* Oh, I'll take care of that!"

Sabrina didn't say anything. She just stood there, enveloped in Lindsay's embrace like a limp, lifeless rag doll.

"I'm going to make my special *fideo* for you." Lindsay chatted excitedly as she took Sabrina's bag and slung it across her own shoulder. "I'll make it with fresh tomatoes from the garden."

"It's okay," Sabrina mumbled softly. "You don't have to."

"Oh, but it won't be a bother."

"But I'm not hungry, Lindsay," Sabrina replied, this time more curtly.

"That's because you haven't had good food," Lindsay said. "Up there at school they don't know everything. But let me—"

"Lindsay!" Sabrina snapped. She rubbed the right side of her temple. "Stop it!" she snapped again. "Just *stop* it!"

Indeed everything just stopped—everything and everyone.

"Oh." Lindsay pulled back from Sabrina. *"Lo siento . . ."* She turned to Evie's mother for guidance. "I didn't, I . . ."

Evie looked over at her mother

"Oh, it's okay," her mother tried to assure Lindsay as she went over to Sabrina. "No worries."

It was unsettling, to say the least. Sabrina's disposition was usually as bright and perky as her name implied. Evie couldn't recall when her sister had ever raised her voice to anyone at all, and especially not to Lindsay.

Sabrina bowed her head onto her mother's chest. Her mouth creased downward at the sides, and small tears percolated from the corners of her eyes. Her whole body began to tremble.

"Oh, oh . . . ," Evie's mother said. She seemed at a loss as to what to do. She quickly handed her own handbag and car keys to Lindsay. "Lindsay, here," she said, "I'm going to take Sabrina up to her room."

"*Sí, claro.*" Lindsay took the purse and keys as Vicki Gomez put her arm around Sabrina and led her up the stone steps toward the front door.

"What happened?" Evie asked Lindsay as soon as they were inside the house. "What's wrong with Sabrina?"

"*Yo no sé,*" Lindsay confessed. "I never wanted to make Sabrina upset or make her cry. I did not want to be the cause of her tears."

At that moment, Evie's father, still in his apron and chef's hat, came from around the side of the house.

"Hey." He looked around and found no heartwarming family reunion in his driveway. "What happened to our little girl?"

Both Lindsay and Evie were too stunned to answer.

11

"SO WHAT DO YOU THINK HAPPENED TO HER?" DEE DEE ASKED EVIE.

Evie, Dee Dee, and Raquel had gathered later that afternoon for another impromptu ER/RE! meeting, again at Evie's request.

Her mother had taken Sabrina upstairs, and the barbecue, of course, was off. Lindsay had gathered up all the food and put it away, and Ruben Gomez's enthusiasm and chef's hat both came down. Evie had taken the opportunity to leave the house and head out toward the far west end of the Rio Estates country club golf course.

Now Evie lay flat on her back on the meticulously maintained lawn, where any passing member might guess that she was just a young girl casually counting clouds or working on her midwinter tan with her friends. Oh, if only life in the Estates were that simple.

"Like I said," Evie repeated, "as far as I know, she and Robert broke up and she's all upset over it."

"But why?" Raquel held her cell phone with both hands inches above her face as she texted. "I mean, who broke up with who?"

"It's not 'who broke up with who.'" Dee Dee exhaled smoke from her flavored California Dream. "It's who broke up with *whom*."

"*She* broke up with him," Evie said.

Dee Dee rolled over on her side to face Evie. "That makes no sense. Then why is she the one who is all sad and crying?"

"I have no idea." Evie waved Dee Dee's cigarette smoke away from her face.

"He probably cheated on her," Raquel said. "And then she broke up with him after she found out."

"How could you say that?" Evie looked over at Raquel. "You've never even met Robert, and why would anyone ever cheat on Suprema? She's, like, perfect." She was surprised that she would even be cheering for Team Suprema, someone who definitely didn't need any more PR work.

"Oh." Raquel looked away from her cell phone and then looked at Evie sharply. "So, you have to be *perfect* in order for a guy *not* to cheat on you? Are you saying that's why Jose fucked around on me? I'm imperfect?"

"No, I'm just saying that Sabrina and Robert were perfect for each *other*." Could Evie have stuck her foot any farther into her mouth? "They had been going out for, like, two years or something."

"Two years?" Raquel's thumbs went back to composing text. "Well, that says it right there. He was probably bored. Big-time."

"Could you *stop*?" Evie slapped Raquel's fingers. "That is *so* annoying when I'm trying to have a conversation with you."

"I'm just shoving it back to Davey," Raquel explained. Despite Evie's irritation, she didn't give her fingers a rest. "We were supposed to hook up today, and *now* he's saying he's not even sure about getting together tonight."

"You know," Dee Dee continued, on the Sabrina saga, "I think there is more to the story. Maybe Sabrina was, like, caught in some illicit love affair with one of her professors or something." She sat up almost excitedly. "Ooh, and then the wife, who, like, worked some menial job to put him through grad school, confronted Sabrina at her sorority house, in front of all her sisters. Oh. *My*. God."

"*You*"—Evie waved away more of Dee Dee's smoke—"read too many of those Mexican soap rags." Between Dee Dee's cigarettes and Raquel's texting, she was getting good and irritated. "I don't believe you guys. I come to you for help, maybe some advice, and all I get is more *novela*."

"Hey," Raquel said. "We only can guess what's happening from what you tell us. You wanted our opinion on what we think is going on with Sabrina. It's not our fault you don't agree with what we think."

"Okay, well, what do you think about this?" Evie challenged. "Lindsay just told me how much it's gonna be to fix that guy's car. You won't believe it."

"How much is it?" Dee Dee asked.

"Twelve hundred bucks," Evie answered.

"*Twelve* hundred? Are you shitting me?" Raquel asked. "I thought you said that the guy you hit had some little piece-of-crap car?"

"He did," Evie said. "And now it's gonna have one little piece of fine-ass bumper. I don't know how I'm gonna pay for it. Grandma Chablis better come through."

"Well, I'd ask for an invoice *and* a receipt from this guy," Raquel said. "He's probably just gonna keep the money and never have his car worked on."

"Yeah, that's what usually happens," Dee Dee agreed as she lay back down on the grass. She took another long pull from her cigarette. "But back to Sabrina. I just don't get it. How could she break up with her boyfriend and then leave Stanford, just like that? I mean, *yo no sé,* it's like she's giving up or something."

Raquel bolted up quickly. *"Shit!"*

"Qué pasa?" Dee Dee looked over at her.

"Friggin' Davey." Raquel fumed at her cell phone. "He's *such* an a-hole. First he flaked on me today, and now he's bailing on me tonight."

Evie couldn't help but feel slightly relieved. One less night with

Davey Mitchell was one more night of safekeeping for Raquel. Evie had finally seen Davey Mitchell, or at least his silhouette. On the days Raquel didn't drive B.J., he'd swing by campus to pick her up, and he never once came out of his truck. It was matte black with gray primered fenders (V-plates: LOCLFE). One disturbing add-on was the stenciled words laid out across the truck's tinted back window in Old English script: *In Loving Memory*. Directly below *In Loving Memory* were the names of three of Davey's friends who had died in who knew what kind of way. When Evie had asked Raquel about them, she'd simply shrugged her shoulders and claimed the three friends had been at the wrong place at the wrong time. Evie couldn't imagine dating anyone who had a condensed obituary on the back window of his truck. She also couldn't help but worry. What if Raquel were merely at the wrong place at the wrong time?

"Hey!" Evie suddenly remembered her own evening duties with the reserve. "What time is it?"

Raquel checked her cell. "Almost six, why?"

"Ah, man, I gotta go." Evie stood up and slipped into her satin-covered Trovata flip-flops. She had to meet Tori in less than an hour.

"And where are you going, Miss Thang?" Raquel sounded suspicious. Lately she was usually the one who had to take off somewhere on a Saturday night.

"Nowhere exciting." Evie cracked her knuckles as she stood up. "I'm on reserve duty."

"Ew." Dee Dee wrinkled her nose at the sound of Evie popping her fingers. "I *hate* when you do that." She put out her cigarette in the grass. "You're going to work on a Saturday night? I thought you had the whole day free."

"I did," Evie said. "*The day*. But tonight I gotta go to some *charro* rodeo."

"You mean a *charreada?*" A smile spread across Dee Dee's face.

"Yes, exactly," Evie said. "How do you say it again?"

"A *char-ee-ada*," Dee Dee repeated slowly. "You're going to one? Tonight? *Qué chido!*"

"What is it?" Raquel asked, still texting.

"It's a rodeo," Dee Dee started to explain. "But a Mexican rodeo, with more synchronized competition, and everyone is dressed in traditional Mexican clothing. It's really festive and colorful. Rocio and I used to go them when we visited his cousins in Jalisco." She suddenly got that "woe is *yo*" look. "But wait, how does going to a *charreada* work into your volunteer credit?"

"You got me." Evie shrugged her shoulders. "But I ain't asking. As long as I don't have to clean up at the reserve, it's fine with me. It's a fund-raiser, and Arturdo said if any of the volunteers wanted to buy a ticket and go, we could still get credit."

"So are you, like, *buying* your donation or *donating* your money?" Raquel smirked.

Evie ignored Raquel. "And this girl, Tori," she continued, "who I volunteer with, is gonna pick me up," she went on to explain. "We're gonna go together."

"If I didn't have to write my essay for Las Hermanas, I would definitely invite myself," Dee Dee said. "*Charreadas* are so much fun. They have live mariachi music and lots of food. You aren't taking Alejandro?"

"I would," Evie said, "but he's decided to drive down to San Diego tonight. He and Gorby, that guy from Buena, are gonna stay the night in SD so they can go surfing in Baja tomorrow morning. Dawn patrol."

As soon as she spoke, Evie could already sense Dee Dee feeling sorry for her. *He's going away. Again. Without you. Pobrecita.* She had mentioned to Dee Dee that she and Alex had talked about going to Baja, but he wanted to go sooner than her work schedule allowed. Of course, it bugged her that he'd actually gone ahead and made plans without her.

"I was actually gonna go with him," Evie lied. "He wanted to do this whole day thing with me, down in Baja, but I gotta go to this fund-raiser."

"Plus," Raquel added. "I really can't see your mom letting you cross into Mexico with Alex. No way would Vicki G. stand for that."

"Right." Evie nodded. Although Raquel's observation supported her little fib, she resented it slightly. Why did Raquel *always* have to point out just how strict her mother was? Just because Raquel's mother, Kitty, was too busy with her software business, her La Madrinas mentoring network, and hosting her over-the-top bunco parties to notice whatever craziness Raquel was up to, it didn't make Evie's mother a complete tyrant.

"But Baja isn't Mexico," Dee Dee pointed out. "Everyone thinks it is, but it isn't. It's really just an extension of California."

"Oh yeah?" Raquel asked. "If it's just an extension, why do *I* get sweated at the border when my Cabo tan and I are just trying to make our way back into SoCal?"

"Maybe it's not your dark tan," Dee Dee mused, "but maybe your dark, moody attitude."

"Yeah." Evie laughed. "Or, maybe 'cause you got caught trying to smuggle tequila in your tote bag."

"Or—" Dee Dee laughed too. "—pot in your panties."

"Excuse me," Raquel informed the both of them, "I do *not* drink tequila. That crap is nasty."

"And"—Evie looked at her—"you don't wear panties."

"You know"—Raquel threw Evie a sideways glance—"I *was* thinking of tagging along with you to your little rodeo, but now I just changed my mind, thank you." She went back to texting.

"Oh, yeah, thanks for the offer," Evie smirked. "Now that Davey's ditched you."

"And Alex hasn't ditched *you?*" Raquel asked.

"Not twice," Evie said. "In the same day."

"Chicas, chicas," Dee Dee interrupted. "How much longer is this juvenile sparring going to continue? If we're done here, I need to get back home and work on my essay."

"No, but really," Raquel said to Evie. "I'll go with you to this rodeo thing. I could be into getting my mariachi on." She stuck out her elbows and flapped them around.

"*Serio?*" Evie asked.

"Why not?" Raquel asked. "Can I catch a ride with you and your horse friend?"

Tori, Evie remembered, was also a classmate of Jose's, and she could only imagine an evening of severe grilling à la Raquel. She made a mental note to warn Tori, *ixnay* on the Jose. But other than that, Evie thought it would be fun to have Raquel to herself for an entire evening. Since Raquel had been going out with Davey, it seemed like forever since they'd had any QT together on a weekend.

"Of course," Evie said. "You should totally come with us."

"Oh." Dee Dee pouted. "I am *so* jealous. You are going to have *un* blast. *Charro* boys are so fine."

"That's enough for me." Raquel slammed her cell phone shut in defiance. "I'm *so* over Davey."

12

EVIE, RAQUEL, AND TORI ARRIVED AT THE CHARREADA JUST AS IT WAS starting, and the small arena was filled nearly to capacity with families, packs of teenage boys, and glassy-eyed men already drunk on Corona. The grandstand walls were draped with oversized *banderas* in red, white, and green, the colors of the Mexican flag, and in the bleachers, hundreds more miniature flags were waved by enthusiastic spectators.

Raquel scanned the bleachers. "Damn, I thought we were going to a rodeo, not some freakin' *futbol* game. We ain't never gonna find a seat."

"There's some space over there." Tori pointed toward the left end of the bottom bleachers with her chin. "I'm sure we can squeeze our fat asses in."

"Speak for yourself." Raquel threw Tori a look as she lugged three large clear plastic bags of kettle corn and *churritos*, as well as three *elotes* slathered in mayonnaise. One bag and one *elote* for each girl, *of course*. Last year Raquel had been somewhat of a super*torta*, but she had skipped the slimming period that often followed a breakup, so now she seemed to have even more belly flapping over her low-rise jeans.

As soon as she sat down, Raquel pulled a small glass bottle of Jack Daniel's from her bag. She took one of the sodas from the tray that Evie had been carrying, looked left, looked right, and then topped it off with the whiskey.

Tori eyed the bottle and smiled. "Woman, I like your style."

"Want some?" Raquel asked.

"You bets!" Tori held out her cup.

Raquel poured Tori even more JD than she had poured herself.

"Want some, Evie?" Raquel waved the glass bottle seductively.

"Uh, no, thanks." Evie winced with disapproval. "Whiskey gives me the runs."

"Ah, poor Eves." Raquel pouted her lips and feigned sympathy as she took a sip of her drink. "*Lo siento*. I forgot to get some of that fancy-ass Veuve for you."

Evie was about to say something to Raquel, but then the whole crowd jumped up from their seats. The first bull rider was released into the arena, and the crowd cheered him on. Evie, Raquel, and Tori followed their lead, with slightly less enthusiasm. It was challenging to get up so quickly with a lapful of snacks.

"This is Little Jess from Fontana!" A booming voice blared from the arena's speakers. "And if Little Jess can stay on Thunder till the whistle blows, well, Jessie is gonna be going home with his own case of tequila, courtesy of one of our proud sponsors, Viejo Gold. Remember, folks, when you want the best, you wanna go for the old gold! What do you say, *hombres?*"

Hombres? Evie found herself cringing. *Where* did they find this MC?

"Give *me* the tequila!" Raquel roared. She held her Styrofoam cup out toward the arena in a military-style salute. "The well's running dry!"

Evie noticed some people sitting near them had turned around and laughed with Raquel. Or, Evie wondered, *at* her?

"I thought you didn't drink tequila," Evie reminded Raquel curtly. She knew she was being a buzzkill, but WTF, she didn't have a buzz and she definitely didn't want to get popped by security just for being with others trying to get one.

Raquel ignored Evie and took a big swig from her drink.

Evie checked the time on her cell phone. The show had just started, and she worried that it might be a long night. She looked over at Raquel and watched her suck the JD and Coke through her straw. Seeing Raquel so intent on getting so much liquor in her system bothered Evie. Why did *every* outing have to have booze involved? Evie wondered if she was being just a bit hypocritical by judging Raquel. After all, it was *because* Raquel was such a party *puta* that she was able to secure free ad bevs for Evie's party, and she definitely didn't mind *that*. But then again, it was a birthday party, her six-teeñera, and didn't it deserve more attentive party planning than just another Saturday night out?

Raquel peered out through her overgrown bangs and nudged Evie. "Man, check out the *hombres* round here! *Qué fine*, right, Eves?"

Evie looked around and had to admit that Raquel was right. *Charro* boys in their snug *charro* suits were *muy*—how do you say FAF *en español*? Plus, tons of other guys were walking around in their own mariachi-inspired duds—bolero jackets and tight-fitting pencil pants with silver conchas stitched along the side seams. They were kinda sexy, in a mariachi-rocker sort of way.

"Damn." Raquel raised one eyebrow and nudged Evie again. She actually removed her lips from her straw to whistle under her breath. "Look at *that* piece of ass!"

Both Evie and Tori looked over. Tori covered her mouth, laughing. The so-called piece of ass belonged to none other than the biggest *nalgón* himself, Arturdo.

Evie almost didn't recognize him at first. She was used to seeing Arturdo at the reserve, cranky and sweaty and wearing a worn-out Pendleton and, of course, *those* boots. But tonight he looked relaxed and was dressed in black jeans, a black shirt, and a black felt cowboy hat. Had anyone called Pablo Montero, because his costume was missing!

"You've *got* to be kidding." Evie also covered her mouth and laughed with Tori. "That's, like, our boss at the reserve."

"What, are you serious?" Raquel leaned forward to get a better look. "Damn, hook a sister up with some volunteer opportunities. I'm suddenly feeling in a very *giving* kind of mood. Ooh—" She lowered her voice. "—he's looking this way." She fluffed her long hair over her shoulders and took another swig of her Jack Daniel's and Coke.

Evie turned her head to the side, hoping Arturdo wouldn't notice her or Tori. She suddenly regretted bringing Raquel to the *charreada*. Not only was she already getting loud and obnoxious, but she was gonna make a fool of herself in front of Evie's "like, boss." And to top it all off, she was getting Tori drunk. Who was gonna drive them home?

Unfortunately, Arturdo did see Evie and Tori. He waved to them. And both offered obligatory waves back. Evie hoped that would be it. Eye contact made, credit *should* be issued. But instead, Arturdo, in all his black-attire badness, made his way over to them.

"Hey." He actually smiled. "You two made it. Nice." He placed his polished boot on the rickety bleacher bench above them and balanced himself on his leg.

Nice? When was Arturdo ever happy to see Evie and Tori? It seemed like every time they were at the reserve, he found it necessary to point out everything they were doing wrong. He was just as bad as Evie's parents.

"My name's Raquel." Raquel held her hand up all dainty-like, as if she were actually expecting him to lean over and kiss it or something. "I'm Evie's best friend."

Arturdo took Raquel's hand, but he merely shook it. "Oh." He smiled. "You're the one who lived in Mexico City."

Evie was surprised that he remembered something she had mentioned weeks earlier. Granted, it was the wrong ADA, but still.

"Uh, *no.*" Raquel raised her eyebrow at Evie. "I'm the *other* best friend." She looked back at Arturdo and sipped her drink suggestively. "The *pretty* one, La Bonita."

Arturdo looked at her cup and laughed. "You mean the drunk one, La Boracha."

That comment made Evie LOL.

Raquel looked over at Evie from the corner of her eyes. "Well it's better than being tagged *Turdo,*" she muttered under her breath.

Oh my God. Evie and Tori tried hard to contain their laughter. He could *so* not hear her say that.

"What did you say?" Arturdo asked as he tilted his cowboy hat slightly forward.

"Hey, Arturo," Evie said, hoping to distract him, "thanks for asking us here. It's pretty fun."

Yeah, right.

"Well, thanks for buying a ticket." Arturdo looked toward the arena. "It all goes to a good cause. A large percentage of the ticket price helps rehabilitate the performance horses that have been hurt. If they don't get better, well—" He paused. "—they don't have the best future."

"What do you mean?" Tori asked.

"I mean, they get put down."

"*What?*" Evie looked over at Arturdo, alarmed. "Are you serious? They get killed?"

"Oh yeah," Arturdo answered in an almost casual tone. "Their owners don't think they're as useful if they aren't performing and making money."

"Wow." Evie looked out toward the arena. A bunch of white and gray horses were forming two lines in an elegant synchronized fashion. "I didn't know that."

"Yeah," Arturdo said. "See that horse down there?" He pointed to a dark caramel–colored stallion just entering the ring. "That's how Chamuco used to be, performing for the *charreadas* and for the drill team, but now he's old and blind. I don't know what's going to happen to him. He's always passed over during our adoption-day clinic."

Evie took a deep breath and looked over at the stallion. She'd had *no* idea stuff like that happened. Sure, Chamuco got frightened easily, and yeah, he was old, but he didn't deserve to be *killed*. She suddenly felt sad.

Just then, to Evie's surprise, Josephina walked up to them. *Of course*, she thought to herself. Arturdo wouldn't dress up just to impress some fellow *caballeros* on a Saturday night.

"Turo?" Josephina asked.

Actually, maybe she wasn't asking but rather just saying Turdo's name. The way she spoke, one never knew with Josephina.

"Ah, Josephina." Arturdo turned to face her. He took his boot off the bleacher and stood up. His energy immediately changed from relaxed to rigid. "You're back already?"

"Why? Am I interrupting something?" She eyed Evie, Raquel, and Tori coolly.

"Uh, no, we were just . . . oh . . ." Arturdo suddenly seemed even more awkward. "You remember Evie and Tori, and this is their friend—"

"Oh, *Turo* just gave me a pet name," Raquel piped. "La Boracha."

Josephina looked at Raquel's cup. "Are you drinking?"

"Yeah, want some?" Raquel held out her cup toward Josephina.

"Uh, no?" Josephina wrinkled her nose. "There are already enough stinky drunks here." She adjusted her tiara—er, gold hair band—and turned to Arturdo. "Turo, I still *have* to use a bathroom, and I'm not about to use the filthy outhouses they have here. Can't you take me somewhere?"

"Somewhere?" Arturdo asked. "We'd have to drive into Moorpark or Camarillo."

"Well, let's go then, anywhere other than here." Josephina looked around. "There's nothing but obnoxious *borachos* around." She looked over at Raquel and Tori.

"*Pero querida*—" Arturdo checked the time on his watch. "—we'll miss the *escaramuzas*."

Josephina looked back at him, her eyes demanding the right answer.

"But I don't want you to be uncomfortable." Arturdo looked around and softened his tone. "I guess I can take you into Camarillo. We'll find a gas station or a Pollo Loco for you." He put his arm around Josephina. "We'll be back," he told Evie and Tori. "Maybe we'll see you later."

"Yeah," Tori said. "Laters."

As soon as Arturdo and Josephina left the bleachers, Raquel dived in. "Oh. *My.* God," she exclaimed. "That girl talks like a total Val, and what's with her getup? Is she gonna go fox-hunting or something?"

"Oh, she always dresses like that," Tori said. "She keeps her horse at the reserve."

"What's her name again?" Raquel asked. "Horsaphina? Talk about an Ugly Betty, and she was all getting in my face as if I wanted her man or something."

"Well," Evie pointed out, "you *were* flirting with him."

Tori almost choked, laughing. "Arturdo and Horsaphina! Perfect! A match made in manure. I can't stand either one of them."

"And how whipped is that Turdo?" Raquel observed. "My mack is dry, *ay, ay.*"

Tori waved her hand aside. "He just doesn't wanna argue with her. She can be pretty high-maintenance."

"Or maybe," Evie suggested, "he wants to be, like, My Super Sweet Boyfriend."

"Please," Raquel said. "No guy is *that* sweet."

"Alex is." Evie didn't have to think for a second.

"Oh yeah?" Raquel looked at her. "And where is Prince Charming now? He's in San Diego, probably hooking up with some surf honeys as we speak. Has he even texted you in the last hour?"

"Of course," Evie lied.

She knew what Raquel said was far from the truth, but she didn't want her thinking otherwise. Evie took a sip of her soda and watched Arturdo and Horsaphina walk from the grandstand arena toward the exit. Arturdo took off his jacket and covered Horsaphina's bare shoulders with it, and even though he was one of her least favorite people, Evie couldn't help but feel a twinge of envy. She couldn't remember the last time Alex had been so chivalrous with her or the last time they had actually gone on a date. Yeah, they surfed all the time, or at least they used to, and sometimes they'd split an order of pancakes at Pete's Breakfast House or a burrito at La Gloria downtown, but those weren't really dates. Now, with her volunteer duties, Evie wasn't even able to do those simple things with him, and it wasn't like he was making any effort to initiate any romance.

"*Vamos a ir, hombres,*" Raquel said, imitating the announcer.

"I *heard* that." Tori echoed Raquel's sentiment. "Now that Arturdo is gone, we can bail. Just lemme finish my drink."

Evie looked over at the stallion that Arturdo had pointed out to her in the arena.

"Hey, Eves, you got your learner's permit on you?" Tori tapped the remaining ice from her cup into her mouth. "Maybe you should drive."

"Uh, yeah, I can drive," Evie offered dryly. Normally, she would have been excited to practice her driving, but her mood suddenly felt damp.

Raquel swirled the last bit of ice in her cup. "Okay, I'm ready to go."

"Wait," Evie said. "I wanna see more. This horse reminds me of this one at the reserve."

Evie looked out at the arena and watched the brown stallion trot to the center of the ring. His rider, a young girl in a cream-colored Victorian dress, tapped his side with a riding crop. He instantly lowered his head as his front legs bowed in a curtsy. This, of course, garnered tremendous applause from the adoring crowd. They were totally *encantados* with him.

"Aw." Raquel clicked her tongue. "He is *so* cute! Wouldn't you love to have a pony like that, Evie?"

"Yeah," Evie answered. The spotlight shone on the horse, and Evie walked down the bleacher steps to get a better look at him. Yes, he was the color of caramel, dark caramel, and his mane was slighter lighter, but it was his eyes that captivated Evie. They were large, perfectly button-round, and so gentle, somewhat like the eyes on the stuffed animals on Sabrina's bed. Ooh, Evie's heart got all gooey. Whether he could do tricks or not, Evie didn't care. And just like the crowd around her, she was completely, totally *encantada*.

13

"BRINA?" EVIE TAPPED SOFTLY ON HER SISTER'S BEDROOM DOOR. When Sabrina didn't answer, she knocked again and then held her ear to the door. But Evie heard nothing, not even the hum of Sabrina's TV or her computer. She was about to knock one more time but decided to give it a rest. She reluctanctly walked to the end of the hall and toward her parents' bedroom. Their door was wide open.

"Mom?" Evie stood at the doorway.

"Come in, Evie." Her mother was sitting on the edge of the bed. Her hair was wet from the shower after her morning swim, and she was drying it with a towel. *"Qué te molesta?"*

"What's wrong with Sabrina?" Evie asked her mother as she entered the room. She took a seat on the linen chest at the foot of her parents' bed. "I knocked on her door, but she's not answering. And it was the same thing last night, when I came back from the rodeo."

"She's probably still sleeping," her mother answered. "It's early."

"Early? It's already nine o'clock." It was unusual that Evie would question someone else's sleeping habits. Until Sabrina arrived, Evie was the sole snoozer of *la familia Gomez*.

"She's going through a tough time." Her mother sighed. "It's something we all go through. Heartbreak, loss, change—but how you handle it is one of the things that separates the girls from the women." She looked at Evie and smiled weakly. "But your sister is going to be fine. She has so much love around her, how could she not get better? And all she really needs is some fresh air and some good old-fashioned Pilates."

"Good *old-fashioned*?" Evie asked.

"You know what I mean," her mother answered. "I'm gonna try to get her to go with me tonight. Why don't you come?"

"Nuh-uh. *No* way," Evie said. "If that's the way to handle a crisis, I think I'll just stay a girl, thank you."

"E-ve-*liina*!" It was Lindsay calling from downstairs.

"You better get down there." Her mother bent her head and rubbed the back of it with her towel. "It's her day off, but she came in just to help you with your driving, Evie. Don't forget to thank her."

"I know. I won't." Evie got up slowly and looked at her mother's hair. "Why don't you just use the hair dryer?"

"Ever since I went blond I try not to," her mother replied. "I don't want any more damage done to my hair." She swung her head up and looked at Evie. "Hey, why don't you practice in my car? Would you like that?"

"Uh, the Benz?" Evie asked. She was *not* about to go there again. "No . . . it's okay, I'm already sorta used to Lindsay's car. I mean, it's the only car I've been using, besides when I'm with Dad and using his."

"What?" Her mother frowned as if she didn't understand. How could anyone turn down her classic burgundy Benz? "No, really," she continued. "As long as you stay in the front and don't leave Camino del Rio, you can go ahead and practice with it."

"No, I'm cool." Evie's stomach slowly made a somersault. "I'd rather just practice with Lindsay, in her car."

"Well, okay." She went back to drying her hair.

Evie went downstairs to meet Lindsay in the kitchen. Why, she wondered, would her mother offer her Mercedes? That was something her mother would *never* do unless, say, maybe things were pretty bad with Sabrina. Maybe she was using her car as a distraction? It was just a bit suspicious.

"*Estás lista?*" Lindsay asked as she took her car keys out of her purse and handed them to Evie.

"Yeah." Evie took the keys from her. "I'm ready."

The last time she had been behind the wheel in Rio Estates was that fateful day when she had gotten in that (cue to lower voice) *accidente*. Evie felt the odd sensation of an unwanted déjà vu. But today would be different, she hoped. For one

thing, she wasn't going to be distracted by a phone conversation with Dee Dee, and for another, it was a Sunday.
According to Lindsay, Jesus put in double time as a copilot for
those needing extra guidance.

"Now." Lindsay fastened her seat belt after she got into her
car (license plate: JKL829K) with Evie. "What's the first thing
you do?"

Evie reached for the radio dial. "Make sure I got some tasty
tunes on?"

"Evelina!" Lindsay tapped her hand.

"I know, I know," Evie teased as she checked the rearview
mirror and side mirror. "Safety belt first and then make sure
all mirrors are adjusted correctly to the driver's height."

"*Correcto.*" Lindsay pulled down her car's sun visor and put
on her sunglasses. It was just a little after 9 A.M., but the sun
was already reflecting off the hood of the car.

As Evie backed out of the driveway and onto Camino del
Rio, she felt a little shaky. She took a deep breath and told herself that she just had to relax.

"*Ay, no te preocupes,* Evelina." Lindsay patted her arm. "Don't
worry so. You're doing so well with your driving. Much better
than when Sabrina was learning."

Evie suddenly sat up in her seat. "Really?" she asked. "You
taught Sabrina to drive, and she sucked?"

"I did *not* say *that.*" Lindsay frowned. "She was just very nervous and timid. You are—I don't know—more of a go-getter."

"Really?" Evie suddenly felt gleeful.

Lindsay shook her head and looked out the window. "*Ay*, I don't know what's going to happen to Sabrina. She is still so sad."

"My mom said it's just a matter of time," Evie said. "She's just depressed."

"I don't know." Lindsay didn't sound convinced. "She doesn't eat, and she just sleeps all the time." She looked out the window. "It's a sensitive time, and you should try to be extra nice and helpful."

"I *am* helpful." Evie frowned at Lindsay. "All the work I'm doing at the reserve. I do a lot, Linds."

"I know, *mija, claro que sí*," Lindsay said. "I know you've been working hard. Everytime I pick you up, *ay*, you look so tired."

"Yeah, I am. Very tired." Evie felt the need to state her case one more time. "And even when I'm not at the reserve, I have to go to fund-raisers and stuff."

Okay, so she had been to only one fund-raiser, and it had been far from being burdensome with work, but even Arturo had said her attendance, her ticket, *helped* the cause.

"Just last night I went to a *charro* rodeo," she told Lindsay.

"A *charreada*?" Lindsay asked. "Oh, we have them all the time in Mexico. My cousins were *escaramuzas*."

"Really?" Evie turned Lindsay. "I've heard that word before. What's that?"

Lindsay reached over and gripped the steering wheel. "Keep your eyes on the road, Evie. *Escaramuzas* are team riders, women. A *charrita* is actually a cowgirl."

"Oh." Evie nodded. "So, I went to one last night and it was *so* cool. They did these tricks—"

"*Suertes,*" Lindsay interrupted. "They are called *suertes.*"

"Oh, right," Evie said. "How come you've never told me about *charreadas*?"

"Evelina, how would I know what might interest you?" Lindsay said. "You are so finicky. One day it's surfing, and now it's suddenly horses? What are you going to do now? Trade in your flip-flops for *botas*?"

"I've *always* been into horses." Evie looked down at her Rainbow sandals. She wasn't about to trade them in for cowboy boots just yet.

"For today, let's just concentrate on the driving," Lindsay said. "The sooner you learn to drive, the sooner—" She stopped herself.

"The sooner what?" Evie looked over at her.

"The sooner you get to drive," Lindsay simply replied.

"No, you were gonna say something else," Evie insisted. "Is it about my car? Are my parents gonna get me my Beetle for my birthday? They are, right?"

"Turn here." Lindsay ignored Evie's question and pointed to Calle Boca Grande. "Evelina, remember to use your signal *every* time you need to make a turn or get into another lane. Give the other driver enough time to know what you plan to do."

"Why?" Evie asked. "So they can speed up and block me?"

The sedan suddenly jumped forward.

"And you don't need to hit the brake all the time," Lindsay said. "Keep *both* hands on the steering wheel.

"Oh, I'm *never* gonna get this!" Evie groaned. "I'm not gonna get my driver's license by my birthday."

"You can get your license any time," Lindsay said. "You don't have to get it by your birthday."

"If I wanna drive away from my party in Cherry Bomb, I do," Evie said.

"Cherry bomb?" Lindsay looked at her. "*Qué es* cherry bomb?"

"That's what I'm gonna name my car," Evie told her. "Cool, huh?"

"Where are you getting this idea that you're getting a car for your birthday?" Lindsay asked. "I thought that you might not get your party."

"Who said that?" Evie asked. "Did you hear that, like, recently?"

"I thought I heard your mother talking to your dad and—"

"And what?"

"I don't know, I don't want to say anything." Lindsay got flustered. "But I thought I heard them talking about going up to Sabrina's school, and I thought they were talking about going up there that same weekend."

"*What!*" Evie couldn't believe what she was hearing. "The weekend of the twenty-ninth? My birthday weekend? You are *not* serious!"

"*Mi'ja*, don't. . . ." Lindsay reached for the gearshift. The car instantly stalled.

"Oh, man." Evie realized that she had shifted too slowly "I'm *never* gonna get it."

"You're never going to get what?" Lindsay asked.

"Take your pick," Evie answered glumly.

14

"YOU SHOULD HAVE BEEN THERE, ALEX." EVIE WENT ON ABOUT THE *charreada* as he drove her to the reserve the next morning. "It was amazing. The horses were so beautiful. They really are these incredible animals. God, I feel like such an idiot. I mean, I've been doing all this work at the reserve, and I guess I really had no idea why. I know why *I* need to work at the reserve, but I had no idea *why* my help was even needed. I can't believe people would just give up on a horse, their pet. Do you know what I mean?"

"Uh-huh," Alex said, but it seemed as though he wasn't really listening. "So, I don't get why you skipped Baja just to be out drinking it up with the girls."

"I wasn't drinking it up," Evie said. "Didn't you just hear me? That was Raquel and Tori's deal. And you know I had to go, to get the credit. It just happened that it turned out to be really cool, sorta educational."

"Educational?" Alex looked at her. "What's next? You're gonna join Mathletes?"

"You know, if I didn't know better"—Evie threw him a sideways glance—"I would say you were jealous."

"Jealous?" Alex frowned. "Jealous of what?"

"That I'm doing different things, learning about different things."

Alex looked at her and smiled. "Eves, no, I am not jealous. For reals. I'm actually glad it turned out okay for you. It just would have been cool if you had come to Baja."

"Well"—Evie looked back at him—"it would have been *cool* if you could have waited and planned the Baja trip on a weekend that I could actually go."

When Alex pulled up at the reserve, Evie was unusually excited about her workday. She wanted to find out more about horses and *charreadas* from Arturdo. But when she reached the stables, Tori had beaten her to the punch with follow-up *charro* chitchat.

"So, did you and Josephina have fun Saturday night?" Tori was asking Arturdo as Evie walked over to pull out flakes of alfalfa and oat hay.

"Oh yes," Arturdo said. "I love *charreadas*. They have them all the time in Pico Rivera, but I rarely get a chance to get out there. My father is a *charro*. So are my brothers."

"And they do all those tricks?" Tori asked.

"They aren't called tricks," Evie joined in. "They're called *suertes*."

"Right." Arturdo looked at Evie, slightly surprised. "You know, the Mexican *charro* was the first cowboy. Not that many people know that."

"Really?" Tori nodded enthusiastically, and it made Evie a little suspicious. It wasn't like her to be so conversational with Arturdo. "That is *so* cool," Tori went on. "How come you aren't a *charro*? I mean, you totally could be one. You know so much about horses and stuff."

"It's the 'stuff' part that's really isn't my thing," Arturdo confessed. "I didn't follow the *charro* tradition. Besides, my whole family is still back in Colorado, and they all practice and perform together."

"You came out to California by yourself?" Tori asked.

"Yeah," Arturdo answered. "I moved out here because I really wanted to go to Thatcher."

"And you left behind your whole family? And all your friends?" she asked.

"*Whoa!*" Arturdo laughed and held up his hand, faking protest. "I didn't know I was the subject of some in-depth interview. Is this part of your extra credit?"

"No." Tori laughed lightly. "I was just wondering, that's all."

Evie couldn't help but feel a bit curious too. Arturdo was a senior at Thatcher and only a few years older than she and Tori. She couldn't believe that someone would move halfway across the country just to work with some horses. She loved to surf, but she couldn't imagine moving to, say, Hawaii, just to be closer to some choice waves. But then again, after that cute little caramel-colored horsie she had seen at the rodeo, oh, who knew. He was just *too* adorable.

"But come on." Tori tilted her head and looked up at Arturdo. "Don't they have horses in Denver?"

Was she actually flirting with him?

"Of course." Arturdo furrowed his brow. "But Thatcher has one of the best horse programs in the country, and if I wanna study veterinary medicine at UC Davis, I need a high school that will give me the best transfer. Hopefully I'll get into Davis."

"Hey, my Grandma Chablis teaches at UC Davis," Evie said. "Wow, you might see her there."

"Chablis?" Arturdo asked.

"I mean, Chavella," Evie said. "We call her Chablis 'cause she teaches viticulture. Winemaking."

"Uh, yeah." Arturdo smirked. "I *know* what viticulture is."

"Turrrro!"

It was Horsaphina calling out for Arturdo. Evie was surprised they hadn't heard her car (V-plates: PRNCESS) pull up.

"We're over here," Arturdo called out over his shoulder. "In Blackie's stall."

Horsaphina stood at the doorway in a formfitting plum-colored satin halter dress, beige fishnets that shone against her tanned legs, and spiky knee-high black leather boots. She'd topped off her whole look with a black velveteen derby hat.

"You're not done yet?" she asked Arturdo. Her annoyed tone was less Valley-esque and more demanding. "I thought you made the reservations? For seven o'clock?"

"Uh, *hello*? How are you? How has your day been?" Arturdo teased Horsaphina for not greeting him. He dropped four enormous pills into the selected buckets of feed.

"Arturo"—Horsaphina checked her slim gold wristwatch—"it's time to *go*." She ground her boot heel into the gravel. "I don't want to be late. If we don't get there on time, we might as well not go at all."

"Josephina." Arturdo stopped what he was doing and exhaled. "We'll make it. I'm the one who made the reservations, remember? And we're only twenty-five minutes away." He looked at Evie. "But I guess Evie and Tori can take over. You don't mind, do you?"

"Uh, no," Evie said. "I don't mind."

What could she really say? He was the boss, sorta.

Arturdo turned back to Horsaphina. "I've got my shirt in my truck. I'll go change."

"Okay, okay." Horsaphina checked the time again. "But do it quickly."

"I hope I didn't interrupt you guys." Horsaphina looked over Tori and Evie as Arturo went out to his truck.

"Huh?" Evie asked. "What do you mean?"

"When I walked up," Horsaphina explained. "It's like you guys were in the middle of a conversation? It seems like every

time I see you two with Arturo, I am barging in on something."

"No, we were just being silly." Evie felt awkward. The last
thing she wanted was Horsaphina *hating* and then complaining to Arturdo about it. She looked over Horsaphina and
assessed damage control. "You look really pretty. Are you
going somewhere fancy?"

"Oh yeah," Horsaphina said as she smoothed out her dress
and adjusted the gold mesh bracelet on her wrist. "Arturo's
taking me to Koi."

"Koi?" Evie asked. She had no idea what Koi was. Was it
a club? A lingerie boutique, as in *coy*? Maybe it was a mis-
pronounced Native American name for another horse
reserve?

"The Teppan Grill?" Horsaphina smiled when she noticed
Evie's confused expression. "They seat you in groups of
twelve, and if we're late? We'll get a regular chef, but I want
Mayru. He's the owner?"

"Oh, right." Evie nodded.

"I can't believe you've never been there," Horsaphina said.

Neither Evie nor Tori said anything.

Horsaphina looked around with an air of disapproval.
"Don't you guys ever get tired of working here?"

"Nuh-uh," Evie said. "Not really." It was half true.

"Me neither," Tori agreed with Evie.

"Well, I would," Horsaphina stated. "I don't get it. Arturo

spends so much time here. But then again, you two *have* to be here? Right?"

"Not really. We're volunteers," Evie pointed out. "I mean, I could have picked any organization for work."

"Hmm-mmm." Horsaphina wasn't convinced. "That's not what Turo told me."

"What are you talking about?" Evie asked.

"He said that your school counselor called to ask if the reserve still had room for you? And they didn't? Turo had already made out the whole schedule for the year, and he's very organized that way. But when he told them no, your counselor went over his head and straight to Lynn. She okayed it."

"Oh, I didn't know that," Evie said. No *wonder* Arturdo had been tough on her from day one.

When Arturdo reappeared, Evie looked up. *Wow.* What a difference a nag made. He had changed from his worn-out old blue-and-green Pendleton work shirt to a gray button-down shirt. His hair was slightly combed back, and Evie noticed that he had put on the slightest hint of cologne (woodsy and eucalyptus-smelling). Did he always wear cologne? Maybe she just hadn't noticed before. She did remember that Alex used to wear cologne (sea breezy and fresh), at least, for the evenings when the Flojos would all go fancy, party-crashing or something. Evie sighed. But that was all *so* last semester, and in a galaxy so far, far away.

158 MICHELE SERROS

"Turo." Horsaphina scowled at his boots. "You *cannot* wear those to Koi. They have a dress code?"

"*Josephina,*" Arturdo started, "there is nothing wrong with my *botas.*" He looked at the ones she was wearing. "You're wearing boots."

"Yes, but mine were, like, four hundred dollars?" Horsaphina rebuffed. "They're not some Red Wing work boots from, like, Gordon's Western Wear."

"Josephina." Arturdo pursed his lips. "If you want me to change, it's only going to make us even more late. Is that what you want?"

It seemed obvious to Evie that Horsaphina was working his last nerve.

"What*ever?*" Horsaphina just looked up at the sky, seemingly surrendering control.

As soon as they left, Tori turned toward Evie and smiled smugly. "Pretty smart of us, huh?"

"Smart of us, what?" Evie asked.

"Kissing Turdo's ass like that, pretending we were all into the rodeo and working here and stuff," Tori said. "That part about your Grandma Chablis just about killed me."

"But I *did* like the *charreada,*" Evie insisted. "And my Grandma Chablis does teach at Davis. What are you talking about?"

"I don't know about you, but I'm behind with my hours. I've been late sometimes, and Turdo subtracts even the minutes. If I don't get the credit I need, I'm gonna have to retake one of my other classes. I'm thinking if I get on Turdo's good side, he might be cool letting me slide. You have all the hours you need?"

"Uh—" Evie hesitated. "Yeah, I don't know. I mean, I think I'm pretty much on the right track." She hadn't really sat down and looked over all her hours, and she'd just assumed that if she showed up, her attendance counted for a full shift. The way her body ached, she at least *felt* that she had put in her share.

"Yeah." Tori went back to work. "I'd hate to be doing all this for nothing."

Evie watched Arturdo and Horsaphina as they headed for his truck. He held the door open as he waited for her to get in the passenger seat, and then went around the front of his truck and got in.

When Arturo finally drove off and his truck was out of sight, Evie excused herself.

"Man, you better be right back," Tori warned her. "I ain't gonna do all this alone, like last time."

"No, I just gotta make a call," Evie said, and went to get her backpack from the supply shed. She pulled out her cell phone and speed-dialed Alex's number. While she waited, she thought of Arturdo. He wasn't such a bad guy. So he was a bit of a *dick*tator at first, but Evie thought it was pretty cool—no, *very* cool—that he cared so much about what he did at the reserve. She realized it might be time to take the *d* out of Arturdo's name.

Again, she got Alex's voice mail.

"Hey, Alex. It's me," Evie started. "Hey, I'm wondering . . . this coming weekend. Do you think we can go out? Like not surfing, but go *out*, out? Do something different? Okay . . ." She didn't know what else to say. "So just let me know."

15

THE FOLLOWING SATURDAY EVENING COULDN'T COME FAST ENOUGH FOR Evie. She had spent the whole week looking forward to going *out* with Alex. He had responded to her phone message with a text:

> **Sat. Nite. Cool.**
> **Smthin diff. TTYL**

"So, no surfing this weekend?" Alex had double-checked one last time with Evie on Friday afternoon as he was taking her to the reserve. "You sure 'bout that?"

"I have to work all day tomorrow and then again on Sunday," she reminded him. "I really have only Saturday evening free.

"Okay, but we *could* do a twilight set. After you're done with your shift at the reserve we can head out to Sea Street. There's supposed to be a south swell."

"Alex," Evie said. "This is California. There will *always* be a south swell coming from somewhere. I wanna go *out*, out, remember? Do something different. You said it was no problem."

"You're right." Alex smiled. "Whatever you say, cutie."

❋ ❋ ❋

By Saturday night, Evie had decided on her favorite halter, the satin one with the yellow and green swirls, and a three-tiered satiny skirt she had bought at Tilly's. She even made the bold decision against wearing flip-flops (*gasp*) and slipped on some espadrilles (*sorta* satiny) that she'd borrowed from Dee Dee. Thanks to all the long hours at the reserve, Evie was gradually (and sadly) losing her tan. She went to her bathroom and looked through her cabinet for some foundation. She wanted a darker cream. Maybe Sabrina had something?

Evie went down the hall to Sabrina's room, but, like always, found the bedroom door closed.

She was about to knock when she heard a sound, a muffled noise, coming from inside Sabrina's bedroom. Evie leaned closer. Was Sabrina *crying?* Evie caught her clenched fist just before it hit the bedroom door.

"But it's *not* getting better," Sabrina sobbed. "My family is driving me crazy. I should have just stayed back at Stanford. Here, I'm surrounded by friggin' idiots."

Evie couldn't believe what she was hearing. *Friggin' idiots?* Who was she talking about?

"No." Sabrina struggled to catch her breath. "I don't even talk to her. She's such a little spoiled brat that I might as well not have a sister at all."

Whoa. Evie pulled back from the door. Was she hearing right? Was Sabrina talking about her? No. She could *not* have heard right. She leaned in closer to the bedroom door and strained to hear more.

"Evelina!"

Evie looked up and found Lindsay in the middle of the hallway, holding a small box of tile samples.

"You do *not* sneak around, trying to listen in on other people's conversations." Lindsay spoke sharply under her breath. "You are being very rude."

"But she's talking about me, us." Evie lowered her voice in protest.

"Evelina," Lindsay insisted. "Leave her alone."

Evie reluctantly moved away from Sabrina's door.

"I have to come into your room." Lindsay heaved the box of tiles to her left hip. "Your mother wants to see which tiles she needs to order for your bathroom."

"Now?" Evie asked.

Lindsay adjusted the box again. "Yes, she wants to place the order first thing in the morning, and I'm going to be leaving soon. We have to do it now."

"O-*kay* . . ." Evie started back down the hall to her bedroom, grudgingly. There was no way she was going to argue with Lindsay. And God forbid she sound like a spoiled *brat*.

Oh, *hurtful.*

As she entered her room with Lindsay, the bedroom's landline rang. Evie grabbed the receiver off the carpet floor.

"Hullo?" she asked.

"Finally." It was Raquel. "What up, girl? I called your cell and it went right to voice mail, and you didn't answer my text."

"My cell's charging." Evie went into her bathroom and walked past Lindsay, who was lining up the tile samples against the wall. She grabbed her makeup bag off the sink's counter and moved out of Lindsay's way.

"And then I've been calling the landline," Raquel continued. "And it just rings and rings. I didn't even get the voice mail."

"Sabrina's been on the phone." Evie was half-listening as she sat on the edge of her bed and squirted a glob of foundation onto her shoulders. She was going to have to settle for the orangish brown offerings of Sunburst.

"What's wrong?" Raquel asked.

"Nothing." Evie tried to shake off the feeling. Sabrina's words stung something fierce. She smoothed the cream evenly across her neck and shoulders. "Raquel," she started, "do you think I'm spoiled?

"What?" she asked. "Who said that? Alex?"

"No. Nobody." Evie lowered her voice again and looked over at Lindsay, but she wasn't even paying attention. In typical "Lindsay Knows Best" fashion, she just stood in the bathroom with a disapproving look on her face as she looked over the tile samples.

"Actually," Evie started, "I just overhead Sabrina on the phone, and she told someone, I think one of her sorority sisters, that I was spoiled. A spoiled *brat*, to be precise."

"She said *that*?" Raquel asked. "I don't know. I mean, I guess someone might think you were spoiled, because you *do* get a lot of stuff that you want."

"*Me?*" Evie was thrown off by Raquel's blunt reply. "That is so far from the truth. Who's the one schlepping horse crap around? Who's the one who may not have her own birthday party? On a year that there *is* actually going to be a February twenty-ninth?"

"It's really how you look at it," Raquel said. "I mean, of course you should get the things you want. And some people might think you are spoiled, but I'm surprised it would be Sabrina saying that. I mean, doesn't she usually get her way?"

"And more," Evie agreed. "That girl gets the grades she wants, the car she wanted, and accepted into the school she wanted. She gets everything her way. Like even now, with her being home and everything, I totally have to walk on eggshells around her."

"Ugh, I could *not* deal," Raquel groaned. "That's why I am *so* glad that I'm an only child."

"You and Dee Dee both." Evie looked at herself in her closet mirrors. Her neck and shoulders looked dark compared to the rest of her. She added some foundation to her face.

"But anyway," Raquel said, "don't sweat over Sabrina. From what you tell me, she's just moody over that Robert dude."

"Yeah, I guess," Evie said. "God. It's just been a complete bummer of a day, of *a week*." She looked over at Lindsay again.

Evie got up from her bed and stood with her back toward the closet mirrors. She looked quickly over her shoulder, à la red-carpet *Teen Vogue* pose. She had to do the checklist. No VPL: *check*. No unsightly bulge of back fat: *check*. No bac— Wait. Evie peered closer into the closet mirror and discovered a small but still very noticeable blemish. It was right below her left shoulder. Argh! The curse of midwinter bacne! She instantly squeezed more Sunburst goop onto her finger and dabbed the offending violator. But the foundation now made *that* section of her skin look blotchy and uneven. She decided to pull off her whole halter and give herself a thorough application of cover-up, but just as she pulled it off, her mother walked into her bedroom.

"*Mom*, do you mind?" Evie held the phone between her chin and shoulder and covered her chest with her arms. "I'm changing."

"Sorry, Evie." Her mother couldn't have cared less. "The

door was open and I already knew that Lindsay was in here."
She brushed right past Evie. "I need to take a look at these
tiles."

It was less about modesty and more about the incriminating *RxE* inked near her left breast. Last semester, she, Dee
Dee, and Raquel had visited La Ley Si, a tattoo artist who
eschewed the "over eighteen" requirement and would ink
anyone with enough of an idea and enough cash. She loved
her little *RxE* in blue-black ink near her heart. It made her
feel so *un*–Rio Estates, a bit *scandalosa* in a secretive kind of
way, but if Vicki Gomez ever found out that her youngest
daughter had a tattoo *anywhere* on her body, there would be
only one kind of party for Evie—a good-bye party.

"Hey," Raquel asked, "did you get that fancy-ass manicure
for your date with Alex?"

"Oh, yeah." Evie looked at her fingernails. They were
painted a deep shade of blue. "I got a hand job from Jonathon,
just like Dee Dee recommended. Oh, man, he's *so* good."

"*Evie.*" Her mother, as well as Lindsay, looked over from the
bathroom. "*Who* are you talking to?"

"Raquel," Evie said calmly. "And I'm talking about the *manicure* I got at Michael Kelley. They call them hand jobs, just in
case you and Linds were eavesdropping and misunderstood
me, *Mother.*"

"We weren't eavesdropping," her mother said as she glanced
over at Evie's nails. "But very nice hand jo—uh, manicure."

"Evie!" her father called from downstairs. "Alex is here."

"Hey," Evie said to Raquel as she gave herself a heavy bronze dusting on her neck, shoulders, back, and face. "Romeo is here, gotta go."

"Hey, Evie," Raquel started.

"Yeah?"

"I've been thinking. If you need to borrow money, you know, for that guy's car, I can totally lend it to you, and you wouldn't have to worry about paying me back for a while."

"What?" Evie asked. "How do you have so much money?" Sure, Raquel got a hefty allowance, more than her or Dee Dee, but twelve hundred dollars was a lot of *lana*, for anyone.

"I dunno," Raquel said. "I've just been spending less, I guess. Probably 'cause I don't have to carry Jose's cheap ass!"

Evie laughed. "Wow, Raquel. Thanks. I mean, that is so nice of you." She was touched by her offer. "But hopefully Grandma Chablis will come through and I won't have to put the *mordida* on you."

"Cool," Raquel said. "Well, just let me know."

"Okay." Evie looked at herself in the closet mirror again. She was still a little taken aback by Raquel's offer. "I better go."

"Lates," Raquel said. "Don't do anything I wouldn't approve of!"

As she headed downstairs, Evie felt fortunate (*not* spoiled) that she lived in a two-story home. There is nothing more

O.C. than descending a staircase into the arms of a waiting surfer boy.

But the minute Evie saw Alex at the bottom of the stairs, her fantasy went from The *O.C.* to *O. U. Gotta Be Shittin' Me.* Yes, Alex was waiting for her in the foyer, but not looking anything remotely like a Saturday-night hottie. He was in his usual tattered camo cutoffs, the ones cut a little below his knees, and he was wearing his plastic flip-flops, the "bin specials" that Evie knew all too well. He had obviously not taken the planning of their date as seriously as she had. He had sand around his ankles, and stank from the leftover medicinal-smelling sunblock he slathered on earlier. Evie guessed that he must've still gone to Sea Street to catch that oh-so-important late afternoon swell.

"Hey." Alex looked Evie over with a puzzled look on his face. "You're all dressed up."

"Yeah," Evie said. He hadn't said she looked nice, just dressed up. Was that supposed to be a compliment? And why did he look so puzzled?

"Yeah, Evie." Her father also looked her over. "And you got some color on you. Were you out in the sun today?"

Okay, maybe "dressed up" and "color" were male-speak for *cute?*

"So, where are you two going?" her father asked Alex.

"I dunno," Alex answered in a tone that was a little too laid-back for Evie. "I've been at the beach all day. I'm pretty wiped out." He turned his head from side to side to prove his point. "I think we'll just take it easy." He looked at Evie. "Right, Gomez?"

Evie managed a weak smile but said nothing. He could *not* be serious.

"Well, have fun, you two." Evie's father walked them to the front door. "And Evie, don't forget your curfew."

"Do you think," Evie started, "that just tonight—?"

"No," her father said. "Twelve thirty."

Evie walked alongside Alex toward his truck, and there was his long board in the flatbed—evidence that he *had* just come from the beach. She felt her chest fill up with heavy disappointment. She looked over at Alex.

"What?" He looked back at her and smiled.

"Nothing." Evie looked away and felt conflicted. Sometimes Alex would look at her, and his dark eyes would just penetrate hers, making her feel the way she had felt at Sea Street on the morning he had given her the abalone necklace. She suddenly felt guilty. Alex really *was* a sweet boyfriend, and maybe she *was* a spoiled brat. Just because he was dressed down didn't mean he hadn't put any thought into arranging a little something special or different. The evening was just beginning. Maybe he'd played it off with her dad, you know, one guy trying to be cool with another guy type of thing? What, was he actually going to go into detail with her father about what he really wanted to do with her?

"Well, first, Mr. Gomez, I'm going to take Evie out to a very

romantic, very expensive restaurant, where I will request the most secluded table in the whole house, just for the two of us. Then I am going to drive her out to the Shores, where we will stroll out to the most secluded area in the sand dunes, and I will spread out a blanket just for the two of us. Then Evie will cuddle up next to me as I crack open a bottle of Veuve (her favorite) and pour it into two glass flutes that I brought with me because I have been planning this evening for a whole week. Then I will make a toast to our evening right before I pull out a book of poems that I have carefully chosen for Evie, but, I have to confess, the minute I look into her dark brown eyes, I'll—"

A long, slow whistle interrupted the satin-halter-ripping scene in Evie's head. The whistle came from the front of Alex's truck. She squinted her eyes in the darkness and slowly made out the glow of a cigarette in the passenger seat of the cab.

No!

But yes. It was Mondo. She could *not* believe what she was seeing.

"Why is *Mondo* with you?" Evie struggled to keep her voice down to a whisper.

"You wanted to do something different," Alex answered earnestly. "And it's just been a while since we all hung out together, and you were saying that—"

"*What?*" Evie forced herself to maintain her composure. "Are you serious?

"Uh, yeah." Alex sounded confused. "Why?"

"I *said*," Evie started, "that it had been a while since you and *I* hung out, spent time *together*. I wanted to go *out*, out, remember?"

"Evie." Alex sounded even more confused. "What exactly does going *out*, out mean?"

"Just *forget* it." Evie was quickly losing her patience with Alex.

Mondo got out of the front cab just as they got to the truck.

"Hey, G." He looked Evie over, making her feel slightly Sangro slutty. "Look at you, all gussied up in all your shiny outfit and shit. What are you, the satin Latin or something?"

Mondo pulled the passenger seat forward so he could get in the back of the truck's cab. "So, you ready to give the horse gig a break and just chill with Alex and me tonight?"

Alex and me? Grrrr. Evie couldn't help but feel hot with anger. What *was* Alex thinking, bringing Mondo along on their date?

"So, check it out." Mondo took off the white knit cap he was wearing to show Evie his hair. "Chop job. I bit your style, from last semester."

Last year, Evie had cut and bleached her own hair herself. She was now gratefully relieved that it was growing back to a length she was comfortable with. Mondo's hair, however, was newly buzzed and bleached Tweety Bird blond.

"Check out the back." Mondo turned his head to show off a

separate dye job, a large question mark in deep jet black, smack center on the back of his head.

Evie couldn't keep from laughing. "Why would you have a question-mark on the back of your head?" She asked, "What, are you trying to create some new Batman villain?"

"What?" Mondo frowned. "*No*. It stands for 'Whaddya need?'" He ran his hand over his freshly shorn scalp. "Check it out, my cousin just got back from Amsterdam and he told me that, like, all the cafés have little areas with designated question mark signs. Like, you can get *anything* you want there. You know what I mean? Cool, huh?"

"Yeah, I guess." Evie fastened her seat belt and couldn't help but roll her eyes. "In Amsterdam."

"So—" Mondo rubbed his hands together and leaned forward between Evie's and Alex's seats. "—what's up for this evening?"

Evie decided to stick to her guns. She was going to get her fancy dinner at Koi if it killed her, or, more appropriately, killed Mondo's date with Alex.

She feigned an earnest smile. "I was thinking we'd go get sushi."

"Sushi?" Mondo smirked. "Uh, no thanks." He held his nose and dropped the sides of his mouth. "I had sushi last night, if you know what I mean." He looked at Alex. The look in his eyes said everything.

You have got to be kidding.

"*Mondo,*" Alex reprimanded him as he started his truck. "Come on, there's a lady present."

"Yeah." Mondo looked at Alex in the rearview mirror. "That's what *I* thought. Last night."

Alex started to pull out of the driveway. "So, you want sushi, Evie?"

Not after Mondo's inexcusable one-liner.

"You know," Mondo chimed in as he flicked his cigarette butt out the window. "I could actually go for some seafood. We should go to Otani's. They got kick-ass tempura."

"*Actually,*" Evie said, trying to lure Alex from siding with Mondo, "I was thinking of Koi."

"Koi?" Mondo frowned as he leaned forward between Evie and Alex. "You mean that fancy-ass place that took over where the E Bar used to be?"

"Yeah," Evie said.

"Nah," Mondo said. "We don't wanna do Koi. It's all SUV vermin. We gotta go to Otani's." He leaned back in his seat and looked at Alex in the rearview mirror again. "Dude, they have a waitress with a rack *this* big." He made a gesture over his chest like he was balancing two imaginary cannonballs.

Alex couldn't help but chuckle as he drove down Camino del Rio.

Evie shot him a look. "*Alex.*"

"Oh, sorry, cutie." Alex straightened his smile and rubbed her arm. "Look, we'll go to Koi. Whatever you want."

"Whatever *she* wants?" Mondo looked at Alex and then at Evie. "Talk about spoiled milk."

Evie crossed her arms over her chest. *Spoiled?*

Was Evie just being *sentida*, or was everything that came out of Mondo's mouth just truly inappropriate?

❋ ❋ ❋

There was over an hour wait for a table at Koi.

"We can't seat you any sooner without a reservation," the host told the three of them. "And—" He looked over Alex and Mondo's feet. "—we have a dress code. No flip-flops."

"You gotta be kidding," Mondo protested. "Dude, this is friggin' SoCal—everyone wears flip-flops."

"Not during dinner hours." The host shook his head.

Evie looked around the restaurant. Outside the patio, a fire roared in a stone fireplace and water trickled from decorative bamboo chutes into a kidney-shaped pond filled with bright orange and yellow koi fish. She noticed that the moon was full, large, with hues of soft yellow, pink, and beige. She couldn't stop thinking how much more romantic it would be to snuggle with Alex on one of the wicker love seats and just inhale the beauty, *alone.*

"Why don't we just wait?" Evie suggested. "We can get some appetizers or something. An hour will go by fast."

"Dude." Mondo pulled Alex aside. "That monkey totally dissed us. I ain't gonna shoot my wad here." He seemed to have already made the decision for the three of them as he started back toward the front doors with his fists deep in the pockets of his baggy cords.

"Sushi is sushi." Alex shrugged his shoulders apologetically. "We can come here another time, Eves. Promise."

❊ ❊ ❊

Alex sat between Evie and Mondo at the counter at Otani's. It was a short counter with yellowed, chipped Formica and a sloppy pile of stained plastic menus at the far end. The diners were far from SUV vermin and were made up more of aging surf *veteranos* and leather-skinned longshoremen. Both groups, Evie noticed, wore tattooed sleeves depicting their lives on (or battles with?) the Pacific.

Otani's was cheap eating, and you could fill up if you had a little cash. *Cash.* Otani's did not take credit cards, and Alex had forgotten his wallet and had only three bucks on him. Evie's pride refused to let her offer any of the twenty bucks she had on her toward the meal. The three of them shared one tempura shrimp boat with a complimentary order of sticky white rice, and it actually turned out to be a good thing that Mondo was tagging along. It allowed Evie to order a diet soda.

As they were finishing up their meal, Mondo looked past Alex and eyed Evie's shoulders as if he were seeing them for the first time.

"What's up with your skin, G?" he asked her.

Evie rubbed her shoulders. "I always get goose bumps when it gets a little cold."

"No." Mondo looked her over. "It looks like you got dirt or something smudged on them." He reached over, across Alex, to brush off whatever he thought was on Evie's skin.

"It's not dirt, Mondo." She pulled away from him. "It's bronzer."

"Bronzer?" Mondo looked confused. "For what? It's getting all over your satiny shirt."

"It's not a shirt," Evie said. "It's a halter."

"Well, whatever it is, you better be careful. You're getting crap all over it," Mondo said.

"Never mind, *Mondo*." Evie hugged her arms across her chest and placed her hands on opposite shoulders. It was cold in Otani's, and she remembered seeing a jacket in Alex's truck.

"Alex," she started, "don't you have a jacket in your truck? I thought I saw one."

"Uh-huh." Alex played with the ice in his Styrofoam cup with his straw. "I thought I'd need it, but I'm okay."

"Do you mind if I wear it?" Evie asked.

"Nuh-uh," he said as put his hand in his shorts pocket and pulled out his car keys. "But try not to get all that makeup on it."

"Oh." Evie didn't take the keys. "Never mind."

"Dude." Mondo nudged Alex to look over at the group of

women who had just entered Otani's. "We're talking boulders at three o'clock. *Your* three o'clock."

"*Mondo.*" Alex threw him a sharp look, but before doing so, Evie noticed that Alex did take a quick glance over toward the women.

"Hey," Mondo suddenly said to Evie. "You ate more than your fair share."

"Huh?" Evie saw that he was now looking over her paper plate.

"Look." Mondo counted the shrimp tails on her plate with the end of his wooden chopstick. "Alex and I only have three tails each, but you've got, like, five."

"Mondo." Evie couldn't believe what he was implying. She looked down on her plate. "It's just batter."

"No, it ain't." Mondo pressed down on the tails with his chopstick.

"What, you want me to burp them back up?" Evie asked. Could the tension between her and Mondo get any fiercer? She pushed her paper plate away from him. "*Stop* it."

"So—" Alex stretched back, oblivious to how annoying Mondo was being to Evie. "—what's up for the rest of the evening?"

Evie hoped that she didn't hear him correctly. Hadn't he planned *anything*?

"Check it out," Mondo started after he had finally stopped counting shrimp tails. "A buddy of mine was telling me about a party over on Hemlock. Should be pretty KB."

"What about my board?" Alex rubbed the space between his eyes and yawned. "I don't wanna leave it out at some party."

"Yeah, I'm not really in the mood for a party, either," Evie said as her stomach growled. Hmm, maybe pride wasn't such an honorable thing. Time to use her twenty? "But maybe, if you really want to go," she told Mondo, "we could drop you off." She looked over at Alex's Nixon. It was only 10 P.M. She still had a good two and a half hours before she had to be home. She and Alex could still have *some* time to themselves.

"*We?*" Mondo looked at Evie. "When did you start sharing Alex's pink slip? You don't even drive."

"I know," Evie said. "I'm just saying that we might do something else."

"But, Eves, if you don't wanna go to a party," Alex asked her. "What do you wanna do?"

"I don't know." Evie hated being put in the position of activities director, and *why* was Alex not backing her up? "I thought we could go to the pier, walk around. There's a full moon tonight."

"Whoa." Mondo pressed two fingers on the side of his neck. "I hope my pacemaker can keep up with this excitement." He looked at Alex. "Dude, come on, let's go check out the party. Hey, you know who's gonna be there?"

"Who?" Alex asked.

"Our boy Jose."

The minute Evie heard the name Jose, her stomach went from empty to numb.

"I haven't seen that clown in weeks." Alex chewed lazily on the end of his plastic straw. "What's he been up to?"

"Maintaining." Mondo casually pulled out a pack of cigarettes. "So he says."

"Alex"—Evie leaned her head to the left and looked up at him—"can't we just go for a walk tonight? Like on the pier? It's so nice out."

There was no way she wanted to see Jose, even at some mellow, kick-back party. Not only had Jose cheated on Raquel, but he had also practically molested Evie at a Sangro party and almost decked her in the school's parking lot. Why would Alex, her own boyfriend, even want to be in the same room with Jose?

Both Evie and Mondo waited for an answer from Alex as he continued chewing on the end of his straw.

"Dude." Mondo stretched his arm around the back of his chair. "You know, I'll do whatever you want." He looked at Evie. "*I'm* easy."

❊   ❊   ❊

At about half past 11 P.M., Evie returned home. Her so-called date with Alex was officially over, and she was dropped off one full hour before her 12:30 A.M. curfew. No such thing had ever, ever, happened before during the so-called best years of Evie Gomez's life.

"The whole evening sounds completely wretched," Dee Dee sympathized. She called Evie as soon as she got her text. "And Alejandro? Did *nada?*"

"Nothing," Evie was embarrassed to admit. She knew that Dee Dee was already comparing Alex to Rocio. "Once he was with Mondo, it was like I didn't even exist. They were too busy yucking it up and checking out girls."

"That is so disgusting," Dee Dee said. "What the hell is wrong with Alejandro?"

"I have no idea." Evie was already in bed, nibbling on a flaky *hornito* and a pumpkin empanada that her father had brought home. "So, what are you doing home on a Saturday night?" she asked Dee Dee. "No Hermana group hug?"

"I have a brunch tomorrow," Dee Dee said. "With some of the other Hermana candidates. I should be in bed already, but I've got this avocado mask on and I wanted to give it another twenty minutes."

"*Another* brunch?" Evie asked.

"No, this is the first one," Dee Dee said. "The last Hermana get-together was an informal meet-and-greet, and after that, the second get-together was more of mixer." Dee Dee took a breath. "*Oye*, have you seen Josephina? Has she said anything about me?"

Ever since Evie told Dee Dee that she had met Horsaphina, Dee Dee was always trying to dig up bits and pieces about her possible future as a Hermana debutante.

"No, *Dee Dee*," Evie said. "I told you, she never talks about *anything*. She just *asks* things. The girl talks in question marks. But have you talked to Raquel?" she asked. "I texted her but didn't hear back."

"I talked to her a few hours ago," Dee Dee said. "She was on her way to some house party. A house *arrest* party."

"Huh?"

"Exactly," Dee Dee said. "One of Davey Mitchell's little friends got in trouble for breaking his probation, so he's tied to his house, with his mother and an ankle bracelet. All the Bard Boys took a party to him."

"Are you serious?" Evie laughed.

"Yeah, he isn't allowed to go anywhere over five hundred feet away from his house without checking in with his PO."

It was funny to hear Dee Dee talk so TV cop shop. "So where was this party?" Evie asked.

"Some place on Hemlock," Dee Dee said.

"On Hemlock?" Evie repeated.

"Yeah," Dee Dee said. "Why?

Evie suddenly felt empty. "No reason."

16

"GO-MEZ . . ." ALEX THREW EVIE A SIDEWAYS GLANCE AS THEY DROVE
to school together. "How long you gonna beef with me?"

It was Monday morning, and Evie was still feeling tender
from the Saturday date fiasco with Alex.

"I'm not beefing," Evie tried to answer casually, but it was
no use faking it. She was still upset. Alex hadn't even *apologized*. Unless, that is, you counted the text message she'd
received the morning after from him.

Mrng Gomez. Cool prty

Srry u mssd it. TTYL

His text was less of an apology and more of an observation.
So he'd gone to a "cool party" and he was "sorry she missed
it"? BFD. She couldn't hide her aggravation from Alex and
had remained silent for pretty much the whole drive. She kept
her arms crossed over her chest and didn't add anything to his

comments except an occasional mild "uh-huh" to something he'd said.

"Saturday night was so not my fault," Alex insisted. "I can't control Mondo."

"But you can control whether or not he comes with us on a date." Evie refused to look at him and instead looked out her window and focused on the fascinating scenery—oil derricks and lemon groves that lined Highway 33 into Ojai.

"How was I supposed to know we were on a *date*?" Alex was perplexed. "You told me that you wanted to go *out*, out, and that you wanted to do something *different*. To me, hanging out with you and Mondo is different. You're my two favorite buds."

"That's just it, Alex," Evie said. "I'm not your bud. I'm your girlfriend."

"But you're also my bud," Alex said. "I don't get it. Why do things have to be so different now that we're a couple? You're not trying to change me, are you? Like mold me into a little version of what you think is ideal?"

"What? Of course not."

Evie didn't want him to change. She liked Alex for who he was and what he was about. And that was the reason why she thought he would make a great boyfriend, *her* boyfriend. So why wouldn't he act like it?

"I don't get it, Evie," Alex continued. "Sometimes I don't get you."

Evie discreetly glanced over at Alex and studied his profile. How could she *not* have noticed how cute he was when they were just Flojo friends? When she had started Villanueva and had been introduced to him, he had a wide bandage adhered across the bridge of his nose. He also had cotton splints stuffed up his nostrils. Evie had figured that he was just like the other type of vanity plates at Villanueva and that he had also gotten a nose job. It wasn't until later that she learned that the bandages were from a surfing accident—some newbie's foam board had flung up right into his face and had shattered his nose and cheekbones. He was supposed to have kept the bandages and splints for at least a couple of weeks after his surgery, but upon hearing that some southwesterly swell was coming in at the Sea Street break, Alex yanked the splints out himself, right in the school's parking lot. He just *had* to catch that swell. The yanking act alone made Evie think he was just about the coolest guy. And cool guys can make cool boyfriends, right? But why, she wondered, couldn't he be cool enough and just tell Mondo that his company was not wanted on their dates? Evie studied Alex's profile more. Sigh. He was quite handsome.

"I'm sorry, Alex." Evie tugged on his elbow. "I just wish, sometimes, we could do things more, I dunno, romantic. You know what I mean?"

But Alex didn't say anything back except "uh-huh" as he turned up Monte Carlo 76 on his iPod.

✳ ✳ ✳

They pulled into Villanueva, and before Evie had even gotten out of Alex's truck, she received a text from Dee Dee.

Lots to tell!

Dee Dee was *so* excited about having Rocio in Rio Estates and she wanted to do a girls-only lunch off campus to tell Evie and Raquel all about him. As if they hadn't heard enough about him already. But Evie figured it would be a good breather from Alex. Eating lunch apart might give them time to think. She texted him by the start of first period.

Goin to O-hi w/
the grls 4 lnch.

To which he responded:

No prob

Of course she read more into his two-word text. *Much* more. "No prob" as in "No problem. I really don't care what you do"? Any textlator could translate Alex's simple six characters (seven, if you included the space) to mean that he was annoyed with Evie, perhaps *over* Evie? It took everything in her power not to follow up with a response. During class, she found herself checking her cell just to reread the two words and see if she could figure out their deeper meaning. Evie looked around the classroom, wishing she had either Dee Dee or Raquel in Civics to help her decipher his cryptic text. Who could she trust with such personal information? She scanned the classroom.

Absolutely no one. For one thing, the timing was bad. It would be such *not* good PR for Evie to be hosting *the* coolest party of the year yet not be cool with her own man. People would definitely talk. She snapped her cell shut. She just would *not* think about it. But four minutes later, she opened her cell again.

"Hey." She leaned over to September Valdez, who sat next her. September was a senior and had had many boyfriends during her reign at Villanueva. She was also the vice president of Villanueva's Senior Sleuths Book Club, so she *knew* how to read between the lines. "What do you think this means?" Evie showed her Alex's message.

"Who sent it?" September took Evie's cell and propped it up inside her Civics book, assuming that Vasquez-Reyes Alarcón didn't have X-ray vision. She studied the text.

"Alex sent it," Evie whispered from the side of her mouth. She kept her eyes focused on Vasquez. The last thing she wanted was her phone to be taken away, not at this crucial time in her life.

"Alex, as in your boyfriend, Alex?" September asked.

"Uh-huh," Evie glumly answered.

"No smiley face or heart." September looked it over and shook her head. "Hmmm . . . it doesn't look good." She handed the phone back to Evie as soon as Vasquez-Reyes Alarcón turned his back to face the dry board. Evie turned her phone off and felt her stomach sink. Yup, September knew what she was talking about.

❋ ❋ ❋

"So, he got in last night," Dee Dee went on about Rocio as she, Evie, and Raquel headed out of the student parking lot in Jumile. "He's staying in our guest room and ay, it was so hard to leave him this morning."

"He slept at your house?" Evie asked, from the back-seat.

"Yes, and it was *unbearable*." Dee Dee cranked up RBD on her iPod. "I haven't seen him in over four months, and I just wanted to sneak in the guest room and be with him the whole night." She pulled out on to Ventura Avenue and made a left, toward O-HI Frostie.

"So why didn't you?" Raquel immediately turned the vol-ume down, way down. She hated RBD. "If I had some fine-ass *papi chulo*, as you claim he is, under my roof, that I hadn't seen for months, you best know I'd be giving him a big ol' grand welcome, *Americana* style."

"Raquel, you're scandalous!" Dee Dee turned up the vol-ume and gave Raquel a look. "I *can't* sleep in the same bed with Rocio. My parents would *freak* seeing us come out of the same bedroom in the morning."

"What you gotta do is set an alarm clock in his room," Raquel began. "Like, set it for an hour earlier, before your par-ents wake up. But you gotta make *sure* you wake up and get out of the room. Also, make sure you don't go in the room wearing any perfume or that hair stuff of yours that's gonna leave girl stink behind."

"You've obviously done this before," Evie said.

"You could say that." Raquel faced Evie with a sly grin. "You know, Eves," she then started, "I think it was pretty shitty how Alex treated you Saturday night. I mean, I don't know, maybe you need to teach him a lesson, like light some fire under his ass."

"And how would I do that?" Evie asked.

"You should go out with some other dude," Raquel said. "Just for kicks."

"Raquel," Evie said. "I am *not* going to do something like that. That is *so* not me."

"Well, you never know . . . ," Raquel said. "But *I* do."

"Didn't you say that Rocio was gonna look into Stanford?" Evie asked Dee Dee.

Evie really didn't care where Rocio went to college, but she just didn't want to talk about Alex anymore.

"Yeah." Dee Dee lit up a Midnight Berry at the first stoplight they came to. "In fact, he should talk with Sabrina. She would be the perfect person to talk with."

"Not right now." Evie looked out Jumile's window. "She's not the best person for anything." Evie still hadn't talked to her sister about what she had overhead her say on the phone and her grudge was still deep.

"Sabrina is *still* depressed?" Dee Dee looked at Evie in her rearview mirror. "I can't believe it."

"I know," Raquel teased Dee Dee. "Looks like there has to be a recount for your American Idol."

"I wouldn't say she's my *idol*." Dee Dee took a pull from her cigarette. "But, well, yeah, she's up there. Sabrina's the best." Dee Dee looked at Evie in the rearview mirror again. "I was actually," she started hesitantly, "sorta hoping that she could write me a recommendation letter for Las Hermanas."

"No way," Evie said. "Like I said, now is not a good time to ask Sabrina for *anything*."

17

O-HI FROSTIE WAS LITERALLY THE LAST BURGER STAND STILL STANDING
on the downtown's main drag. Unlike the majority of new
eateries that had overtaken the area, it offered outdoor dining
without pretentious heat lamps, multiple-page menus, or
linen napkins. A handwritten menu board hung above the
order window, and if it got too cold outside, you ate inside.
And as far as tableware went? No forks, spoons, or knifes.
Only tissue-thin paper napkins were offered to wipe off the
thick grease their burgers left behind. By the time Dee Dee
pulled up, O-Hi Frostie's wooden picnic tables were already
taken over by backpacks and skateboards, courtesy of nearby
Vista Sierra public high school students.

"Ew." Dee Dee looked them over. *"Vista Sierra."*

Evie looked at Dee Dee in surprise. Such private school
snootiness was unlike her.

"So when do we get to meet Rocio?" Raquel asked Dee Dee as they all got in line to order.

"Definitely at Evie's party." Dee Dee pulled up her sunglasses and studied the menu. Evie wondered why she even bothered to look at the menu. The three of them always got the same thing: A guac dog, which, of course, was a grilled Jody Maroni hot dog smeared with thick guacamole and wrapped in a flour tortilla, and one large chocolate frostie each.

"Wait, Evie's *party*?" Raquel squawked. "We gotta wait until *then*? What, you ashamed of us or something?"

"*Por fa.*" Dee Dee furrowed her brow and shook her head. "Don't be so *pinga*. It's just that he is going to be so busy researching colleges and universities that I'm barely going to see him myself."

As they all stood in line, two boys, both dressed in low-rise, supertight black jeans and scrappy skater tees, approached Evie.

Raquel covered her mouth with her hand and muttered under her breath to Evie, "*Wassup*, rockers?"

"Are you Evie Gomez?" the one boy with eyeliner asked.

"Uh, yeah," Evie answered cautiously. She looked over at Dee Dee and Raquel. "Why?"

"We wanna know if your party's open," the other kid said.

"Open?" Evie asked.

"Uh, yes." Raquel suddenly took over and leaned across Evie. "It is. You can buy an invite if you want. We have a few left. Fifty bucks each. *Cash*."

"Fifty bucks?" the boy with eyeliner asked. He looked back at his two other friends, similarly garbed skater boys, who were sitting on one of the picnic tables.

"Yeah, we ain't talking entry to some skatepark." Raquel looked over at his friends. "This is the *panchanga* of the year."

"No, it's just I gotta just tell my other friends," he said. He went back over to the picnic table.

As he left, his friend stayed in line with Evie, Dee Dee, and Raquel. He crossed his arms and checked out Dee Dee. It never failed. No matter what set a boy was with, Dee Dee was *always* checked out.

"Are you *all* gonna be there?" he asked.

Evie looked down. She was used to feeling invisible when blond and blue-eyed Dee Dee was near. Dee Dee never went near the beach, let alone got in the ocean, yet everyone always claimed that she had the classic "California Girl look."

"Of course, we're *all* gonna be there," Raquel said. "And what about you guys?" She looked over at the guy with eyeliner. "Will *Jared* be in attendance?"

"*Who?*" The kid looked back at his friends. "Stevie? Yeah, he'll be coming."

Raquel smiled and whispered to Evie, "In more ways than one."

"*Raquel!*" Evie covered her face in embarrassment.

"Yeah." Raquel put her arm around Evie. "My girl here, her boy's been slacking off, so you guys make sure you show some love to the birthday girl."

"Raquel!" Evie got even more embarrassed.

"There's gonna be booze, right?" the kid asked. He couldn't care less about deadbeat boyfriends.

"We ain't charging fifty bucks for Hawaiian Punch." Raquel frowned. She took her arm off Evie. "Of course there's gonna be booze. Haven't you heard? It's an *open* bar. Why do you think I just said it's gonna be the party of the year?"

"Okay." The boy now tagged by Raquel as Jared Leto came back with a wad of crumpled twenties. "How about one forty for all four of us?"

Evie looked at Raquel, and Raquel looked back at her. Dee Dee rolled her eyes and went back to looking up at the menu board.

"Sold!" Raquel grabbed the money from Jared's hands.

"So, don't we get a receipt or something?" the other boy asked.

"You want a receipt?" Raquel looked at them. She pulled out a small slip of white paper from her wallet and wrote: *Good for Four Entries.* She blotted her lips on the paper, leaving a deep, dark red smack print. "How's *that?*"

"Cool." The kid took the paper, not terribly impressed. Both boys went back to the picnic table to join their friends.

Dee Dee pulled Evie aside and looked over toward the boys. "Evie, you do *not* want those guys coming to your sixteeñera. They're going to expect a lot for all that money."

"Oh, they're harmless," Raquel said as she counted the

bills. She glanced over at the boy with eyeliner. "And that Jared Leto one is *fine*. Besides, if they show up at all, they'll probably all be so lit that they won't even remember this transaction."

Raquel gave Evie the money and went back to looking up at the menu board. "Lunch is on you, Eves."

18

LATER THAT EVENING, DEE DEE CALLED EVIE ON HER BEDROOM'S landline. Evie welcomed the call more than Dee Dee would ever know. Alex had been rubbing ice on her all day, and she desperately wanted to talk to Dee Dee about it, *without* getting Raquel's two cents. But before Evie could get into it, it seemed that Dee Dee had her own *novela* brewing.

"I need you to keep something on the DL," she told Evie.

"Sure." Evie lowered her voice and her iPod. She loved playing the confidante. "What's up?"

"So, you know how Rocio is here," Dee Dee started, "and how his parents are coming out in a few days, right?"

"Right."

"And this is all a big deal for him, to find a school out here. I mean, he's basically doing this for me, for us to be together."

"Uh-huh," Evie answered. Could it also be that California

had some of the best business schools to offer—better than, say, Mexico?

"So anyway," Dee Dee continued, "my dad and Graciela want to have a little dinner party for Rocio and his parents and," she paused, "I really want to invite you and Alejandro."

"Oh." Evie was taken off guard. She'd been expecting some big grand announcement. Like, maybe Dee Dee and Rocio were engaged and were going to run off together, and maybe Dee Dee wanted her to make crepe paper flowers for their get-away car. But it was just dinner, a dinner party, at the de LaFuentes'. Cool enough. Very adultlike. "We'll definitely come," Evie said. "Sounds swanky."

"But one thing," Dee Dee added. "You can't tell Raquel."

"Huh? Why?"

"It's not like I'm keeping something from her, to be mean or anything. I just . . ." Dee Dee searched for the right words. "I just don't want to feel uncomfortable or embarrassed. You know how Raquel can be coarse and sometimes make a scene. I can't have anything go wrong at this get-together."

"But can't you just tell Raquel that?" Evie felt awkward. She didn't like keeping things from among the three of them. "Can't you just make it clear to her that she has to be on her best behavior?"

"I wish it was that easy." Dee Dee sighed. "But you know Raquel. You know how she can be, and now that she's all with Davey Mitchell, I don't know what do expect from her anymore."

It was true. Davey Mitchell had passed Raquel's two-week mark and neither Dee Dee nor Evie had even been introduced to him. *That* was very telling.

"You know," Dee Dee said, "I wasn't gonna say anything, but Raquel called our house, drunk, twice last week."

"Are you serious?" Evie asked.

"Uh-huh," Dee Dee said. "And I'm not taking about D-dialing my cell. She called on the landline, like at three in the morning, and woke up my father and everything. In fact, he was the one who said it might be better if Raquel didn't come to the get-together."

"Are you effing with me?" Dee Dee's father was the most accepting of Raquel, more so than Evie's own father, who she had thought was very forgiving of Raquel's antics. Evie herself had received the drunk dials and tipsy texts from Raquel, but they had all been very amorous chatter, consisting of Raquel going on and on about how much she loved Evie and how Evie was her "bestest, bestest friend in the whole wide world." But thank God she never D-dialed the Gomez's landline. Her mother would shit *stone*.

"So, you won't tell her, right?" Dee Dee asked Evie in a hopeful tone.

"I guess not." Evie still felt a bit deceitful. "I mean, I won't."

"Don't even mention it to your mother," Dee Dee said. "She might say something to Raquel's mother and, you know."

"Oh, don't worry," Evie assured Dee Dee before hanging

up. "I *definitely* won't tell my mother about your dinner party. Promise."

"Whose dinner party?"

It was Evie's mother, and she was standing in the doorway of Evie's room. Keeping dinner plans on the DL might become quite a chore when you were dealing with ears as big as Vicki Gomez's.

"Mom, you were *so* not listening to my conversation!" Evie was furious.

"I was not listening in," her mother insisted. "I'm just bringing this in." She held up Evie's student driving manual. "You left it in Lindsay's car." She put it on the dresser and then continued to stand, aimlessly, in Evie's room. "So who's having a dinner party?"

"I promised Dee Dee that I wouldn't say anything." Evie couldn't believe that her mother could be such a buttinski, but worse, she couldn't believe how loose her own lips could get.

"Frank and Graciela are throwing a dinner?" Her mother sat down, uninvited, on Evie's bright blue canvas butterfly chair. "I saw Graciela at Pilates the other night, and she didn't mention anything to me."

Graciela? Pilates? Ew. Now *that* was a union Evie never wanted to see.

"It's not really a party," Evie tried to explain. "It's just a little get-together for Rocio and his parents."

"Well, whatever they are calling it, I would think that after the welcome-home brunch that I threw for them Frank would want to return the gesture," her mother said. "Something like this would never have happened if Margaret were still alive."

Evie couldn't believe her mother was comparing Margaret, Dee Dee's dear departed mother, to Frank de LaFuente's new wife, Graciela. Her mother's cattiness belonged less in her bedroom and more near Alejandra de los Santos's scratching post.

"Mom," Evie started, "it's not even about or for the parents. I'm just going for support. For Dee Dee."

"Sure, but why wouldn't Frank or Graciela invite your father and me to even that?"

"Mom, like I said, it's really not an adult thing." Was Evie *really* having this conversation with her mother?

"You know, Evie," her mother said in a tone that Evie knew meant she had an idea. And it would probably be a lousy one. "Why don't you take Sabrina with you to the dinner?"

Yup. Lousy.

"What?" Evie looked at her mother. The last thing she wanted was mopey ol' Sabrina barging in on her date with Alex. "Why would I take her?"

"Because it would be a nice thing to do," her mother said. "Dee Dee and Sabrina have everything under the sun in common. Sabrina was a Hermana, and now Dee Dee is going to be one too."

"We don't know that yet." Evie found herself feeling oddly

jealous. What *was* so great about being a Hermana anyway? "Dee Dee still has to be nominated."

"Oh, Dee Dee's a doll." Vicki Gomez waved her hand aside. "Of course she'll be nominated. Also, didn't you say that Rocia will be attending Stanford?"

"It's *Rocio*," Evie corrected her mother. "And I didn't say he was *attending* Stanford. I said he was going to look into it. Checking out a school is much different than attending one."

"I *know* that, Evie," her mother said. "I just thought you'd want to help get your sister out of her rut. But speaking of school . . ."

Uh-oh. Here it comes.

"How is your volunteer work coming along? Is your GPA going to be up before the next quality check? Your father asked me about it the other day, and I'm feeling a lot of pressure, Evie."

She's feeling pressure?

"Mom, I've got it under control." Her mother was getting under her skin. Fortunately, the landline rang again.

"I hope you got it under control, Evie," her mother said as she reached for the phone. "It would be a shame if we didn't get to have your party. But if we do have it"—she raised her eyebrow—"I just *hope* I don't forget to send Frank and Graciela an invite."

20

"YOU LOOK REALLY NICE," EVIE TOLD ALEX AS THEY DROVE TO THE de LaFuentes' house. She was feeling the brown cords and cream-colored dress shirt that he was wearing. And she loved that he had surrendered his standard "bin special" flip-flops for the evening. He had on actual shoes, black canvas Winos. *Too* cute, in a *cholo* kind of way.

Yes, the dinner party at the de LaFuentes' was perfect for mending the friction between her and Alex. Granted, it wasn't a night out at a superswanky Japanese restaurant, or a super-romantic poetry reading at the beach, but still, it was dinner, a dinner date, and he had dressed up. He had *planned* to look nice for her.

"Thanks." Alex looked over at her and smiled. "You do a good job cleaning up yourself, Gomez."

Evie put up the armrest and snuggled close to Alex. So far, so good. She could even overlook being called Gomez.

"You know what?" Alex lowered the volume on his iPod. "I haven't been to Dee Dee's since last semester. Remember? When I went over to give her swimming lessons, and Alejandra de los Santos and her little pack of *fresitas* were there?"

Evie grimaced. "Ugh. How could I forget? I showed up thinking it would be just you, me, and Dee Dee, and you're, like, in the swimming pool, drooling all over Xiamora."

"I *really* don't remember that." Alex smiled jokingly.

"Well, I do."

"But I *do* remember," Alex started, "that the de LaFuentes had a pretty tight pad. They're probably gonna have some good grub tonight."

"Totally," Evie agreed. "But I can tell you one thing they aren't going to have."

"What?" Alex asked.

"They aren't going to have Koi sushi." Evie playfully pinched his side.

"Evie." Alex frowned over at her. "Let it go, will you?"

"I was just messin'." Evie cuddled up closer to him.

"No, you weren't." He shrugged a little. "You keep making these little jabs, like you're trying to make me feel guilty or something."

"No, I'm not." Evie could feel his arm tense up. She looked up at him. "Seriously, I was just joking."

Alex sighed. "You *keep* blaming me for that night. You know, maybe you were just expecting too much."

"Expecting too much?" Evie leaned over and turned down Monte Carlo 76. "What, that I wanted to go out, alone, with my own boyfriend for once?"

"I dunno," Alex said. "It's like I feel like all this pressure that you want me to act a certain way."

Evie let go of Alex's arm and sat up in the seat. "Alex," she started, "if I'm supposed to be your girlfriend, sometimes I wanna be treated like it."

"So, what, I treat you like crap or something?" he asked. He was now turning onto Camino Pacifico and was a few blocks from Camino Cortez, Dee Dee's street.

"I didn't say that," Evie said. "It's just seems that you treated me with more chivalry when I was just a friend."

"What is that supposed to mean?" he asked.

"I mean, you were more of gentleman—"

"I know what chivalry means," Alex snapped.

"Look," Evie tried to explain, "all I'm saying is when you were trying to get my attention, you were all nice and everything, but now that I'm your girlfriend, you, like, totally take me for granted."

"For granted?" Alex asked. "Like what? When?"

"Jeez, where do I begin?" Evie shook her head in bewilderment. How could he possibly be so clueless? "Like you flake on me, *a lot*, and—"

"I don't flake," Alex interrupted. He leaned over and turned up the music. "Maybe I change my mind or my plans change, but I never just don't show up. I never just leave you hanging."

"So you think you didn't leave me hanging that night at Otani's?" Evie raised her voice, if only to talk over the music that Alex had so rudely turned back up.

"Uh, *no*." Alex looked at her, puzzled. "We asked you to go to the party with us. You were totally invited, but you *chose* not to go."

"Oh, so let me get this straight," Evie said. "You and Mondo were kind enough to invite me to the party with the both of you. You *two* invited *me*. Wow, gee, Alex, I hope I didn't intrude on your little date with Mondo."

"You know," Alex said, "you're acting like a bitch. Like how Raquel would always nag on Jose."

"A *bitch*?" Evie snapped at him, her eyebrows practically rising off her forehead. "Well, *you're* beginning to act like Jose. When you're not dribbling over big-chested waitresses, you're acting like some lazy-ass *flojo*. Why can't you ever plan something for us to do? All you wanna do is surf and who knows, maybe you're seeing Alejandra de los Santos behind my back."

"Hey!" Alex pulled up in front of the de LaFuentes'. He didn't turn off the engine. "I'm not the one who made out with my best friend's *significant other* in a photo booth behind her back."

Evie was now legally livid. "Alex, how could you say something like that? You know what happened that night. Jose

attacked *me*! You know that's what happened, and now for you
to use it against me is complete shit. God, Alex!" Evie leaned
to the far side of the seat. She crossed her arms and shook her
head. "I thought I knew you. I thought I really, really knew
you, but I guess I don't."

"That makes two of us," Alex bit back.

Evie could not believe what was happening. Tonight was
supposed to be such a special night, a makeup night for the
Saturday evening before. She looked up at Dee Dee's
house. The Malibu lights on the front lawn showcased the
de LaFuentes' three-tier stone fountain. Water cascaded
down to each tier, and Evie was reminded of the back patio
at Koi, where water had trickled from the decorative bamboo chutes into the koi-filled pond. And now, here was
another night that was going to be ruined because Alex was
being so insensitive.

Evie felt tired. She was tired of arguing with Alex. Was this
what it was like to go out with someone? Always in arguing,
defending, or accusing mode? She was not feeling it. She took
a breath as she reached around her neck and unhooked the
clasp of her abalone necklace. "Here." Her hand was shaking
as she gave the necklace to Alex. "Just take it."

Alex looked at the necklace, then at her. "Evie . . ."

"No, just take it." She didn't look him in the eyes, but rather
at the necklace itself. The knots that held the pieces of abalone
shell in place were hand-twisted and looked like a third-grade

attempt at high fashion. How could she have *worn* something so hideous?

"Obviously, it's too hard for you to say or do nice things for me anymore," she told Alex. "Obviously, it's too much of a challenge. Here." She held out the cord. "Just take it."

Alex took the necklace. "So what is this supposed to mean?"

"I don't know," Evie said. "Maybe we should just take a break."

"A *break*?" Alex asked

"Yeah," Evie said curtly. "Time off."

"Okay." Alex looked out his side window. "Then why don't you just give me back the headphones? I gave those to you too."

"Fine." Evie's heart sank. The Bose headphones? *Ouch.* "I *will.*"

"Whatever." Alex leaned over and stuffed the necklace into his glove compartment. It looked completely out of place crammed between his empty jewel cases and miscellaneous paper trash. "If that's what you want . . . time off. Now, that's a plan that I wish *I* had thought of!"

Evie got out of his truck and slammed the door. "Well, let's see how long you *plan* to carry it out!"

21

WHEN EVIE SHOWED UP IN DEE DEE'S ROOM, SHE WAS PUFFY EYED and bare necked.

"Hey." Dee Dee's face dropped when she saw Evie at her doorway. "*Qué pasó?*" She looked over Evie's shoulder. "What's wrong? Where's Alejandro?"

Before Evie knew it, she was crying all over again. "We got in a fight. He just dropped me off and then took off!"

"What? *Serio?*" Dee Dee led Evie to the edge of her bed. "Here, sit down." She grabbed a box of blue tissues from the shelf under her night table. "What happened? Tell me."

Evie went into the horrid details about her argument with Alex—how Alex had accused her of being a bitch, a nag, and a two-timing best friend.

"And what did you say to all that?" Dee Dee asked.

"Nothing," Evie said. "I said nothing. I just gave him back his stupid necklace."

"You gave him back his necklace?"

"And the headphones." Evie blew her nose. "I mean, I'm gonna give those back to him when I get them."

"*Híjole.*" Dee Dee looked around her room in shock. "I'm really, really surprised, especially the part about Alejandro saying all that stuff about you and Jose. Alejandro has always seemed like such a gentleman."

"He is, or was, I guess." Evie said, "I mean, he's not horrible, but he just acts so flaky, and sometimes he treats me like just a dude. He's always calling me Gomez, and his texts—he always types, 'talk to you later.' Why doesn't he ever want to talk to me *soon*? I've just burned out. Is that so wrong?"

"Of course not." Dee Dee handed her more tissues. "You are the cutest girl, and you deserve a guy who is going to treat you like a *princesa*."

Princesa.

"You know Horsaphina?" Evie wiped her nose. "At the reserve? The senior Hermana?"

"Uh-huh, *claro*." Dee Dee moved in closer to Evie, perhaps hoping that she had the inner scoop about her potential Hermana-ship.

"Well, Arturo is totally sweet to her," Evie said. "I mean, he just dotes on her, and I just don't understand why *I* can't have a boyfriend like that." She wiped the corners of her eyes.

"Arturo?" Dee Dee frowned in confusion. "I thought you said that he was a jerk, like a total control freak."

"Not to her he isn't." Evie said, "Arturo is totally sweet and romantic to her."

"Evie," Dee Dee said, "you were totally talking smack about him, like just a month ago, and now you're saying that he's the ideal boyfriend?"

"I didn't say he was *the* ideal."

"In not so many words you did," Dee Dee said. "And when did you start calling him Arturo? I thought he was Ar-*turdo*."

"Huh?" Evie didn't know what Dee Dee was getting at. "No, everyone calls him Arturo."

"Everyone but you," Dee Dee said.

"Dela?" Marcela interrupted Evie and Dee Dee as she tapped on Dee Dee's bedroom door. *"La familia Fontes están aquí."*

"Oh!" Dee Dee jumped up from her bed. *"Ay, güey!* They're already here!"

Evie was so lost in her own sorrows that she had forgotten the whole reason she was at Dee Dee's. She heaved a deep sigh. She was not in the mood to spend the entire evening faking pleasantness.

Dee Dee waved her fingers in the air like she was trying to make wet polish dry on her fingernails. "I am *so* nervous." She twirled around for Evie. "Do I look okay?"

Evie looked up at Dee Dee. She hadn't noticed how truly adorable she looked. Dee Dee was wearing a soft pink knee-length dress with a cream-colored tulle edge. Her blond hair had been curled into ringlets and moussed to perfection.

"*Yes.*" Evie managed to smile. "You look beautiful. No, better than beautiful. You look just like . . ." Evie looked around Dee Dee's bedroom for inspiration. "Anahí."

"*Anahí?*" Dee Dee's face lit up. There was no higher praise. She looked at herself in the bedroom mirror, placed her hand on her hip, and drew down her face, a total Anahí pose. "Really? You're not just saying that?"

"No," Evie promised. "And yes, *really.*"

Anahí from RBD was Dee Dee's favorite, favorite singer/actress/chica *rubia* in the whole wide world of *telenovelas*. Dee Dee idolized Anahí and RBD.

Evie watched Dee Dee continue to fuss in front of the mirror, and then she caught a look at herself. Her face was red, puffy, and tearstained. The three coats of mascara she had applied earlier had collected in the outer corners of her eyes. There was no way she wanted to meet Rocio and his family looking all *la llorona.*

"Dee Dee?" Evie got up from the bed and wiped her cheeks with the edge of her palms. "Can I borrow some concealer? For my eyes?"

"*Claro,* of course." Dee Dee went over to her bathroom and brought out a professional-looking black leather makeup case that possessed every item CoverGirl and M.A.C. could possibly carry.

"*Sientese.*" Dee Dee patted the cushioned stool in front of her vanity table and mirror. As Evie sat down, Dee Dee laid out a line of small tubes, pencils, and a concealer brush on the mahogany table. It reminded Evie of being at the dentist's office, where Dr. Mizraji lined up every shiny important-looking instrument on the dental tray, ready to tackle any problem.

Dee Dee stared at Evie's face. "Ooh, you've lost a lot of your tan. We'll definitely have to go with something *mas blanca*."

Evie tried to relax and just let Dee Dee take over. It felt soothing, almost therapeutic, to have her softly rub creams and lotions under her tired eyes.

"Drama should never drain the diva." Dee Dee smiled proudly as she stepped back to admire her work. *"Bien. Mira."* She let Evie look at herself in the vanity mirror. "Now you look more like Dulce Maria to my Anahí."

Evie looked in the mirror. She thought she resembled RBD's Maite more than Dulce Maria, what with her dark hair and all. But either way, she would rather look like a Sweet Maria than a Weepy Evie.

❋ ❋ ❋

When Dee Dee finally felt both girls were Rocio-ready, she led Evie down the stairs, where they were met by Rocio himself. He was waiting in the foyer. He *was* quite the *papi chulo*. He looked just like the pictures Evie had seen of him with Dee Dee in Mexico City. He had a slight build and seemingly freshly cut hair. His eyes were very dark and intense and topped with thick, bushy eyebrows, almost like Dee Dee's father's. And he was wearing a casual dark blue dinner jacket that made him look cosmopolitan and mature. Evie had seen boys dress similarly, but posing on motor scooters or in front of ancient fountains in the fashion magazines that Dee Dee had lying around her room, never in person.

"Dela." Rocio smiled as he took her hand and helped her with the last step. *"Te ves muy hermosa."*

"Oh!" Dee Dee covered her embarrassed smile with her hand. *"Really?"*

"Yes." Rocio's eyes widened as if she were crazy to question him. "Really."

"Oh, Rocio, I—" Dee Dee stopped herself and looked over at Evie. "Oh, I am *so* sorry! This is Evie." She placed her hand on Evie's shoulder. *"Recuerdas? Mi amiga del alma?"*

"Sí, sí." Rocio took Evie's hand and actually kissed it. *"Estoy encantado.* You are even lovelier in person."

Lovelier? Evie couldn't ever remember being called lovely. Did people, boys, even talk like that? She guessed in Mexico City they did. And they kissed hands too? Wait until she told Raquel. Oh, wait, she couldn't. She glanced down at her hands, relieved that her hand job from Michael Kelley still looked intact.

"Muchas gracias, Rocio." Evie smiled. "I've heard so much about you."

"Good things, I hope." He smiled back. "Or at least interesting."

Dee Dee looked over Rocio's shoulder and into the great room. "Where are your parents?"

"Listen, they're already out in the backyard." A large grin continued to expand across Rocio's face. "There was immediate respect. I felt it, first thing."

"Really? Oh, Rocio." Dee Dee linked arms with him. "I am so happy you are here." She linked her other arm with Evie's. "I couldn't be *mas feliz*. My two favorite people *en todo el mundo!*"

As the three of them headed outside, Evie couldn't help but wonder where Raquel fit in between Dee Dee's "two favorite people in the whole world." She felt a bit ashamed, as though being at this dinner party was betraying Raquel. But, Evie had to admit, Raquel *had* been getting a little crazy with her party patterns. Then again, they all got a little crazy in their own way. *Were* there levels of acceptable craziness? Last year had been a pretty wild semester, and Evie wondered, would she have been invited to the special dinner with fancy-pants Mexicans if she still had her choppy blue hair?

Dee Dee's parents, Frank and Graciela, were out in the backyard, under the large *palapa* lounging area, with another couple who were obviously Rocio's parents.

"Dela!" Rocio's mother stood up and held her hands out to Dee Dee. "Long time no see, *mija*. We miss you in El Districto."

She wore a sleeveless black linen dress suit, accented by a dramatic red raw silk *rebozo* that Evie recognized from Studio

Tres Rios. Her wavy dark hair was pulled back into an elegant bun and secured by a large simple silver barrette.

Dee Dee went over to hug her.

"Oh, I miss you too, Herminia. I miss D.F. in general. How are Fred and Ofelia? Oh, and what about Café Blanca? Have you been there lately?" Dee Dee stopped herself and covered her face again, in bashfulness. *"Lo siento,"* she apologized. "I sometimes go on and on about Mexico."

Sometimes?

"It's just that I have such a love for D.F.," Dee Dee explained anxiously. "I really miss the nightlife. The U.S. is nothing like Mexico, and California can be, *cómo se dice, opressor?* I mean. No theater, no culture . . ."

No culture? Hadn't Evie just taken her to Skate Punk to look at their new line of knitted skull bags? And what about the mural that was just dedicated to Rell Sunn on Sea Street? Where was all this coming from? And why hadn't she been introduced to Rocio's parents yet? She felt awkward just standing there.

Dee Dee finally glanced over at Evie. "Oh, *lo siento,*" she said, as if she had just read Evie's thoughts. "I forgot. This is my dear friend, *mi amiga mejor,* Evelina."

"Hello." Evie nodded toward Mr. and Mrs. Fontes and followed Rocio's cue with his Spanish. *"Estoy encantada."*

"Estamos encantados." Rocio's parents nodded and smiled back.

That was pretty much the only exchange between them and Evie for the rest of the evening, and she was a bit relieved. The night seemed to be all about cosmopolitan culture, proper social etiquette, and correctly pronounced Spanish, none of which were her strong points. Besides, her eyes throbbed like two enormous soggy tea bags, and she just felt *so* exhausted.

❋   ❋   ❋

Dee Dee sat down next to Rocio on one of the rattan benches, and Evie followed. She watched Rocio and Dee Dee and couldn't help but notice how perfect they seemed together— Rocio practically finished Dee Dee's sentences, and Dee Dee advised Marcela on what to keep out of Rocio's pasta (peppers, pine nuts). It was like they were already mini-adults, and it made Evie anxious. She was going to be sixteen years old. Would she *ever* meet the perfect guy for her?

"So, have you gotten used to the time change?" Dee Dee's father asked Rocio's dad.

"We are getting along okay. Thank you," Señor Fontes replied.

Rocio's father had a slight build, like Rocio, and he also wore a sports jacket. Evie noticed that he was wearing impeccably shined leather shoes. She looked over at Señora Fontes. She had on pricey-looking leather shoes, too—black slingbacks with a slim heel. Thank *God* Evie hadn't worn her flojos to dinner.

"We're getting used to the time change much better than we're getting used to this American tequila." Rocio's father playfully held up his drink. "I was expecting, since you are such the big *chingón* out here in California, you'd be serving up Tequila Oro or something."

"This is actually Temequila." Frank held up his own glass. "I couldn't resist seeing how it compared to the real stuff—or, should I say, tequila manufactured in Mexico."

"Oh, really?" Rocio's father looked at his drink again and nodded his head with a newfound interest. "So it *was* distilled here. *Qué interesante*. But you know, you can't mess with tradition."

Graciela suddenly chuckled to herself.

"What is it?" Rocio's father looked over at her.

Graciela looked down in embarrassment as she tried to cover her smile with the edge of her own silk rebozo. "Oh, nothing," she said. "I don't want to be mean."

"Now you *have* to tell us," Rocio's mother nudged with encouragement.

"It just reminds me"—Graciela looked over at Evie—"and I hope I don't upset you, Evelina."

"Me? Why would I get upset?" She had no idea what Graciela could be talking about.

"I was just thinking about your father and when we had brunch at your parents' house, remember that?"

"Oh, yeah," Evie said. "I mean, yes."

As Evie's mother had mentioned earlier that week, she had

hosted a small intimate brunch to welcome the de LaFuentes back from Mexico. It was given just last October and the morning after the big party that Raquel's mother had thrown, also for the de LaFuentes.

"And your father—" Graciela started to chuckle again as she turned away from Evie and looked at Rocio's parents. "Evelina's father owns a *panadería*, and he makes, or *did* make, *pan*, pan dulce *sin manteca*."

The eyebrows of the Fonteses rose simultaneously, and soon both Rocio's parents joined Graciela in laughter.

"*Sin manteca?*" Rocio's mother looked at Evie. "Without lard? *Fíjate?*"

But it was Graciela who answered. "*Sí, sí.*" She started to laugh so hard that soon she started coughing. She quickly covered her mouth with a cloth napkin. Evie secretly hoped that the napkin would stay put.

"Now, Graciela, *stop* it." Frank de LaFuente put his plate down on the glass table and came to Evie's aid. "*Mira*, we never know anything until we take chances. Right, Evie?"

"Right." Evie smiled meekly. Could she feel more like an ugly American?

"*Right.*" Dee Dee shook her head with a pronounced nod. "And *I* liked it. I couldn't even tell the difference, that much."

❊ ❊ ❊

As the dinner plates were cleared and the three couples continued to reminisce about the fabulously wonderful city life in D.F., Evie found comfort by retreating to the kitchen. She figured she could hang, at least for a little while, with Marcela and the assistant that the de LaFuentes had hired to help her prepare and serve food. Evie pulled out a kitchen stool and sat down to check for cell phone messages. There were none.

"Qué te pasa?" Marcela asked Evie. It was apparent that she was hiding out. After all, why would a guest be in a hot kitchen when she could be enjoying a balmy evening outside?

"Nothing," Evie lied. Ever since she had been spending more time with Dee Dee, she had gotten to know Marcela better. Marcela was a lot younger than Lindsay, almost thirty years to Lindsay's sixty. Evie sometimes felt Marecela's contemporary chica insight was more helpful than Lindsay's matronly *madre* judgment. "It's just my boyfriend and I—"

Marcela's cell phone suddenly vibrated from her hip. "*Ay, lo siento*, Evelina," she apologized as she unclipped it from the waistband of her stonewashed jeans. She read the text. "Oh, it's my baby's *papa*. I have to call him."

"No worries," Evie said. "Go ahead, make your call."

As soon as Marcela turned her back and got on the phone, Evie found a cheese knife and cut herself the tiniest sliver of the Spanish *membrillo* from the slab on a serving tray. She looked over at Marcela, who now held her cell close to her ear. She had a big smile on her face and was looking over her

French manicure. God, did *everyone* have *someone* in his or her friggin' life? Evie cut herself another piece of membrillo, this time with cheese.

"*E*-vie?" Dee Dee came into the kitchen. "I wondered where you were. Come on." She took Evie's hand and pulled her off the stool. "We're about to have dessert. Why are you being so antisocial?"

Evie had no choice but to quickly swallow the quince and cheese she had crammed in her mouth and follow Dee Dee out to the backyard. The glass hurricane lamps on the main patio table had been lit, and now both Graciela and Rocio's mother were fully draped in their rebozos. Surely for show, Evie guessed—it was such a warm night, and no cover-ups were really needed.

Marcela's helper soon came out with the tray of quince paste and cheese. Thankfully, each slab looked perfectly intact. *Whew.* Evie had done a good job with the cutting. No one would suspect that she had indulged in therapeutic snacking.

"Oh, *this is just wonderful*," Rocio's mother raved as the helper set the tray down. "The whole dinner was *excelente*." She put her hand over Graciela's. "And the *bolillos* you served? *Muy blanditos!*"

"Gracias, Herminia." Graciela smiled as she poured hot water from a small teapot into delicate teacups.

"So, tell us, Rocio," prompted Frank de LaFuente, "how has it been looking at schools? You know, I have to say," he ribbed playfully, "I'm a little offended you haven't looked into Channel Islands."

"No, no, sir." Rocio placed his fork on his dessert plate as though a long explanation on his part was going to commence. "It's nothing against C.I. I would love to attend Channel Islands. The campus is so beautiful, and I'd be closer to Dela." He looked at Dee Dee and squeezed her hand. "But I need to get my MBA from a university that has the best department available. I can't waste time if I want to start a business and a family by the time I'm in my midtwenties." This time he did not look at Dee Dee, but Evie noticed he squeezed her fingers again.

"Well, that's very admirable," Frank said in a tone you'd expect to be followed by a pat on the back and the lighting of a cigar. "Very admirable. I can respect that."

Evie looked Rocio over. He was so mature and just, well, *capable*. He was barely eighteen years old and already thinking of a future with Dee Dee? In a way, he sorta reminded Evie a little bit of Arturo. Rocio was also moving away from his family and home to follow a dream, whatever that dream was. Was he moving to California to attend an American business school, or was he moving to California to attend to his American girlfriend? Either way, he was making plans. He was doing something to benefit both him and Dee Dee.

Evie opened her evening bag, discreetly checked her cell phone, and sighed. No text or message from Alex.

22

THE FIRST THING EVIE DID ON MONDAY MORNING AT SCHOOL WAS return her beloved Bose headphones to Alex. She decided to leave them in his locker with no note, no explanation, no *nada*.

It was two days since their fight, and he still hadn't called or texted her, and she wasn't about to phone or text him either. After all, he was the one who had left her hanging at the de LaFuentes' dinner party. If anyone deserved an apology, she did.

"I can't *believe* he wants your headphones back." Raquel leaned against the lockers. "What an asshole. Weren't they, like, a gift?"

"Yeah." Evie placed the headphones under his gray-and-white Señor Lopez pullover. She looked at the pullover and felt slightly deflated. They both used to wear their pullovers together on cold mornings at Sea Street. "He's just being a jerk," she remarked. "He asked for them back as soon as I gave him back my necklace."

Raquel peered past Evie and into Alex's locker. "You know, we could do some serious damage here. I could plant some lawn and then call the school, anonymously. Friend or not, I ain't got no loyalty when it comes to some dude messing with my girl."

"Raquel, *no.*" Evie slammed his locker door shut. "He's not that big of a jerk. Besides, he has the combination to my locker, and who knows? He might be talked into retaliation via Mondo."

"Yeah," Raquel reluctantly agreed. "He ain't worth it anyway. It's a good thing you don't have any classes with him. That would be a major drag. I remember with Jose, I'd have to see his ugly mug in Spanish and then his skinny white-ass legs in P.E. That's why I now *refuse* to date anyone who goes to the same school."

"Or someone who even *went* to school," Evie found herself teasing.

"Excuse me?" Raquel cocked one eyebrow. "You know, if I wasn't such a caring ADA, I *could* say something, but I won't. You're La Sad Girl now, so I'm just gonna be all nice and supportive." She put her arm around Evie, and they started down the hall for their first-period classes. "But check it out: now you and I can be a team—*the* team. Forget last semester and all that Flojo crap. We're *Solas Patrollas.*"

"But you still have Davey," Evie pointed out. "And Flojo or not, I won't give up wearing my flip-flops."

"I know, neither can I." Raquel looked down at her own jewel-encrusted flip-flops. Two of the green Swarovski gems had fallen off. "You know what?" Raquel said. "I say we skip the rest of the day and head on down to L.A. Let's go shopping. I could use some new flojos."

"Nuh-uh, no way." Evie turned the corner, toward first period. As good as a shop day in Los sounded, she couldn't afford to skip class and get in trouble. Her party depended on her being the perfect student. "If I get caught ditching my—"

"I promise, you won't get caught," Raquel said confidently.

"How you gonna promise that?" Evie asked.

Raquel opened her binder and flaunted a wad of slips. They were official Villanueva slips, three-by-five sheets of paper for every excusable reason to be out of school—off-campus slips, tardy slips, absentee slips—and they were all signed, seemingly, by Headmaster Covarrubias.

"How did you get those?" Evie couldn't believe what she was seeing.

"I've got my connections," Raquel bragged as she pulled down her Utopia Cop Out sunglasses and shut her binder. "Come on, let's go find Dee Dee and get out of here."

* * *

Dee Dee found a parking space for Jumile right in front of Decade on Robertson Boulevard. Dee Dee had suggested they shop at Fred Segal, and Raquel had wanted to go to Mud D., both on Roberston, but Evie was the one who needed to mend her heart and had first dibs on where they shopped. Her naked neck announced to everyone that she was Alex-less, and she wanted that to change, and so she picked Decade.

"You are *so* much better off without him," Raquel insisted as she got out of Jumile with Evie and Dee Dee. "Alex is such a punk ass. I told you how he was at that party, right? The one on Hemlock?"

"Yeah, you did tell me about that party," Evie reminded Raquel. She didn't want to hear about that night all over again.

Evie hit the buzzer near the front glass doors of Decade, and a clerk inside the shop let the three girls in. As soon as they entered, they were all sent back in time via the shop's exquisite midcentury interior—polished blond wood floors, zebra-skin throw rugs, and space-age swag lamps hanging from the ceiling created a sophisticated glamorous mood that you just didn't find at, say, Forever 21. Decade on Robertson supposedly had an ample inventory of designer vintage couture, and Evie had seen enough red-carpet poses to know that a lot of her favorite stars shopped at Decade. It would be fun to browse, and a little retail therapy would definitely get her mind off Alex.

"Yeah, so there I was," Raquel went on anyway as she

followed Evie and Dee Dee into the shop. "Just kicking back, blazing some one-hitters with some new friends, and here comes Jose, with Mondo and Alex. They don't even know any of the Bard Boys. I mean, *I* know the Bard crew, but they were acting as if they were part of the G-unit or something."

"I really don't think Alex thinks *that*," Evie said. Sure she was mad at Alex, but he didn't deserve to be sorely misrepresented.

"Welcome to Decade." A tall, slender salesclerk in a long-sleeved shirt and vintage silk ascot looked over at the three girls. He was helping a woman with the plumage on a felt hat. "I'll be right with you."

"Oh, thanks." Evie smiled at him and pulled the hood of her orange Roxy hoodie off her head. She immediately wished she had dressed nicer. She stood out like a sore beach bum.

"You know, Evie"—Raquel looked through the heavy bracelets arranged on a pale mannequin's arm—"you need a man. A *real* man. You know what? I'm gonna hook you up with one of Davey's friends. He's got lots of cool friends."

Evie looked over the simple but elegant dresses. There were only about ten dresses on each display rack, a sign that they were most definitely out of her price range. She carefully pulled out a short black strapless dress and glanced at the price tag. Eek, *so* many zeros for *such* a little amount fabric! Evie immediately put the dress back.

"I am *not* going out with some Bard Boy," she told Raquel. "There is *no* way in hell."

"Oh, *my*." Raquel pulled her sunglasses halfway down and peered at Evie. She put on a Southern accent and placed her hand on her chest. "Well, ess-cuse *me* . . . Muss Evie. I do declare, I overspoke."

"Evie needs a gentleman, a caballero, right, Evie?" Dee Dee took down a quilted metallic bag from one of the glass shelves. Each shelf had only four or five handbags on display, totally unlike Tilly's, where the totes were crammed on racks near the boogie boards and vintage rock tees. Dee Dee placed the chain strap over her shoulder and looked at herself in one of the oval full-length mirrors. "You know, as soon as Rocio moves out here, I'm sure he'll make lots of new acquaintances who will be dying to date someone as cute as you."

"Why do I have to date anyone at all?" Evie exhaled. Dee Dee and Raquel were talking like grand *tías*, deciding between themselves what was best for her, and she didn't want any of it. "It's like the both of you think that all I *need* is some boy to make things all better," she told them. "Look at Sabrina. She was with Robert for, like, two years and he was, like, perfect for her, but look what happened to her."

"You know, I just thought of something," Dee Dee remarked as she continued to look at herself with the bag. "If you're not talking to Alex, who's going to take you to your party?"

"Dee Dee!" Raquel looked over at her in amazement.

"Didn't you just hear Evie? It's not like she's having some backwards friggin' *quinceañera* and she has to have some boy escort her."

"*Right,*" Evie said. At least Raquel was getting where she was coming from.

"I know," Dee Dee agreed. "But she can't be at her own party all by herself."

"She's not *going* to be by herself," Raquel said. "We'll be there, and we'll be so loaded from freebie ad bevs, who'll care if Alex is there or not?"

"Yeah," Evie said. "Besides, you guys are acting like I'm never going to talk to Alex again. I mean, it's not like we're officially broken up." It helped her to say it out loud. She and Alex had *not* break up. They were just on a time-out. *Big* difference. "Besides, it's not like my party's tomorrow. Who knows what will happen between now and then."

"Yeah, but you did give him back his necklace," Dee Dee said.

"And the Bose headphones," Raquel added. "Besides, we don't even know if your parents are gonna let you have the party."

"Right." Evie's mood dropped again. She had yet to check on her horse reserve hours or get Dee Dee to start on her essay. She had better step up if she was serious about having her sixteeñera. Eve shook her head, as if she could shake off the worry.

The salesclerk finished helping the other customer and came up to Evie just as she pulled out another dress, a Chanel. "Would you like to try that on?" he asked.

"Um . . ." Evie glanced at the price tag. It was a little *too* couture, even for fun's sake. Knowing her luck, she'd snag the fabric or break the zipper and she'd have to pay for the damages. After the fender bender, she couldn't afford any more avoidable accidents. "I don't think so. It doesn't look like my size."

"You can't go by label sizes with vintage couture," the clerk said. "You just have to feel whether the dress works or not."

"Feel?"

"Yes." He looked Evie over. "We have quite a large collection of petite sizes. What are you looking for?"

"Um, I don't really know," Evie said. She was really just looking to have fun.

"Something fancy," Dee Dee said.

"Anything rock star–like?" Raquel asked.

"We do have a few Ossie Clark pieces," the clerk said. "Why don't I set you up in a dressing room and I can bring a few pieces out from our gallery?"

Collection? Pieces? Gallery? Evie thought they were looking at clothes, not bidding for art.

"Yeah, bring some out," Raquel answered for Evie.

"Of course," the clerk said. "I'll be back shortly." He left for another room in the back of the shop.

"So when is your driving test?" Raquel asked Evie.

"Next week," Evie answered.

"And you're all ready?" Dee Dee asked. "Right?"

"I think so," Evie said confidently, if only to convince herself. "I've been practicing with my dad and Lindsay for, like, the last month."

"And then you just gotta finish your horse credit. Speaking of which, how is that whipped-ass Arturdo doing?" Raquel asked.

"Has Josephina said anything about me?" Dee Dee wondered.

"You mean, Horsaphina?" Raquel snorted. "She's such a Sangro in horse clothing. I pegged that the minute I met her."

"No," Evie answered Dee Dee. "Horsaphina hasn't said anything yet. But don't even sweat it, Dee Dee. You don't need ol' Horsaphina. You'll totally be nominated for Las Hermanas on your own."

"Yeah, and when you are—" Raquel laid a yellow shift with a hemline of bright yellow boa feathers flat against her body. "—that's one celebration party I best be invited to."

As soon as Raquel spoke, Evie couldn't help but feel guilty. She knew that Raquel would be hurt if she knew about the de LaFuentes' dinner party. *How* could Dee Dee not have invited her? But worse, *how* could Evie have promised never to say anything about it? She hoped that Raquel would never find out.

The clerk came back with three dresses enveloped in clear plastic garment bags.

"I thought you said you had a lot of small things." Raquel looked over the bags.

The clerk looked at her blankly. "Yes, we do have an adequate stock of petite evening wear; however, these are couture. They can be very delicate pieces. They are nothing that can be thrown over my arm and lugged out."

"Oh, right." Raquel looked embarrassed and took a seat in a large Lucite egg chair.

Evie took the three dresses from the clerk and went into the dressing room.

The first dress that caught her eye was long and hot pink. It was less a dress and more a gown. She had never worn a *gown* before. She had always thought that if she and Alex went to prom together, she would wear a long dress, but would it be a gown? The prom was still two years away, *and* she wasn't even with Alex or anything. *Alex.* Ugh. She *had* to stop thinking about him.

Evie slipped out of her sandals, her shorts, and hoodie and slipped on the gown. She came out of the dressing room and walked over to the full-length trifold mirror.

"Man, you look *so* cool," Raquel said.

"Yes," the clerk agreed. "It's a very body-aware gown."

"Uh, well, I don't know if I want to be so aware of my body." Evie modestly crossed her arms. But she had to admit the gown was cool, very cool. It was a halter gown, and the back went down superlow. It had a slit that practically went up to her left armpit, and, as if she wasn't showing enough skin already, there was a diamond-shaped peekaboo opening right in the middle of her chest. God, she'd never imagined that she could look so—dare she say it?—*hot* in a dress.

"No, no," Dee Dee said. "It looks good, gives you hips."

"Really?" Evie looked in the mirror. "You thinks?"

"Evie," Dee Dee said. "Your hips are speaking *Spanish!*"

Evie covered her mouth and laughed.

"Oh my God." The clerk also laughed. "I *have* to use that line. There's someone who *needs* to make my hips speak Spanish, and I'm not even bilingual!"

Suddenly the shop door's buzzer rang.

"Oh, it *never* ends." The clerk rolled his eyes as he went to release the front door.

"You *gotta* get it." Raquel looked Evie over.

Evie glanced at the tag. "Oh my God. I shouldn't even be wearing this!"

"Why?" Dee Dee asked. *"Cuantos?"*

"It's like two thousand dollars!"

"And?" Raquel asked.

"And, *hello,* I don't know about you, but *I* don't have two thousand bucks for a dress or anything, especially after the whole Lindsay fiasco. *Please.*" Evie started back into the dressing room to take off the gown. "I'm just trying on things for fun."

"Evie, do you *like* the dress?" Raquel inquired.

"Well, yeah. But that doesn't mean—"

"Do you *love* the dress?"

"Well, yeah," Evie said. "No question." She looked at herself in the mirror. Her hips, for sure, did not lie. The gown actually gave her curves. Not quite hourglass, but there was some concave action going on at her waist.

"Then you *are* getting the dress." Raquel opened her Roxy tote.

"Raquel!" Evie exclaimed when she saw her pull out her wallet. "You are *crazy*. You are *so* not buying me this dress!"

"Why not?" Raquel nonchalantly pulled out her credit card. "It'll be my birthday present to you."

"Raquel, *no*." Evie covered her entire face. She couldn't believe what she was hearing.

"Evie, *yes*. I can't have my ADA looking all *scrapa* at her own party. Right, Dee Dee?"

"Uh, right," Dee Dee said. Even she looked a little awkward about the whole transaction that was about to take place. "Now I feel bad. The present I got for Evie sucks compared to the gown."

"Well, if you want," Raquel said, "you can pay for half of it."

"Uh, I don't feel *that* bad," Dee Dee said.

The clerk came back. "So have we made a decision?"

"Yes." Raquel handed him her credit card. "We'll take it. And we'll take that for her." She directed him toward Dee Dee, who still had the quilted bag draped over her shoulder. "And we'll have them both wrapped," Raquel added. "They're gifts."

23

WHEN EVIE GOT HOME FROM L.A., SHE IMMEDIATELY WENT TO HER room to try her gown on again. *What* would she tell her mother? The gown was far from being a "great find" at one of the *segundas* downtown, but then again, what did her mother know about vintage couture?

As she was zipping up her gown, she heard her cell phone ring and fumbled in her bag to look for it. But before Evie found her phone, it stopped ringing and then her bedroom's landline rang. It was Dee Dee.

"I've got something major to tell you," Dee Dee said. Her voice sounded serious.

"What? Don't tell me that Raquel's credit card was stolen and we gotta return everything?" Evie teased. She looked herself over in her closet mirrors. *Damn.* She was *caliente!*

"No, don't say that." Dee Dee laughed. "I would hate to have to return my purse. God, don't you just love your dress?"

"I'm wearing it right now," Evie confessed sheepishly.

"Are you serious?" Dee Dee asked. "So why do you think Raquel has all this extra *lana*?"

"From not having to cover Jose's ass all the time," Evie said. She actually liked that she knew something about Raquel that Dee Dee didn't. Sure, they were all ADAs, but she could be a bit of a control freak when it came to having first-run information on either friend. "Remember?" she asked. "Raquel was always paying for him when he ran out of his trust money."

"I guess," Dee Dee said. "I mean, I didn't know him when they were going out, but she had said he was pretty on the *codo* side. I'm taking my purse to school tomorrow. Wait until Alejandra de los Santos sees it."

"Yeah," Evie agreed. "Wait until—" She stopped herself. She really had no one to impress with her sexy hot pink halter gown. Alex might not even *be* at her party.

"So anyway . . ." Dee Dee sighed. "I have to tell you. Rocio came back today, from looking at schools in the Bay Area."

"Cool." Evie continued to look at herself again in the mirrors. "Has he made any decisions?"

"Yeah," Dee Dee admitted slowly. "And it looks like he doesn't want to go to college out here at all."

"Oh, no. Are you serious?" Evie knew Dee Dee must be bumming hard. She was surprised that she hadn't requested an ER/RE! meeting.

"He doesn't want to leave D.F.," Dee Dee explained. "And

I don't blame him. So—" She cleared her throat. "—I'm thinking I'll move back to Mexico too . . . so I can be closer to him."

"*What?*" Evie laughed. "Yeah, right. Dee Dee, you are *so* not moving back to Mexico City. You're crazy."

"No, I'm not," Dee Dee asserted. "I already talked to Graciela about it. She said I could stay with her family in Coyoacán." She paused. "That's where Frida used to live, with Diego."

"Yeah, I *know* that, Dee Dee." Evie felt irritated. "But wait, I don't understand. How can you just move back to D.F.? You just started at Villanueva, and what about Las Hermanas?"

"I know." Dee Dee sighed. "I feel really bad about that."

"Feel *bad* about it?" Evie asked. It now seemed clear that Dee Dee was serious. "Dee Dee, are you saying you don't want to be a Hermana anymore? I can't believe this."

"No, I'm not saying that. I definitely want to be a Hermana, I'm just saying that I don't think I can be one at this time. I'm going to have—"

"*At this time?*" Evie couldn't believe what she was hearing. "So when do you think you can *become* one? When you're like thirty years old or something?"

"You didn't let me finish," Dee Dee interjected. "Evie, I need to make a decision, and right now my decision is that I want to be closer to Rocio."

"But Las Hermanas is all you've been talking about forever.

What about the first dance, with your dad? And your mom? She *wanted* you to be a Hermana."

"Evie," Dee Dee said. "I don't know what to tell you except that it's really my own decision, and for you to bring up my mom like that . . ." Her voice got soft. "I . . . I just don't want to get into it right now."

"Yeah, but Dee Dee," Evie protested.

"Evie, I really don't want to talk about it with you."

Dee Dee then practically hung up on Evie. Evie was stunned. How could so many things change in a matter of days? First she had lost her boyfriend, and now her best friend was leaving! She called Dee Dee back, but her call went straight to voice mail. Evie then texted Raquel with the emergency code of ER/RE! but didn't hear back from her all night.

24

"HELLO?" ARTURO WAVED HIS HAND IN FRONT OF EVIE'S FACE. "Anyone there?"

"Oh, I'm sorry." Evie looked up. She was feeding Chamuco and had no idea that Arturo had even been talking to her. "I wasn't paying attention."

Evie was still in a bit of a daze. Dee Dee's announcement of the night before was still weighing heavily on her mind. How could she even think of moving back to Mexico? On their drive to school, Dee Dee had refused to discuss it, and Evie hadn't pushed the subject. It was a long day at Villanueva for Evie. Raquel hadn't come to school, and she was without Alex's shoulder to lean on. *Alex*. His absence was sinking in.

"So, do you want to?" Arturo asked.

"Want to what?" Evie asked.

Arturo cocked his head down in confusion. "Take the

horses out. We're pretty much done here, and I know your housekeeper doesn't come for another hour, so I was thinking we could take them out."

"You mean to *ride?*" Evie asked.

"No," Arturo smirked. "Take them out on a date."

Evie laughed. Actually, what Arturo had said wasn't *that* funny, but somehow his mild sense of humor was rubbing off on her. "I totally want to go riding." Evie patted Chamuco. "But wait, I thought volunteers weren't allowed to ride the horses."

"They can't unless they have seniority. Seniority in *experience, not* age." He smiled. "And I know from your file that you used to spend time with horses up here, when you were a kid, right?"

"Uh, right," she told Arturo. Evie wasn't about to admit that she had colored her file just a wee bit. She had gone horseback riding one time, and one time only, when she was, like, ten years old. But Arturo didn't need to know specifics.

"Why don't we take Chamuco out?" she asked.

"Nuh-uh. No way," Arturo said.

"No, come on," Evie insisted. "We're totally friends. Look." She pulled a carrot out of her front pocket and fed it to him. "Ah, dun't choo like that, huh, Cha-muu-co boy?"

Alex winced.

"What?" Evie asked.

"The baby talk," he said. "It's gotta go."

Evie looked at him. Did she hear right? "Okay, boss. Whatever you say. Let me just go get my pullover and I'll be ready."

"We can take Sprinkles and Panchito out," Arturo said. "They could use the exercise. You can take Sprinkles," he suggested. "He's just about the most gentle horse we have."

Evie gave Chamuco a hug around his neck and then sprinted to the supply shed. Just as she grabbed her Señor Lopez pullover from her backpack, she noticed the light on her cell phone was blinking. She couldn't resist. She opened up her phone and, yes, it was a text from Alex.

Can we talk?

Evie's heart dropped. *Oh.* She wanted to text him back, right away.

"Evie!" Arturo called out. "Come on, we're losing the sunset. There's this great ridge to see it from."

Sunset? Arturo hadn't said anything about a sunset.

She looked over Alex's text. What to do, what to do? Evie closed her phone and tossed it back into her backpack. She would text Alex as *soon* as she returned from her ride on Sprinkles.

When she came out of the shed, Arturo was already saddled up on Panchito and held the reins to Sprinkles. She was a bit taken by the way he looked, high up on Panchito. Arturo looked *nice*. He looked somewhat manly and definitely in charge. Maybe there *was* something about a boy in cowboy boots. Being high on a black mustang couldn't hurt either.

Evie felt a little nervous as she started toward Sprinkles. She hadn't been on a horse in years. She lifted up her left foot, stuck her sneaker in the stirrup, and clumsily hoisted herself up onto Sprinkles. *Oomf!* She flopped ungracefully onto poor Sprinkles's back. She immediately sat up in the saddle and took hold of the reins.

Arturo looked over. "You look good." He nodded. "He agrees with you." He tapped Panchito on his side and pulled the reins to the left. "Come on."

Evie nudged Sprinkles with the inside of her sneaker, but he did not move. She nudged him again. Still nothing. Arturo was already a few yards ahead of her and heading toward a trail that led from the reserve.

"Wait, Turo," Evie called out. "You didn't give me a gentle horse. You gave me a dead one!"

Arturo looked over his shoulder. "Give him a good kick."

"Kick? I don't want to hurt him!"

"He can take it," Arturo called back. "Your foot's gonna feel just like a little baby pat to him."

Evie nudged Sprinkles's side a bit harder, and he suddenly got himself (and her) into gear.

"Whoa!" Evie wasn't quite prepared for his *giddyup*, to just get up and go so quickly. She held on to the saddle horn and tried to keep her balance, but it was a bit of a challenge, to say the least. Sprinkles wasn't the most steady ride. His body fell into a rhythm that Evie couldn't follow, and her bottom was already getting more of a workout than she'd been planning on. Had Arturo said they were gonna ride for a whole *hour*?

But fifteen minutes later, the four of them—Evie, Arturo, Sprinkles, and Panchito—were already deep in the chaparral of the riverbank, among flora and fauna that Evie had never even known existed. Even though it was midwinter, cactus tunas were in bloom and Evie caught a family of cottontail rabbits scurrying across the dirt path. How *long* had she lived by the river, in a neighborhood and on a street *named* for the river, and yet she hadn't spent any time near the actual river that ran through the whole county?

"Oh my God," Evie marveled. "I *love* it out here. I can't believe I've lived here all my life, and not once have I ever come up this way."

Arturo also looked around. "Yeah, a lot of people forget what's in their own backyard. Especially"—he looked at Evie and smirked—"if you live in Rio *Gates*."

"Hey," Evie teased back, "I can't help where my parents bought a house."

"Yeah, but you can help where you spend your time," Arturo said. "But besides, I think because I'm not from around here, I make it a point to explore more than the average person. Sometimes, after my shift, I come up here on Princesa and take a sunset ride."

"Princesa?" Evie asked. "And who does Hor—er, Josephina ride?"

"Oh, Josephina won't go horseback riding. She's never been out here."

"What?" Evie asked. "You are *not* serious."

"Yeah, I am," Arturo said casually. "I'm the one who takes Princesa out for exercise. Josephina got Princesa for her sixteenth birthday, but I can't remember the last time she even worked out with her." Arturo sighed and shook his head. "That's the problem with some people. They think that horses are really cool and that they make cute pets. They don't realize how much work they are. Oh, hey—" He looked ahead. "Check it out." He pointed out a grassy field they were just riding up to. "See where it's all matted down over there, in the middle of the field?"

Evie looked over. "Uh-huh."

"That's where coyotes were sleeping," Arturo said. "From the size of the impression, you can tell it was a large pack of them."

"*What?*" Evie looked around nervously. "Coyotes? You're kidding, right? There was *no* mention of river coyotes at orientation. God, something is *always* out to get you!"

"What do you mean?" Arturo asked.

"I mean, when I'm surfing, I worry about sharks, and now that I'm horseback riding, I have to worry about coyotes!"

"You don't have to worry." Arturo laughed. "They only come

out at night. We have a little bit of time before the sun goes down, and besides, I'd protect you."

"I can protect myself, thank you," Evie teased indignantly.

"So, I didn't know you surfed." Arturo reined to the left, leading Panchito, as well as Evie and Sprinkles, down a smaller trail.

"Uh-huh," Evie said. "Well, I haven't actually for a while." She realized it had been over a month since she had gone to Sea Street with Alex. "I used to surf a lot with my boyfriend. I mean, my sorta boyfriend."

"Is he the one who gave you that necklace you always wore?"

"The necklace?" Evie asked. She hadn't thought Arturo would notice something like the accessories that volunteers wore.

"Yeah, the shell one," Arturo said.

"Yeah," Evie said. "But I gave it back to him."

"Did you break up with him?" he asked.

Just a tad privado, *don't you think, Turo?*

"No, not really." Evie didn't feel like going into the details, especially with Arturo, who was in a solid steady relationship and wouldn't understand the gloominess of sudden single-dom. It had been about four days since her argument with Alex, and his absence from her life had become painfully apparent. She missed the little conversations they'd have on their way to school and she missed how he'd always take her to the reserve. It was really very sweet and considerate of him to always ask how she was getting home from work. He really *could* be the concerned boyfriend at times. She kept rethinking what had gone wrong the night they were going to the de LaFuentes'. Had she been giving him annoying jabs? Had she been trying to make him feel guilty? God, maybe she *was* a nag.

"Poor guy." Arturo clicked his tongue. "I can relate."

"What do you mean, *poor* guy?" Evie frowned. "You don't even know him, and you don't even know my side of the story."

"But I know all about yo-yos."

"Huh?" Evie asked.

"When Josephina and I first started dating," Arturo started to explain, "I gave her a bracelet. It was supposed to mean that we were going out. Wasn't your necklace like that?"

"Yeah, I guess," Evie said. "I mean, yeah, it was."

"Exactly," Arturo said. "But every time Josephina would get mad at me, she would break up with me, which was like every other week, and then she would take the bracelet off and give it back. At first it used to piss me off, but then it all became so routine. We'd have a fight, she'd take off the bracelet, and well, you know the story. She just gave me back her bracelet," Arturo said. *"Again."*

"Oh no," Evie said. "I'm sorry."

"And you know what? If she asks for it back, I'm not going to give it back to her. I'm fed up. I'm over it. I'm over her. So, yes, I actually *can* relate to your boyfriend, or whatever you are calling him now."

"Well, I don't plan on asking for the necklace back," Evie insisted. "And I didn't break up with him officially."

"Does he know that?" Arturo asked.

"I'm sure he does," Evie said. "I mean, I didn't say, 'Here's your necklace back, I never want to see you again.'"

"Good." Arturo nodded. "Like I said, there is nothing worse than a yo-yo relationship."

"I know that," Evie agreed. She had never been in any other relationship, yo-yo or not, but she wasn't about to admit that to him.

Arturo pulled the reins to the right and Evie saw that he was leading them back to the reserve. Their quick little ride was ending too soon.

"So hey," Evie asked cautiously. "What's gonna happen to Chamuco?"

"Well, we got another adoption day coming up. Hopefully someone will take him."

"And if someone doesn't take him, what happens to him?" Evie wasn't sure if she really wanted to hear the answer.

"He'll just have to stay at the reserve longer . . . until the next clinic," Arturo said. "We have them four times a year."

"Why do you think he hasn't been adopted yet?"

"Because people always want younger, healthier horses," Arturo said. "Chamuco has already passed his prime."

Evie felt bothered by this news. "Well, at least he has the reserve."

"Yeah, and we all take care of him. You know, even when you're done with your school credit, the reserve can always use more help. I hope you've thought about staying on."

"Actually, I have," Evie said. She really had been thinking of continuing to work at the reserve. Not only had she grown to love the horses, but she was really liking the people she was meeting at the reserve too—including Arturo.

"Yeah, when I leave for Davis," he started, "we'll be short one more hand."

"You got accepted into Davis?" Evie asked. "Wow, congratulations!"

"Thanks." Arturo smiled. "I'm not starting until the spring, with early enrollment. I'm really looking forward to it."

"That is so cool," Evie said. She felt a little conflicted. She was truly happy for Arturo, but also a bit sad that he would be leaving the reserve. It seemed that everyone was bailing or had bailed on her. What was the total so far this week?

"And if you start working at the reserve, you can learn more about horsemanship," he said.

"I know about horsemanship." Evie's ego felt a sudden need to defend itself.

Arturo looked at her dangling feet. "One of the most basic things to know is how to ride a horse properly."

"Right." Evie didn't understand his point. "That's a given."

"Yeah, for one thing," Arturo said, "you can't have your feet hanging off the side of a horse like that. You need to keep your shoes *in* the stirrups."

* * *

By the time they got back to the stables, the sun had already set. Evie remembered she hadn't seen the sunset from the ridge Arturo had mentioned.

"I'll show you next time," he promised. "I was sorta getting worried that it was gonna get dark on us and, you know, *los coyotes.*"

Evie rolled her eyes at him.

"So, did you have fun?" Arturo asked as he got off Panchito.

"Oh yeah," Evie said. "Definitely. This has been one of the best days I've had in a long time."

"I was thinking that maybe we could go get coffee or something," Arturo said as he took the reins for both horses. They were now at Sprinkles's stable. "And if you want, I can give you a ride home."

"Oh, my housekeeper is probably already on her way." Evie suddenly felt regretful. She was having fun with Arturo and would have liked to hang out with him longer. He had been so cool and friendly during their ride. Plus, it didn't hurt that he was easy on the eyes and that he was quite the caballero, as Dee Dee would say.

Evie started to dismount from Sprinkles, and as she swung her left leg around, she couldn't help but lose her balance. She grabbed for the saddle horn, but still stumbled off Sprinkles.

"Whoa!" Arturo caught her before she fell. "Careful there."

"Oh, how embarrassing!" Evie sagged in his arms. She quickly stood up on her own. "Yeah, guess I could use a lesson in horsemanship."

Arturo looked at her and smiled, an almost shy smile. "You're really cute."

"Yeah, for someone who doesn't know much about horses," Evie joked. She straightened her shirt and pulled up her low-rise jeans. She suddenly felt the oddest sensation in her stomach. *No, this cannot be happening.*

"I'm going to be direct . . . ," Arturo started.

God, why did her stomach feel so weird?

"Would someone like me even have a chance with you?"

"What are you even talking about?" Evie tried to play it off and kept her head down as she wiped the dust and Sprinkles's horsehair off her jeans. She *loved* having a boy ask such a direct question. Unlike Alex, who had shyly come up from behind to offer affection, Arturo was front and center.

"You know what I mean." Arturo placed his fingers under her chin.

Now it wasn't just her stomach. Evie's whole body tingled. Her mouth felt dry.

"I don't know, Arturo," she said softly. She didn't want to

look into his eyes for fear that he might know what she was feeling. "I guess you'd have to find out."

Did I really just say that?

"Oh yeah?" Arturo pursed his lips and then smiled. "Is that a challenge? Well, I *live* for challenges." Before Evie knew it, he had lifted her chin and started to kiss her.

Evie couldn't resist. She placed her hands on Arturo's shoulders and reached up for more. He was tall—taller than Alex, that was for sure—and his kiss was deep and long, different from Alex, who gave quick but gentle kisses. Evie instantly felt that vaguely familiar light-headed feeling.

"Evie?"

Both Evie and Arturo looked up.

It was Alex. He was at the entrance of Sprinkles's stall.

"Alex!" Evie immediately pulled back from Arturo. She wiped her bottom lip with the back of her hand.

"I . . . you didn't answer my text," Alex started. "And Lindsay said you were still here, and so I just came by." He was speaking to Evie, but his eyes were on Arturo.

"Oh, yeah." Evie nervously fluffed her hair forward and started toward him.

"No, *don't*." Alex held his palms out toward Evie and took a few steps back. "Alex, wait," Evie called.

But it was too late. He was already heading back to his truck. He got in and drove away.

25

4getit.

Excuse me? Had she read Alex's text correctly? And what did it mean? Evie held her cell close and reread his text on its screen. *4getit?* It was nearly 1 A.M., and she had been waiting, dying, to hear from Alex, and now this was what she got? *What* did it mean? Did he want to forget about talking to her or did he want to forget their relationship? She went through the complete text message history between her and Alex. How had their relationship shifted from *Nite, QT* to *4getit* in just a matter of days? Of course, she knew how. One word: Arturo.

After Lindsay had picked her up from the reserve that afternoon, Evie asked her to drive by Alex's house, but his truck wasn't parked in his driveway. He didn't return any of her phone calls or texts, and his cell phone went straight to voice mail. It was clear to Evie, very clear, that he didn't want to talk to her. It couldn't be true. But maybe it was. Was Alex not her boyfriend anymore?

Of course, she wasn't able to sleep. Her mind was racing with worry, confusion, and fear. Alex (worry), Arturo (confusion—what *had* happened between them?), and her driving test (fear, major). Then some of the players changed, but the theme continued: Dee Dee (worry), Raquel (confusion), and of course, the driving test (fear, still major). Alex and Arturo, of course, were always floating around in the background. Evie tucked her cell phone under her pillow, turned over, and closed her eyes in determination. She *had* to sleep. Her driving test was in less than four hours.

Get to sleep. Sleep! Don't think about him or him or her or . . . them. Your driving test is the most important thing right now. The first thing you do is check your mirrors. No, you put on your seat belt. Stop it! You need rest. Fall asleep already!

Arturo, Alex . . . Arturo. *Argh!*

Evie turned on her other side and hugged her other pillow when she heard what sounded like Davey Mitchell's truck. She *knew* that staccato rumble anywhere. She pulled her cell phone out from under her pillow and checked the time. Could it really be him coming down Camino del Rio at one thirty in the morning? She pushed away the sheets, got up from her bed, and looked through her bedroom shutters. Yes, it was Davey. He was bringing Raquel home from God knew where. Evie crossed her arms and watched Raquel step down from his lifted four-by-four and sneak around the side of her house.

Evie immediately texted her:

Cn I cme ovr?

To which Raquel replied:

Now?

Evie:

ER

Raquel:

K. Ktch dr. Shh!

Evie quickly threw on some sweatpants, a hoodie, and her Juicy Couture flip-flops. She crept downstairs and went through the side door of the kitchen before cutting across to the Diazes' backyard. When she entered the Diazes' kitchen door, she found Raquel tearing through the refrigerator's freezer.

"I totally have the munchies," Raquel announced, as if it weren't already obvious. She pulled out two Trader Joe's green-chili-and-cheese tamales and tossed them in the microwave.

"Raquel," Evie moaned as she pulled up a stool, "you won't believe it. Alex just broke up with me. He broke up with me by text."

"I thought you guys had already broken up," Raquel said nonchalantly. She hit two minutes on the microwave's timer.

"Not officially," Evie said. Her eyes started to water. Her body felt numb.

"But I thought you gave him back his necklace," Raquel said. She took a soda from the fridge. "Want one?"

"No." Evie shook her head and wiped her eyes. Wasn't Raquel listening? "I mean, we never really talked about it. We just said we were going to take a break."

Raquel sipped her soda and frowned. "But what was there to talk about? You gave him back the necklace. Isn't that how people do it when they're 'going steady'?" She made air-quotes with her fingers.

"What's that supposed to mean?" Evie asked

"I mean, you get into all these rules and regulations, the 'decorum' of relationships, and please, why can't people just do whatever the hell they want?"

The microwave's timer went off, and Raquel pulled out her tamales.

"Raquel, are you even listening to me?" Evie asked. "It's like you're more interested in your food."

"*Sorry*, Evie." Raquel unwrapped the corn husks from her tamales and slid them onto a paper plate. "But I'm starving. Do you mind if I eat? It *is* my house."

Evie hated that she was being so *sentida*. Raquel wasn't known for being the most compassionate person, but tonight Raquel was being downright in-*sentida*.

"Raquel, why are you being so mean to me? I'm telling you that Alex just broke up with me, and it's like you don't even care."

"Evie, I'm *not* being mean. And of course I care. I'm just hungry. Go on, please. I'm listening."

Evie exhaled. "So, I was at the reserve, and Alex caught me—"

"Caught you?" Raquel asked. "Caught you doing what?"

"I was with Arturo," Evie started. "And Alex came by and caught us—"

"Doing *what*?"

Evie pulled her stool closer to the counter. The jack cheese oozing out of the corn tamale looked good, but she was far from hungry. "Nothing, really. I mean, we were just kissing, sorta."

"*Just* kissing?" Raquel's mouth dropped. Evie could see the mouthful of corn masa spread across her teeth and tongue. "Did he have his hands down your pants?"

"No! We were just—"

"Up your shirt?"

"Raquel, *no*! Quit interrupting!"

"But you *were* making out with him?" Raquel took another bite of her tamale. "Shit!" She spat under her breath as she opened her mouth and let a wad of masa drop onto her plate. She took a quick swig of soda and waved her hand over her opened mouth. "It's fucking *hot*!"

"Are you all right?" Evie asked.

"*No!*" Raquel continued to wave her fingers over her mouth. "I friggin' burned my tongue. *Sheeyat.* Whatever, go on."

"We had *just* started to kiss," Evie continued. "It didn't seem like we were making out. It was more of a first kiss that got some, I dunno, extended play."

"*Wow.*" Raquel cut a small piece from one of the tamales with a fork. This time she blew on it lightly before putting it into her mouth. "When did this happen?"

"Today, I mean, at the end of my shift at the reserve. I've been texting you all night, but you never texted me back," Evie complained. "I even texted the emergency code."

"Evie." Raquel rolled her eyes to the side. "Lately all your texts are so-called emergencies. And besides, I was with Davey. It's not like I was just gonna take off and have him drive me all the way back to Rio Estates."

"Where were you?"

"We were kicking it," Raquel said.

"Where?" Evie asked.

Raquel looked at her. "At Hobo Jungle."

"Hobo Jungle?"

"Yeah. Why?"

Hobo Jungle was a part of the river that was known for its, how would one say, challenged population. Whatever you called the people living in Hobo Jungle—river people, transients, or actual hobos—they had been living on the river for years, generations. As a little kid, Evie was always curious about those who lived in Hobo Jungle. Whenever her family would drive on the bridge that crossed that section of the river, she'd crane her neck in vain, hoping to catch a glimpse of a hobo roasting a hot dog pierced by a twig or eating beans out of a can. But Evie's father told her and her sister that Hobo Jungle was not some cute little village of hoboes all getting along together and eating hot dogs on a stick. Hobo Jungle was a place to avoid if they knew what was good for them. The area, he said, was full of ex-cons, drug users, and aimless transients. He warned them that if he found out that either of them ever went even *near* Hobo Jungle, he would give them a spanking to remember.

And now here was Raquel, *kicking it* in the Jungle.

Evie watched Raquel as she scarfed down the rest of her tamales, and it was then that she noticed how bad she looked. Not "It's one in the morning and I've been partying all night" bad, but rather "It's one in the morning and I've been partying hard for the last four semesters" bad. Raquel's skin was flaky, and she had two small scabs on the right side of her face. She looked oddly puffy in her face and her fingers. Not necessarily fat, just bloated.

"Raquel," Evie started hesitantly, "are you okay?"

"Yeah, why wouldn't I be?" Raquel drank more soda. She didn't look Evie in the eyes.

"I don't know." Evie didn't know how to say that she thought Raquel looked bad without sounding insulting. "You just look, I don't know, tired."

"Well, it's almost two in the morning, Evie. And to be honest," Raquel bit back, "you don't look so hot either."

"That's because I haven't slept." Evie got up from the kitchen stool. "And I have my driving test tomorrow—I mean, today—and I just know I'm gonna fail. Everything is turning to crap."

"Well, things can't always go the way we want them to in life."

"God, Raquel!" Evie raised her voice. "Why do you have to be so negative all the time?"

"I'm not negative," Raquel insisted. "I'm just being honest. If you ask me, people should be more honest." She got up to shut the kitchen door. "And *you* need to keep your voice down. You're gonna wake up my mom."

"Okay." Evie put her hands on her hips. "I'll be honest." She somehow found the courage to say what had been on her mind for some time. "I think you have a problem. I think you party too much, and to be honest, you're not looking really good."

"*Excuse* me?" Raquel looked at Evie, almost amused.

"And I'm not the only one who thinks that," Evie remarked. "Dee Dee and I think you drink too much, way too much."

"Dee Dee and *you*?" Raquel repeated in a sarcastic tone. "Oh, and when did you two get together and decide this? That's a pretty bold observation coming from the two of you."

"It's a *realistic* observation, Raquel," Evie said. "An observation that's making me worried."

"You know, Evie?" Raquel crossed her arms and cocked her

head. "Maybe *you* should have a drink once in a while. You run around worrying about everyone, trying to get them to be or act a certain way, and maybe you should just let people be. Quit being so judgmental."

"Judgmental?" Evie snapped. "I'm not judgmental. I'm just concerned, Raquel. Excuse me if I get concerned about people I care about."

"Yeah, you sure showed concern for Alex."

She did *not* just say that.

Raquel scraped the remaining melted jack cheese from her plate and crammed it into her mouth. "Okay, you want to be so honest, all things in the clear?" she asked with her mouth full of masa. "Well, I wanna know something, the honest truth."

"What?" Evie asked.

"What *really* happened between you and Jose in the photo booth, at that Sangro party last semester?"

"*What?*" Evie squealed. "You gotta be kidding me!"

"Well, I'm not. Do you have a problem with me asking that?"

"Yeah," Evie said. "I do have a problem because you know what happened. I told you."

"But why *exactly* were you even in the booth with him?'

"I *told* you!" Evie's voice rose again. "I saw his flojos and then I saw Alejandra's flojos and I thought they belonged to you. I thought it was the both of you, but it wasn't. And when Jose saw me, he pulled me in."

"Pulled you in, huh?" Raquel asked suspiciously. "And you just couldn't say no?"

"I didn't have *time* to say no! He just pulled me in and, like, grabbed me!" She couldn't believe what Raquel was insinuating!

"The thing is," Raquel remarked calmly, "Alejandra de los Santos doesn't wear flip-flops."

"I *know* she doesn't," Evie said. "But that night she . . . I mean, Jose had bought her some. These red Roxys an—"

"*He* bought her sandals?" Raquel asked.

The kitchen light went on.

"What *is* going on here?" It was Raquel's mother. She was in a terry robe, and her eye mask was pushed up to her forehead. She was *mad*. "Evie, what are you doing here? At this hour!"

"I was just . . . ," Evie started. She hadn't seen Kitty Diaz look so angry in such a long time. Actually, the last time she'd looked so pissed was back when she discovered that Raquel had forged her name on a business check, but that was some time ago.

"Raquel!" Kitty Diaz leaned into Raquel and sniffed. "You stink like booze! What the hell is going on?"

Raquel propped her hand against the kitchen counter and leaned back. She looked at Evie and said dryly, "Thanks a fucking lot, *Evie*."

26

THE NEXT AFTERNOON, EVIE WAS GIVEN HER WALKING PAPERS. Literally.

"I'm sorry." Her driving instructor wrote a big fat zero in red ink on the score sheet. "I had to remind you to put on your seat belt. That's an immediate fail."

Evie didn't say anything as she reluctantly took the paperwork from her instructor and headed back into the DMV office, where her mother and Lindsay were waiting. She swung open the glass door, and they both stood up from the plastic chairs they had been sitting on. They both looked confused.

"What happened, *mija?*" her mother asked. "Why are you back?"

"I didn't pass." Evie held out her score sheet. "I got an instant fail. I forgot to put on my seat belt." She was on the verge of tears. Evie nervously rubbed the side of her face and looked around the DMV. People were either slouched over the main counters, lamenting to stone-faced clerks, or they were slouched over paperwork and pulling their hair out as they struggled with the written part of the driving test. Yes, the DMV was an evil, ugly place.

"*What?*" Her mother took the score sheet and clicked her tongue. "How can that be? How could you forget to put on your seat belt?"

"I don't know," Evie started. "I just—"

"So you'll take it again," Lindsay said abruptly. "No problem." She pulled out her car keys to drive them home. Evie couldn't help but look down at the key ring. Did Lindsay *have* to flaunt them *so* soon after her failure?

They left the office and went around the side of the DMV building to get Lindsay's car. Evie took a seat in the back and looked out the window. *How* could she have forgotten to put on her seat belt? How, how, how? Her parents had paid the California Driving School a lot of money to teach her how to drive, and she had spent a lot of time practicing with her father and Lindsay. She must have forgotten, she figured, simply because she'd had practically only three hours of sleep. She had left Raquel's house at nearly 2 A.M. and didn't fallen asleep until about five in the morning. *Of course.* She was in a daze from sleep deprivation. It was not her fault. She *was* a good driver, but how could anyone have expected her to pass a driving test in her condition?

As Lindsay drove downtown, every driver on the road

seemed to be boasting their independence as they whizzed along down Vineyard Avenue in their cars. They were free and liberated, not confined to the backseat as she was, and Evie wondered, would she *ever* be allowed to participate in such an exclusive parade? Her stomach started to hurt.

"Mom?" She leaned forward from the backseat. "Do you think I could just go home?"

She was so not in the mood for school. Raquel would definitely still be pissed off at her, and Dee Dee most likely wouldn't even be in classes but was probably off somewhere with Rocio, picking out china patterns. And Alex? Yeah, right. Mr. 4getit. Like he really cared.

"Evie." Her mother turned around to face her. "You can't miss school just because you didn't pass your driving test."

"It's not that." Evie held her side and leaned into the backseat's pleather upholstery. "I just really, really don't feel good. I didn't sleep at all last night, and I feel sick."

"Oh, I don't know." Her mother looked at Lindsay and then back at Evie. "But you do look really tired."

When they arrived home and pulled into the Gomez' driveway, Lindsay kept her sedan running as Evie got out.

"We're going to meet your father," her mother told her. "It's better if he doesn't know that I'm letting you skip school, so don't say anything when he gets home."

"I won't." Evie got her backpack from the car's floor. "Are you gonna tell him I flunked my test?"

"I'm going to have to," her mother replied. "Are you going to be okay?"

"Yeah." Evie yawned. "I really just need some sleep."

"Okay, *mi'ja*." Her mother looked worried. "I have my cell, and you know your sister is home if you need anything."

"Okay," Evie said.

Yeah, right. Sabrina would be the *last* person she would go to if she needed anything.

When Evie got inside the house, all she wanted to do was go to the den, grab the multicolored afghan, à la Lindsay, and snuggle in front of the plasma. Maybe *People's Court* was on. Now that would be great. The way Judge Milian dished out Cuban *dichos* and costly penalties to poorly prepared defendants always made Evie feel better about her own problems.

But when she stepped down into the den, Evie was surprised to find Sabrina there. She was in a pajama top and sweatpants, spread out on the den's brown leather couch *and* covered with Lindsay's crocheted afghan. Her feet were propped up on the coffee table.

"What are you doing here?" Evie asked as she stepped over her sister's legs.

She didn't mean to come across as accusatory as she might have sounded. It was just that since Sabrina had been home, she *never* left her room. And of course, Evie still held a grudge over the smack she had overheard Sabrina say about her on the phone.

Sabrina didn't bother to look up. "Last I checked, this *was* my house too."

"No, I mean, you're usually in your room." Evie flopped down on the matching leather love seat and kicked up her own feet on the coffee table. Their mother had insisted there was to be no "flopping" or "kicking up" on the den's expensive California Mission furniture. But their mother wasn't around at the moment.

Sabrina kept her eyes on the plasma screen. She was watching a Korean soap opera with no subtitles. She laughed along with the programmed laugh track.

Evie looked around. "Where the remote?" she asked. "I wanna watch *People's Court*."

"Evie, don't." Sabrina reached for the channel changer on the coffee table. "I'm watching this."

"Like you can really understand what's going on."

"Of course I do, or else I wouldn't be watching it," Sabrina replied.

"Wait, don't tell me," Evie said sarcastically. "You're now president of the Korean Club?"

"Evie." Sabrina still didn't look at her, but rather reclined her head farther back onto the couch. "Just let me be. I've been in my room all morning, and I just wanted to take advantage of no one being home today. Or I *thought* no one was gonna be home. Why aren't you in school?"

"I'm sick." Evie cleared her throat for effect.

"You don't seem sick." Sabrina finally looked over at her. "And if you are, shouldn't you be in bed?"

"Well, you don't seem sick either," Evie snapped. "Shouldn't *you* be back at Stanford? So you don't have to be here? Surrounded by *friggin' idiots*?"

·"What is that supposed to mean?" Sabrina asked.

"You know what I mean," Evie said. "I *heard* you."

"Heard me what?" Sabrina asked.

"I heard you, the other week," Evie continued. "You were on the phone basically talking smack about me, saying how much you hate being here and calling me a spoiled brat."

Sabrina turned away from Evie and looked back at the TV. She said nothing.

Evie counted in her head. *One Mississippi, two Mississippi . . .*

"Evie," Sabrina finally sighed, "you just wouldn't understand."

"Oh," Evie said. "And that's because I'm such a friggin' idiot or a spoiled brat?"

"No, Evie, it's just," her sister started, "I've been having a really, really hard time and—"

"And what?" Evie wasn't convinced that Suprema could ever have such a hard time at anything.

"Evie, I don't want to get into it," Sabrina continued. "For the last month, I've had to have an answer for everything and everyone. *Why* was I breaking up with Robert? *Why* was I going back home? *When* was I going back to school? It's like everyone wanted a tidy little answer tied up in a perfect little bow, and you know what? I don't *have* the answers. I'm tired. I just want to, I don't know . . . chill."

Chill? Did that word actually exist in Sabrina's vocabulary?

"You don't know," Sabrina said. "Maybe you don't understand. I mean, you've always been the baby of the family, the favorite and—"

"The *favorite?*" Evie gawked. *"Me?"*

"Uh, yeah," Sabrina said. "You."

"You're crazy," Evie told her. "You're the one everyone just idolizes. Mom, Dad, Lindsay, Dee Dee's dad . . . even A through H."

"A through H?" Sabrina pursed her lips and slowly cracked a smile. "You mean the counselor? I haven't heard that name in years. He's still at Nueva? You call him that too?"

"Uh, yeah." Evie felt the ice thawing. "I mean, everyone does."

"Does he still clean his glasses, over and over again?" Sabrina asked. "Like obsessive-compulsive?"

"Oh my God." Evie laughed. "Yes. I don't think he ever pays attention to what anyone is saying."

"Oh, he's paying attention, all right," Sabrina said. "But only if you're a female student. He's the biggest perv."

"What?" Evie sputtered. "A through H? Gross! He's like three hundred years old. That is *so* not true!"

"It *is* true," Sabrina insisted. "We used to say that *A* and *H* stood for Ass and Hiney. That was his specialty."

Sabrina slapped her hands together and let out a high-pitched laugh. Evie knew that laugh. It sounded like a baby seal crying out for his mother, and it was annoying enough to make anyone around Sabrina wince. But to Evie the laugh made Sabrina seem less *suprema* and actually more human.

"Oh my God," Sabrina said. "Those were some fun times, back at Villanueva. I wish I was back there, when life was much more chill."

There was that word again.

"Chill?" Evie asked. "Are you sure we went to the same school?"

"You just have a different circle of friends than I had," Sabrina said. "I was always with the square kids, the future CPAs of the world." She rolled her eyes. "I don't know, I think maybe because I am the oldest, Mom and Dad were tougher on me. Mom was so strict with me when I was at Nueva. I wasn't allowed to date or hang out at Sea Street. And to be running around with someone like Raquel when I was fifteen? No way."

"Fifteen and three quarters," Evie corrected her. "I'm almost sixteen."

"*A little less sixteen.*" Her sister smiled at her.

"Hey, I love that song," Evie said. She was surprised that her sister knew of it.

"Yeah, one of my sisters at Stanford always played Fall Out Boy," Sabrina said.

She suddenly turned down the volume on the plasma. "Eves, I'm sorry about what you heard that day on the phone. I've just been out of my mind. I don't like being here, but it really doesn't have anything to do with you. Mom and Dad are really getting on my case. Mom especially. She can be so stifling."

"Tell me about it." Evie was surprised that her sister shared the same sentiment. She had always thought that the two "*Go*-mez Girls" consisted of her mother and Sabrina. She was the odd one out.

"I just feel like I'm letting everyone down," Sabrina continued. "I don't need to be reminded how much Stanford is costing Mom and Dad, or how I didn't love Robert enough."

"Is that why you broke up?" Evie asked. "You don't love him anymore?"

"No, I do love him." Sabrina sighed and curled her legs onto the couch. "But he was going to start grad school this spring, in Massachusetts, and he wanted me to transfer schools so I could be closer to him. At first I was into the idea, but then I just felt like I was losing a part, a big part, of myself. I wasn't Sabrina Gomez anymore. I was Robert Ramirez's girlfriend." She shook her head. "I wasn't about to leave my sorority sisters, my friends, my family . . . California."

"In that order, right?" Evie smirked.

"No." Sabrina threw Evie a sideways glance. "But God, Evie, Robert was, like, so insulted, and he would go on and on about me not going with him, as if I didn't love him enough or something. I grew up wanting to be a Stanford grad, not some grad student's girlfriend in friggin' Massachusetts." She sighed again. "It takes a lot of compromise to be in a relationship, and maybe I'm just not ready to be in such a serious one. And I feel sorta selfish, because I really want to do what *I* want to do, and sometimes people can't understand that."

"Right." Evie nodded. It made sense didn't it? But then she thought about Alex. It seemed that sometimes he wanted to do what *he* wanted to do, and she wasn't letting him. Ooh, was she as bad as Robert?

"So anyway, I really just want to rest." Sabrina pulled the afghan up to her chin. "At least for one quarter, and then I'll go back to school. I want a fresh start. Fresh starts are always good, no?"

"Uh, no. I mean, yeah," Evie agreed as she rubbed her arms. "Everybody needs a fresh start once in a while."

"Are you cold?" Sabrina asked.

"Yeah." Evie stretched. "I'm gonna go get a blanket upstairs."

"You can share the afghan with me."

"Oh." Evie was surprised by her sister's offer. "Okay."

She got up from the love seat and joined her sister on the couch. Sabrina spread the blanket over the both of them.

"So what do you wanna watch?" she asked Evie.

"Uh, I don't care."

"Are you sure?" Sabrina asked.

"Yeah," Evie said. "We can watch whatever you want."

27

WHEN THEIR MOTHER AND LINDSAY GOT BACK, EVIE AND SABRINA WERE still in the den. They had created a feast of canned bean dip and bagel chips and were watching old episodes of *Laguna Beach* that Evie had TiVo'd. Both of them had taken their feet *off* the coffee table.

"One of my sisters went out with Jason," Sabrina told Evie. "Just one date, but it was enough. She said he was *really* cheap."

"No way." Evie dunked her chip into the bean dip. *"Serio?"*

"Yes," Sabrina said. "He practically wanted her to order from the kid's menu, and *then* he asked for a doggie bag for their *bread.*"

"Oh. *My.* God," Evie laughed. "That's messed up."

"And he was so short!" Sabrina laughed with her. "Talk about trial size."

"It is so nice to see you out of your room, *mija*," their mother told Sabrina as she came down into the den and joined both girls on the couch. "I'm going to call your father. Maybe we could barbecue tonight."

"None for me." Sabrina lifted her pajama top and patted her belly. "I'm already full."

"Yeah, me too," Evie said.

"Oh, I think we should," their mother insisted. "We could barbecue some tri-tip."

Sabrina looked at Evie and discreetly held her neck with her hand, in a choking position.

"But what about your SoCal diet?" Evie asked her mother.

Vicki Gomez waved her hand aside. "Oh, I'm not concerned with that anymore." She took a large bagel chip from the bag and dipped it into the can of bean dip.

This instantly worried Evie. It was not a good sign that her mother was off her diet. She had started the diet because of Evie's sixteeñera, almost as a reason to get more into shape. Why wasn't she concerned about looking her best anymore? Because there would be no guests to impress because there would be no party?

Just then the phone rang, and their mother got up from the couch to get the cordless from the kitchen counter.

"Hi, Kitty!" she sang into the receiver. "You know, I was going to call you, I was at—"

Evie sank into the couch. *Uh-oh.* She'd been wondering

when Kitty was going to call to complain about her being over at her house so late—or rather, so early in the morning.

"What?" Evie's mother looked over at her in complete astonishment. "Kitty, *no.* I am so sorry."

Evie squirmed deeper into the den's couch. Should she make a run for her bedroom . . . window? Her mother was obviously hearing about last night's activities.

"Kitty, no, of course not," Evie's mother continued. "I won't say a word. You have my promise. Yes, she's right here." She looked over at Evie again, just as she was getting up to leave.

Evie was confused. What was going on? What *was* Kitty telling her?

After a few more "oh nos" and "of course nots" Evie's mother hung up the phone.

"What happened?" Evie cautiously asked her mother. "What did Kitty say?"

"Raquel hasn't been feeling well," her mother said hesitantly. "So, Kitty's going—" She paused. "So Kitty's going to check her into Isla del Mar."

"Isla *del Mar?"* Evie was taken aback.

"What?" Sabrina looked up. "Why?"

Isla del Mar was a center on the northeast hills of the county that treated people for addiction or depression. Sometimes, last semester, the Flojos would cram into Mondo's Marauder and make their way up the winding road to Isla's parking lot. It was relaxing to sit and lean against the long, high stucco wall of the in-patient entry building and take in the panoramic view of the city and the ocean. If you went at night, which they often did, you could see the offshore oil rigs twinkling in the distance. However, Evie never dreamed that one of *their own* would be on the inside of the same building.

"Kitty said Raquel got in trouble again."

"In trouble with what?"

Her mother didn't answer.

"Mom," Evie said, "tell me. She's my best friend."

"Evie, I told Kitty I wouldn't say anything, but now I'm thinking that you need to know and that I need to know."

"Need to know what?" Evie asked. Why was her mother talking in riddles?

"Did you know that Raquel was dealing drugs?"

"What?" Evie exclaimed. *"No!"*

"Are you being honest with me?" Her mother looked at her sternly. Even Sabrina looked at Evie, wide-eyed with curiosity.

"Mom, *no*," Evie insisted. "I swear I didn't. What are you talking about?"

"Evie, don't swear," her mother said.

"No, I mean, I promise, *promise* that I didn't know anything about this. I had no idea."

"None of your friends do or deal drugs?"

Uh-oh. Evie thought of Mondo. He sold pot, but was he really a friend? Sure, they had hung out in the same clique last semester, but was Mondo really a friend now? Not that much, really, anymore.

"Friends?" Evie asked. "No, I do know of people at school who sell pot and stuff, but they aren't my friends."

Evie's mother put her hands on the kitchen counter and took a deep breath. "Evie, it's pretty serious. Raquel could end up at the CYA or something, so it's better she get help now. Kitty and Charlie want to curb it before it gets out of control, but frankly, I think they should have done something a lot earlier."

"Mom, how could you say that?" Sabrina shook her head. "You just said that Raquel's in serious trouble, and now all you can be is critical of Kitty and Charlie?"

"I'm just saying it might be too late," their mother tried to explain. "Raquel has had problems long before this, and you'd think, with Kitty being the head of Las Madrinas and everything, that she would have been a little more proactive."

"What's gonna happen to her?" Evie asked.

"Kitty's taking her to Isla tomorrow morning."

"Tomorrow?" Evie asked. "Already? What's the rush?"

"I don't know exactly," their mother confessed. "They wanted to take her in today, but they needed to get some things at home in order first."

"Well, I'm going over, then." Evie got up from the couch and started for the kitchen door.

"Evie, don't." Her mother blocked her with her arm. "You need to leave her alone."

"*What?* My best friend is going away, and you're telling me I can't see her before she leaves?"

"Evie," her mother said, "you can't go over now. Give this time to Kitty and Charlie. That's all I'm saying."

Evie brushed past her mother and stormed up to her room. Could this day get any more jacked? Just as she was about to flop onto her bed (on which flopping *was* allowed), her mother called out from downstairs.

"E-*vie*! Vi-si-*tor*!"

Visitor? Her mother practically sang the announcement, something that usually only her father or Lindsay did. Who would be visiting now? Why did her mother sound—? Wait, it *must* be . . . *Raquel.*

Evie rushed from her room and headed downstairs, but, to her shock, she didn't find Raquel in the foyer. It was Arturo.

"Hey, Evie," Arturo said nervously as she came down to meet him.

What was *he* doing at *her* house? Did stalkers wear cowboy boots?

"Oh, hey, Arturo," Evie answered. "Um, how did you know where I lived?"

"Your address was on your file card," he explained. "I'm sorry to just drop by, but you forgot your backpack." He lifted Evie's bag from the foyer's wooden slat bench. "You took off so fast yesterday."

"Oh, yeah. Sorry about that." Evie took her backpack from

him. Okay, so he wasn't a stalker, but he *had* hunted her down, sorta. "I hadn't even noticed it was missing."

Arturo laughed. "Oh, so I can see why you need extra credit for school."

"No"—Evie felt embarrassed—"I didn't go to school today, so I just hadn't noticed, and it's been a rough two days."

"Oh. Sorry." Arturo looked down at the floor and then down the hallway. "I didn't want to make things complicated. I hope I wasn't disrespectful, you know, about—"

"No, it was okay," Evie said.

"Just *okay?*" Arturo winced playfully.

"No, I mean, it was nice." Evie lowered her voice and looked down the hall. She didn't want her mother overhearing what was up with her. Had her kiss with Arturo really been nice? It had seemed to be, while she was doing it, but it was so not worth it, obviously, in the long run.

"I meant all those things I said," Arturo told her. "I don't want you to think that you were some kind of rebound or anything. I have always been, I don't know, sorta *intrigued* by you."

"Intrigued? By *me?*" Evie couldn't quite believe him.

"Yeah, why not?" he asked. "From that first day I met you, I thought you were really cute, but I didn't know what to do. I was still with Josephina, and I knew you were with someone."

"How did you know I had a boyfriend?" Evie asked. "I don't think I ever mentioned it."

"That shell necklace," he said.

Evie raised her eyebrows.

"It looked homemade," Arturo explained. "And seemed sorta special to you. Girls usually don't wear the same necklace every day."

Evie smiled. "Sure they do—that is, if the necklace *is* special."

"My point exactly." Arturo looked around Evie's house. She felt that she should ask him to hang out for a while, but she really didn't want to ask. She just wanted to get over to Raquel's as soon as possible.

"So, are you gonna be at the reserve on Wednesday?" Arturo asked.

"I don't know," Evie said. "I mean, my best friend is going away and—"

"Back to Mexico?"

"No. I mean, yes. Dee Dee might be going away too. I've just got a lot of things on my mind, and my birthday is coming up, and I'm not having the party I thought I was going to have. Everything is just a mess."

"Your birthday?" he asked. "When is your birthday?"

Was Arturo the only person in Ventura County who didn't know about Evie's birthday and possible party at Duke's?

"In about a week and a half," she said. "But I don't know if it's even gonna happen. I have so much work to do, and I haven't started any of it."

"Well, if you're not gonna be at the reserve this week, at the very least let me take you out for your birthday. Can I call you on your cell?"

"Yeah," Evie said. "That would be cool. Lemme give you my number."

"Oh, I already have it."

"Huh?" Evie asked. Maybe stalkers did wear cowboy boots. "Why do you have my cell number?"

"From *the file*," Arturo told her. "I'm no stalker, Evie."

"I know that." Evie laughed, slightly relieved. "But yeah, you can text me."

"I don't do text," he claimed. "Besides, I'd just rather hear your voice."

After Arturo left, Evie's mother joined her in the great room.

"Is that your boss? From the reserve?" she asked. "He's very handsome. I like his cowboy boots!"

"He's not really my boss," Evie said. "He's just in charge of things."

Unlike Alex, Evie thought. With all that had been going on, she suddenly missed him even more. Alex was really great when it came to listening to her problems. So he didn't know how to really plan evenings out on the town, or sometimes he didn't know how to dress, but he was really a sweet person. How could she have gotten into a lip-lock with Arturo? She had made a big mistake. She wanted Alex. She had to get Alex back. But how?

28

"I KNEW SOMETHING WAS UP WITH RAQUEL," DEE DEE TOLD EVIE THE next morning. They were both on the Diazes' doorstep at 7 A.M. "Didn't I tell you?" Dee Dee continued as she rang the bell again. "Remember in the counseling office? That day we were looking for a job for you?"

"I know," Evie agreed somberly. She remembered that day very clearly. She had also felt that Raquel was going a little off the deep end but had hoped that maybe Alex was right when he said that perhaps Raquel was just going through a phase.

"No wonder she had so much money lately," Dee Dee said. "Oh. My. God. Do you think she used drug money to buy my purse and your gown at Decade?"

"Ew." Evie winced. She didn't like the idea of wearing a dress that came from some drug deal. "I didn't even think of that."

"I can't believe her parents are sending her to Isla. I mean, don't you think that is a little severe?" Dee Dee clicked her tongue. "Oh, God, poor Raquel. I would just think that her mother—"

"Hi, Kitty." Evie looked up as Raquel's mother answered the front door.

"*Lo siento*, girls." Kitty Diaz shook her head at Evie and Dee Dee. "Raquel's still sleeping."

"What time is she leaving for Isla?" Evie asked.

"We're gonna leave around ten," Kitty answered. She looked tired. Very tired. Her eyes each had a half moon of darkness underneath. Her hair, cut in a bob style, was flat on one side.

"Can we wait until she gets up?" Evie felt anxious. "Or maybe you could wake her up and tell her that we're here?"

"No, Evie, I can't." Kitty yawned, forgetting to cover her mouth. "You girls go to school. You'll be able to see Raquel soon enough."

"*Ay*, Kitty." Raquel's father came to the door. "Let them see Raquel. They are her best friends, her *amiguitas*."

"Charlie . . ." Kitty looked up at him.

"Just let them see her." Charlie widened the door. "Come in, girls. Go see Raquel."

When Evie and Dee Dee got to Raquel's bedroom, her door was slightly open. The window shades, as usual, were pulled down, and only the computer's screen saver, a photo of the three girls on the hood of B.J., offered light.

"Raquel?" Evie whispered through the darkness.

Dee Dee pushed the door open, and both girls peered in. Raquel lay on her side in bed, under an array of black clothing, her stuffed Molly Monster, and a couple of *Kerrang!* magazine scattered about.

"She's asleep," Dee Dee whispered to Evie. "We should just go."

"Wait." Raquel turned over under the collected mess on top of her.

Dee Dee looked at Evie wide eyed. They both wanted to see Raquel, but neither of them had actually rehearsed what they were going to say to her. They walked into the room toward her.

"Hey, Raquel," Evie said softly as she sat down on the side of Raquel's canopied bed. "How you doing?"

"How do you *think* I'm doing?" Raquel answered dryly. "My parents are trying to get rid of me." Her head was on its side on the pillow.

"Raq, your parents aren't trying to get rid of you," Evie said. "They just want you to get better."

"And I'll get better in some friggin' psycho hospital?" Raquel asked. "Why don't they just send me to Hawaii for a few months? Yeah, I could hang with that."

"Why?" Evie found herself asking. "You have connections there?" The words had slipped out before she knew it. She felt angry. Raquel had screwed up, big-time, and she was trying to be all funny about it.

"What's that supposed to mean?" Raquel looked at Evie.

"Raquel," Evie started, *"why* were you dealing? Is that how you bought my dress? With your drug money?"

Raquel rolled her eyes and clicked her tongue. "Oh, come on. You don't have to be all dramatic, *drug money.* I put your dress on my credit card. Dee Dee's purse, too. I don't deposit *cash, tonta.* Is that what you are so concerned about? That your two-G gown didn't come from the right kind of money? *Please.*"

"Were you selling with Mondo?" Dee Dee asked.

"Mondo?" Raquel rolled her eyes again. "Hell, no. And I wasn't doing anything major, just peddling some pot now and then for Davey."

"Davey?" Evie exclaimed. "Raquel, you have *got* to get a grip. I mean, why the hell are you helping *Davey?"*

Raquel put her head back on the pillow, closed her eyes, and sighed.

"Raquel," Evie started, "I don't get it. I mean, we can all go off the path once in a while, but what's going on?"

Raquel still didn't answer. She pulled her blankets up to her neck, and although her eyes were closed, Evie could see that they were starting to tear up. "You guys wouldn't understand," she said.

Evie felt another one of those moments coming on. Hadn't Sabrina just told her the same thing last week? Why did people, people with whom she *thought* she was close, think she couldn't possibly understand anything that they were going through?

"Raquel—" Evie started.

"No, I mean it," Raquel interrupted. "You guys are all into your own things. Dee Dee's with Rocio, and you've got your surfing and horse thing. I don't have anything. Before, I used to have Jose, and we were Flojos, and we used to hang out and it was fun. But now I don't even have that. And, I don't know, sometimes I really miss Jose. I miss being Jose's girlfriend."

"Jose?" Evie asked. "How could you possibly miss him? He was a *jerk*."

Raquel looked at her. "Don't you think that Alex was a jerk at times, and don't you still miss him?"

"Yeah, but—" Evie began.

"Yeah, nothing," Raquel said. "I'm not saying how I feel makes sense. I'm just telling you how I feel. I don't know. Jose just made me feel good. Not all the time, but a lot of the time he did."

"And so now selling dope makes you feel good?" Evie asked. "Don't you think that's a little too stupid *barrio*, Raquel?"

"Evie." Dee Dee looked at her. "Give Raquel a break. We came here to be supportive, not to be judgmental."

"I'm not being judgmental." Evie tried to defend herself. But in a way, she knew that she was being critical. She looked at Raquel. "Yeah, I guess you're right. I guess I don't understand."

"It's sorta like how Sabrina is depressed and she just sleeps a lot," Dee Dee tried to explain. "But maybe with Raquel, she had to do something different, something that's more Raquel, I don't know."

"I wasn't doing anything *that* jaw-dropping," Raquel defended herself. "I mean, who doesn't sell pot once in a while?"

"I don't," Dee Dee said.

"Yeah, and neither do I," Evie added. "Raquel, you were getting out of control."

Raquel frowned and shook her head.

"Raq," Dee Dee started, "I wasn't gonna say anything about this either, but my dad got really mad that night you called our house and you were drunk."

"Oh, well, yeah." Raquel looked awkward. "Of course, but I apologized to him. Remember, I called the next day. He was cool about it."

"Yeah, but I mean, he was really put off, and I wasn't gonna say anything but he and Graciela had a dinner party for Rocio and—" Dee Dee seemed unsure whether she should continue.

"And what?" Raquel asked. "What's the big mystery?"

"They had this dinner for Rocio and his parents, and my dad, he didn't want you to come. He was afraid that you would make a scene or something."

"What?" Raquel's eyebrows rose. "Your dad thought that? That I would make a scene?"

"Uh-huh," Dee Dee admitted.

"Was Evie invited?" Raquel looked over at Evie. "Did she go?"

"Well, yeah," Dee Dee answered.

"Don't be mad, Raq," Evie told Raquel. "I didn't want to hurt your feelings."

"Wow, I feel like shit," Raquel said. "I always thought your dad liked me."

"He *does*," Dee Dee emphasized. "But he doesn't like the way you can act sometimes. It didn't help that you were spending so much time with Davey."

"Yeah." Evie said, "He hasn't been the best influence."

"The lady I was talking to at Isla said that I should also stop making boys the priority," Raquel confessed. "But I mean, I *like* boys. Why is that a problem? Giving up boy booty would be like Evie giving up her flip-flops."

"But flojos aren't my life," Evie said.

"They *aren't?*" Raquel looked down at Evie's feet. She was wearing brand-new silver Trovata flip-flops. The straps were braided with strawlike fabric and encrusted with tiny white seashells. Evie loved them and had had to have them the second she saw them at A Shore Thing.

Evie looked down at her flip-flops. "Okay . . . I see what you mean. But it's one thing to love sandals and another thing to be consumed by them."

"I don't know," said Raquel. "I've seen you get all crazy at Walden Surf Shop whenever their new shipment from Roxy comes in."

"Okay, okay," Evie laughed. "Look, so you know, what you're saying, about that lady at Isla saying that you cut boys from the menu for a while? It's sorta like what Sabrina was telling me."

"Suprema?" Raquel propped her pillows and sat up slowly. "She's talking now?"

"Yeah, and she's taking a break from boys." Evie said, "Well, I don't know about boys, but definitely from Robert. He wanted her to move to Massachusetts with him 'cause he's gonna go to grad school out there. That's why she broke up with him."

"Really?" Dee Dee looked over at Evie.

"Yeah, but she didn't want to go with him," Evie continued. "He got all mad at her. And now she's just taking a break from him and just about everything. She says she needs to focus on who *she* is and what she wants."

"Which is?" Dee Dee asked.

"I dunno, I guess being a good president for her sorority, doing better on the tennis team, stuff like that."

"But that's easy for her," Raquel said. "I'm not good at anything. I mean, what could I possibly focus on?"

"Raq," Evie started. "*Of course* you're good at stuff. I mean, think about it, last semester, as Flojos, all we did was hang out. We really did nothing. I would *think* about surfing, but now I'm actually doing it. It's just a matter of *doing* what you're *thinking* about."

"Well, I think about doing boys," Raquel said matter-of-factly.

"Then we gotta work on finding you a new hobby." Evie shrugged her shoulders. "Seriously."

"But *I'm* serious, Evie," Raquel said. "You have two dudes totally in love with you, and I have no one."

"I wouldn't say that," Evie said. If two boys were so totally in love with her, why did she feel lonely? "Alex isn't talking to me, and I don't know where I stand with Arturo. But he did say that he might take me out to dinner for my birthday."

"What's going on with your party?" Dee Dee asked.

"I'm still working on it," Evie said. But in reality, she knew she had some major work ahead of her. She still had to tally up her hours at the reserve and then finally, *finally* work on her essay for Harrison.

"So, you ain't into Turdo?" Raquel asked.

"No." Evie shook her head. "I mean, I'm into a guy who's gonna treat me sweet and special, but I really wish *Alex* was that guy. I mean, I just think that Alex is just so cool and nice and I gotta admit, as dorky as it sounds, I really love the fact that he made the necklace for me. I don't know. I think I like Arturo more because of what he stands for, but I'm really not into *him*. Does that make sense?"

"Yeah," Dee Dee said slowly. "It does."

"Girls?" Kitty knocked on the doorjamb of Raquel's room.

"You better get going if you don't want to be late for school, and we need to get Raquel ready."

"Okay." Evie looked at Raquel and exhaled. "We better go. We'll call you the very first day they let us." She leaned in to hug her good-bye.

"The *very* first day?" Raquel asked. Her eyes suddenly had a profound look of fear in them.

"The very first day," Evie said. *"Promise."*

"Okay." Raquel sighed. "Hey, Evie?"

"Yeah?"

"You do believe me about your dress, right? That I'm paying for it with my saved-up allowance, right?"

Evie looked at Dee Dee and then at Raquel. "Yeah, Raquel, I believe you."

"Okay," Raquel said. "I really need you to know that."

Dee Dee and Evie both continued with their long good-byes and then reluctantly left.

"I hope Raquel is gonna be okay," Dee Dee said to Evie as she got into Jumile. "I mean, she seems okay to me, making little jokes and stuff."

"Yeah." Evie threw her backpack in the backseat and got into the passenger seat. "But I just hope she takes things seriously."

"So, I don't understand. Why wouldn't your sister just move with Robert?" Dee Dee started Jumile. "I thought she loved him? I just always imagined they were, like, the college sweethearts that would get married and live happily ever after."

"I'm sure Sabrina wants to live happily ever after, but she also wants to live happily right *now*."

"Hmm . . . interesting." Dee Dee headed toward the main exit gate of Rio Estates. As she drove past the gate, the morning mail truck was just entering. Evie looked after it. She wondered, exactly *when* did QCs get sent out in the mail? Dee Dee hadn't even started writing her essay, and she had yet to turn in her hours to Vasquez-Reyes Alarcón. Evie calculated the calendar days in her head. She had so much work to do, yet it was Alex who remained front and center in her thoughts.

"Hey, Dee Dee," Evie asked. "You still like to write a lot, right?"

"Yeah," Dee Dee answered. "I told you. When I was in Mexico, Rocio and I were always writing each other back and forth."

"In Spanish and English, right?" Evie asked.

"Right," Dee answered.

"Good," Evie said. It was time to put Dee Dee to work.

29

ON WEDNESDAY, EVIE SKIPPED WORKING AT THE RESERVE AND ASKED
Dee Dee over after dinner.

"You have to help me write this," Evie said as she pushed
aside her mother's clothing and kitchenware catalogs and
placed a bag and some pens on the dining room table.

"*Help* you?" Dee Dee placed her metallic vintage quilted
bag on one of the dining room chairs. "I thought I was going
to write the whole essay for you." She looked at the pens.
"And we should be at your computer. I'm not doing it by
hand."

"No." Evie pulled out two flat boxes from the Lautzenhiser's
bag. "Didn't you get my text?"

"Yeah, why do you think I'm here?" Dee Dee took a seat.

"No." Evie shook her head in frustration. "Dee Dee, I need
to write a letter, to Alex."

"A letter? To Alex?" Dee Dee's eyes widened. "*What? La reina* de text is actually going to *write*?"

"*Yes*, Dee Dee," Evie answered. "Is that so hard to believe?"

"An actual letter? *Sin* abbreviation?" Dee Dee teased. "How *are* you going to manage?"

"I'm going to manage quite nicely, thank you," Evie retorted. "Since *you* are gonna help me. You said you used to write all those letters to Rocio when you lived in Mexico, and this is my last hope. Alex won't answer my texts, or my IMs, or my phone calls. I'm thinking I could write him a letter and tell him how sorry I am and what a stupid mistake I made. I don't know, I just need to tell him everything that I feel bad about."

"But what about your extra-credit essay?" Dee Dee asked. "You have to give me adequate time if you want a good paper."

"I know, I know," Evie said. "But I'm sure you'll be able to just whip it out, you're good like that. Right now you gotta help me write this letter to Alex. I haven't had a decent night's sleep since he broke up with me."

"Are you going to mail it?" Dee Dee asked. "That's what Rocio and I did."

"I don't think so," Evie said. "If for some reason he doesn't get it, I would never know. It would just *kill* me. And then what would I do? Ask him if he ever got my letter? That would just defeat the whole purpose of wanting to do something so unexpected and personal. I think I'm just gonna slip it in his locker."

"*Oh!*" Dee Dee's mouth formed a syrupy, pouty smile. "This is *so* romantic." She looked over the boxes of stationery. "This is the paper you picked out?"

"Yeah." Evie showed her the two different styles. "This one"—she pointed out one box that had a border of pineapples and mangoes—"is like the 'fun Evie.' It'll remind him what he's missing out on."

"Or make him crave fruit salad," Dee Dee mused.

Evie ignored her. "And this"—she held up the other box—""this is, like, the 'romantic side of Evie.' I know guys don't go for all the pink girly stuff, but I don't want him continuing to think that I'm just his bud, like, another dude dropping him a note."

Dee Dee laughed. "I don't think *dudes* write each other, Evie."

"Dee Dee." Evie frowned. "Quit making fun! This is serious to me!"

"Okay, okay." Dee Dee put her hand on Evie's shoulder and squeezed it. "So sorry, ADA."

"So which one should I use?" Evie asked.

"I say use a sheet of paper from your spiral," Dee Dee said. "It's more you."

Evie took Dee Dee's hand off her shoulder and slumped back in her chair.

"I'm sorry, I'm sorry!" Dee Dee raised her hands in protest. "I couldn't resist. Besides, Raquel isn't around. Someone has to keep up with the yuk-yuks."

"Well, not at my expense." Evie sat up in her chair and started to open both boxes. "So, what kind of stationery did you use when you wrote to Rocio?" she asked.

"Oh, I wrote him on parchment-like paper. It was peach colored and scented."

"Scented?" Evie asked. "Like what?"

"Like peaches, *duh*." Dee Dee said, "And then I would spray some of my own perfume in the air and wave the paper through it."

"Ew!" Evie grimaced. "How do you think it smelled after a few days in the mail?

"I guess it smelled very *enticing*—" Dee Dee smiled. "—because he *always* wrote back."

Evie decided on the stationery with the fruit border. Just as she and Dee Dee were working on composing a letter that would lure Alex back to her, Evie's mother and Sabrina came into the kitchen.

"Hello, Dela," Evie's mother called out from over the counter.

"Hi, Vicki." Dee Dee looked over. "Hey, Sabrina."

"Hey, Dees." Sabrina helped herself to some *pan dulce* from a box on the counter. "Long time no see."

"Yeah." Dee Dee smiled, somewhat nervously. "So, how's Stanford?" She appeared to Evie to be "Sabrina-struck."

"I love it," Sabrina said simply. "I love that it's far away right now."

"But who's running your sorority while you're out here?" Dee Dee asked.

"Oh, we got a VP to take care of that." Sabrina crinkled her nose and waved her hand aside. "As the president, you pretty much just delegate. It's nothing like when I was a Hermana. We were all running around doing everything on our own— fund-raisers, workshops, community services. Now *that* was a lot of work, but all so worth it. I loved those times."

"Dee Dee's going to be a Hermana," Vicki Gomez said.

"Really?" Sabrina's face lit up. She started toward the dining room table. "Wow, congratulations! Wait, when did you get nominated?"

"Well, I haven't yet," Dee Dee admitted.

"And you can't be nominated if you're living in another country," Evie said. Okay, just a *little* jabby.

"What do you mean?" Sabrina took a bite of her sweet bread and looked at Dee Dee. "Are you going somewhere?"

"Well," Dee Dee started timidly, "I might have to go back to Mexico."

"*What?*" Vicki's mouth dropped. She joined them at the dining room table. "You're moving back to Mexico City? I just saw your father at the country club today, and he said nothing about this. *Nothing.*"

"No," Dee Dee said. "My whole family wouldn't be moving. It would just be me."

Evie tilted her head and looked at her sister. "Dee Dee

wants to move back to Mexico so she could be closer to Rocio, her *boyfriend.*"

"*What?*" Vicki let her mouth drop again, this time lower. "Dela, *m'ja*, you're only sixteen years old. You can't move in with your boyfriend."

"No, I wouldn't be living with him," Dee Dee explained. Evie could tell that she was getting frustrated. "I would live with Graciela's family in Coyoacán."

"You might as well be living with him." Sabrina shook her head and casually took another bite of her *pan.* "Because if you're going to another country to be with a boy, you're basically gonna be living *with* him and *for* him. You're not gonna be a Hermana?"

Dee Dee sighed. "I don't know. Everything is just so confusing right now. Rocio's gonna be going back to Mexico soon, and I gotta decide."

"I would really give it some thought, Dee Dee," Sabrina told her. "I mean, if it doesn't work out in Mexico with him— what's his name?"

"Rocio."

"Okay, if it doesn't work out with Rocio, you can always come back and you'll always have your family here, but you definitely can't be a Hermana. Not if you don't get nominated in time."

"I know . . . ," Dee Dee said reluctantly.

"I would really think about what Sabrina is saying," Vicki

said to Dee Dee. "If it's meant to be with Rocio, he'll still be there. But with Las Hermanas, they have a deadline."

"I know . . . ," Dee Dee repeated.

Evie's mother looked over the stationery on the table. "What is all this?"

"I'm writing a letter," Evie announced, "to Alex."

"A *love* letter?" Sabrina teased as she picked up one of the boxes.

"No." Evie glanced over at her mother. "Just a letter."

"Oh, I used to love writing letters to your father." Her mother picked up the other box of stationery. "But the best was getting letters back from him. That's something you kids don't have nowadays. You exchange your little texts that have no soul, no heart."

"Soul?" Sabrina laughed. "We're writing messages, not composing some RB jam!"

"So, which stationery do you think I should use to write my letter to Alex?" Evie asked Sabrina.

"I think—" Sabrina eyed both boxes as she took another bite of her *pan dulce.* "—you should just use a piece of scrap paper," she teased. "It's *so* much more you."

30

BY THE TIME EVIE ARRIVED AT DUKE'S, SHE WAS ALREADY FEELING LIKE
a princess. In her hot pink halter gown, hot pink jeweled flip-
flops, and, perched on top of her head, an elegant but under-
stated tiara, how could she not feel like one? A hot pink toe
and hand job completed her royal look.

And to top it all off, her father had rented the copper con-
vertible Camaro (V-plates: ANGELS) like the one used in a Super
Elegantes video just to drive Evie, Sabrina, and Dee Dee to the
party. When all three girls got out of the Camaro at Duke's
valet station, Evie caught a glimpse of herself in one of the
restaurant's glass doors. Forget princess, how about rock star?

And really, what do rock stars do? They rock. Which is
exactly what Evie had done the last week and a half. As soon
as she got her hours verified for the SCHR, she ran them over
to Vasquez-Reyes Alarcón and then immediately settled down

with Dee Dee to work on her essay for Harrison, which, to her surprise, she found herself wanting to write more than she thought she would. And then the three of them—Evie, her mother, and her father—had to wait, and wait, until her highly anticipated QC arrived. And then, *yes*, a glorious yes! Evie had done it, and the proof was in the mail. She was currently earning a B-minus in Civics and a B in English. The party was *on*.

Now as she, Dee Dee, and Sabrina made their way through the lobby's entrance, Evie was overwhelmed as the throngs of people—friends, family, even A through H (ew, how did *he* get in?)—crowded around her, tugging on her arm and wishing her happy birthday. People had to scream over DJ Chancla's bass-driven surf music just to be heard.

"Eves!"

"*Feliz cumpleaños!*"

"You look *hot!*"

"Happy birthday, *mi'ja!*"

Evie looked over and saw the tiny white-haired lady in a cream-colored pantsuit among a mob of Hawaiian-print shirts and short vintage muumuu-style dresses.

"Grandma?" Evie was caught off guard. She couldn't believe that Grandma Chablis would take a break from college lectures and her *qitana* lifestyle just to attend a grandchild's birthday party. "What are *you* doing here?"

Grandma Chablis frowned. "That is no way to greet your *abuelita!*" She pushed past Big Bulge and Jared Leto to give

Evie a tight hug. "I wasn't going to miss my own grand-
daughter's *quinceañera*."

"Uh, Grandma?" Did her grandmother really think she was
turning fifteen, and that was why she had made the trip down
from Davis? "This isn't my *quinceañera*. I never had one,
remember? I'm turning sixteen. This is my sixteeñera."

"*What? You're sixteen?* Then how old does that make *me*?"
She glanced over at Jared Leto. "Not too old . . . for *some*
things."

"Grandma!" Evie leaned in to hug her grandmother tighter.
Maybe she should hook her up with A through H?

Evie felt a nudge. Her grandmother had slipped a small
white envelope into her hand.

"Grandma . . ." Evie knew what was in the envelope.
Sabrina looked over at her and arched one eyebrow knowingly.

"Take it," her grandmother insisted as she patted the small
envelope in Evie's hand. "But do something *fun* with it."

But Evie didn't need a birthday check to have fun at her own
party. She could barely catch her breath for all the people
wanting her attention. She was pulled by one friend from one
side of the dance floor only to be yanked by another friend to
the other side of the restaurant. After all that had happened in
the last couple of weeks, it was just so refreshing to have an
entire evening just devoted to dancing, laughing, and of
course *eating*.

The buffet was out of control: a mad fusion of *lechón*, Huli

Huli chicken, mango BBQ pork ribs, and pineapples filled with Mexican rice.

Even Sabrina couldn't resist. She was the first guest to help herself to a plate.

"Damn," she remarked, looking over the spread. "I think I've gained, like, ten pounds just *looking* at all this."

Later, Evie danced in a circle with Dee Dee and some other friends from school. The dance floor had become so hot that Evie's curls were limp and stringy and her back and neck became drenched with sweat. Every now and then, she'd grab her grown by the back zipper and tug at the silk fabric a bit, hoping to get some circulation going, but it just wasn't cutting it. She glanced down and noticed mango BBQ sauce spattered smack center on her pricey silk gown. Oh my God, how long had that *mancha* been there? She was formally defeated. She *had* to take a break from dancing. She left the dance floor and grabbed a cocktail napkin from the bar, dipping it into one of the many glasses of water next to it. She then worked on the splotch, but it only spread out into a bigger and darker stain. Oh, well, Evie figured. Just add a dry cleaning bill to her already growing debt.

Evie surveyed her party. As the birthday girl, she had taken the first whack at the custom-made piñata, cut the two-foot-high mango-and-whipped-cream birthday cake (from her father's bakery, *claro*), and introduced the line of sexy Polynesian dancers, and she still had to unwrap the pyramid

of gifts piled up on one of the large banquet tables. She damp-
ened another napkin and wiped her neck as she headed outside to the balcony. Some fresh air was in order.

"Where are you going, Evelina?" Lindsay asked. She was
sitting with her husband, Alfredo, at one of the small booths.

"I need some air."

"Are you okay?" Lindsay looked alarmed.

"Oh, yeah, Linds," Evie assured her. "Don't worry. Oh, also,
don't worry about the car bill. My grandma gave me the
money for—"

Alfredo turned away from looking at the dance floor and
looked up at Evie.

"Okay, Evelina," Lindsay interrupted as she directed a sharp
glance toward her husband. It was clear that she didn't want
him to know what had happened a month and a half earlier.
Perhaps she never told him that she had paid for bodywork at
Williams. "*Pues*, enjoy the sea breeze!"

"Okay." Evie smiled knowingly and headed out toward the
balcony.

Once on the balcony and even with the waves roaring
below, Evie picked up on the sound of soft laughter. She
looked over and realized that she wasn't alone. Tori was at the
other end of the balcony with a boy. Evie recognized him as
one of the skater boys from O-Hi Frostie who had paid in
advance just to attend her party.

"Hey, Eves," Tori said. "Epic party. I mean, it's like, *the best.*"

"Oh, thanks!" Evie smiled. "Hey, sorry about the booze thing," she started to tell both of them awkwardly. "It sorta all just fell through."

Once he learned Raquel wasn't coming to the party, Bartender Petey wasn't so eager to please a bunch of kids he didn't know. He still had the stash of liquor that Raquel secured weeks earlier, and Evie was almost tempted to approach him about it, but after everything that had happened with Raquel, she figured everyone at her party could go *one* night without fired-up ad bevs.

"No problemo." The boy lifted his Lava Flow, one of the many specialty nonalkie drinks from Duke's. "We partied before we came here."

"It's actually *no hay problema,*" Evie corrected him.

"Huh?"

"Nothing." Evie smiled. She felt relieved. "But I can totally give you and your friends your money back."

"Nah, don't even worry," the boy said. "Think of it as our birthday gift to you."

Tori put her arm around the boy's waist. "Well, we're gonna head back in."

"Oh yeah?" Evie forced a smile. "Well, I'm glad you're having fun. I just came out for some air."

After they left, Evie turned away and faced the ocean. Suddenly her chest felt heavy, and despite all the food she had eaten earlier, her stomach felt oddly empty. Alex wasn't with her at her own party, and it was hitting her hard. When she had decided to have her sixteeñera at Duke's, she had fantasies of sharing a romantic moment out on the balcony, just like Tori and her skater boy. Now, Alex was nowhere near the balcony, and she was obviously nowhere near his thoughts. He'd never responded to her letter. He hadn't even acknowledged its existence even after she had poured her entire heart onto paper. Stationery paper lined with mangoes and pineapples?

She looked back at her guests through the picture windows of Duke's. She had so many cool friends, yet not one of them really knew how she was feeling. Evie turned back to look out over the balcony's ledge. She folded her hands, rested her head on them, and took a deep breath. It was great, *awesome,* to have the sixteeñera of her dreams, but the fun she was having just made her more aware of the party's two big gaping holes. Alex was not with her, and neither was Raquel.

All of a sudden, Evie heard a long, low whistle. She *knew* that whistle. *Ugh, Mondo.* She was not in the mood for him at the moment. She pretended not to hear him and didn't turn around.

Go away, Mondo. . . .

He whistled again.

Evie pushed up from the ledge. She got ready to throw him a smirk and a smart remark, but when she turned around, she couldn't believe who was standing in front of her.

It was *Alex*.

Evie's stomach flipped, and then it flopped. And then it flopped again.

"Hey, Evie." Alex smiled, hesitantly. "I'm sorry. I'm sorry that I haven't returned your calls and texts and everything." He looked around the balcony.

"No, no," Evie started. "*I'm* sorry!" She wanted to reach out and embrace him but wasn't sure if she should. He just stood there and she just stood there, as if they both really didn't know what to do.

"Please, Alex," she begged. "You have to know that it was nothing with Arturo. I know that sounds cliché, but really, I was just stupid, and maybe I was a little mad about that night with Mondo and the night—"

Alex held up his hand. "No, no. I haven't been the best boyfriend. Really. And *I'm* sorry."

"No, *I'm* sorry," Evie practically cried.

"Okay." Alex laughed. "We're *both* sorry."

Alex reached for Evie and put his arms around her shoulders. He held her tight, and Evie was overwhelmed with how good he felt. His hair was slightly damp, and she smelled the tiniest hint of cologne (fresh and sea breezy!). He was wearing an oversizedd sports jacket and dark slacks that had that painfully stiff brand-new look to them. Evie glanced down and saw he was wearing flip-flops, brand-new O'Neills. *Cute.*

"Oh, Evie," he whispered into her ear. "I got your letter. I have never gotten anything like that before. I mean, all the things you said, what you wrote. I couldn't believe it, and I didn't know how to respond. I mean, I didn't wanna just call or send a stupid text. I wanted to see you in person. I guess I wanted it to be perfect, and I wanted"—he paused—"to give you this."

He reached into his jacket pocket and pulled out a small white box. His neck instantly turned pink. Evie knew that shade of nervous pink. "I think this would *really* go with your outfit." He looked her over. "Wow, Evie. You look *so* beautiful. Really."

Evie now felt as though *her* neck was turning nervous pink. Alex had never called her beautiful. He had called her cute, and one time, in a text, he had called her sexy, but never beautiful. She loved hearing him say it. She took the box from him, and when she opened it, she couldn't believe what she found. Set on a blue velvet backing was a single gold charm: two miniature flip-flops, one slightly over the other, and each topped with a small pearl where the straps connected. The charm was attached to a thin gold chain.

"Oh my God, Alex!" Evie's mouth dropped open. "This is *so* cool. I can't believe it. I've *never* seen anything like this."

"I was hoping you'd say that." He scratched the side of his face nervously. "I drove down to L.A. after I got your letter, and I was looking through all the shops on Roberston, trying to find the right thing. I know you've been into horses lately, and I wasn't sure if I should have gotten you a horseshoe or something."

"No, I *love* it. And I'm glad you didn't get me a horseshoe or something. I mean, I love horses, but flojos are, like, *our* thing."

"Yeah," Alex said as he removed the necklace from the box. "I found it at this place called Dakine. It was totally a cool shop. Even Mondo thought so."

Evie smiled. "*Mondo* went with you? To shop for *me?*"

"Yeah, but he's never gonna be with us," Alex explained quickly. "Like when we are together on a date or something."

She looked at the charm. "Will you put it on me?"

"Totally." Alex moved behind Evie and fastened the chain around her neck.

"Evie?"

Dee Dee had pulled the sliding glass door open. "I'm not interrupting anything, am I?" She looked at Alex and seemed unsure of how she should react.

"No, not anymore." Evie looked away from Alex. "Look!" She held out the necklace for Dee Dee to see. "Look what Alex gave me!"

"Oh my God." Dee Dee looked at the charm. "That is the cutest! It goes perfectly with your gown."

"I have to admit," Alex said, "Mondo was trying to talk me into getting you a flip-flop navel charm."

"Friggin' Mondo." Evie laughed. "But that *is* a charm Raquel would wear."

Raquel!

"Dee Dee, what time is it?" Evie suddenly felt panicky.

"That's why I came out," Dee Dee said. "We should get going if we're gonna make it back in time for you to open presents."

"What, you're bailing on your own party?" Alex asked.

"We gotta go to Isla del Mar," Evie told him. "Raquel's there."

"What?" Alex's face dropped. "Are you serious? Since when?"

"Since last week," Evie answered somberly. "We *have* to see her tonight. I need her to see that I'm wearing the gown she got me. She needs to know that I believed her when she told me she bought this with her own money."

"Raquel *bought* you this?" Alex looked Evie's gown over. "Man, makes my gift look like no expense."

"Yours and mine." Dee Dee nodded in agreement.

Evie shook her head. "Look, we just gotta go see Raquel."

"Uh, can I go with you?" Alex asked.

Evie looked at Dee Dee. She didn't know how to answer him.

"I don't know," Evie said. "It's sorta just a girl thing."

"Come on, Evie," Alex asked. "Raquel's my friend too. Can't you make it, like, a Flojo thing?"

"Hey, but then *I* wouldn't get to go," Dee Dee said.

"Okay, okay," Evie laughed. "Let's all just go, but let's go *now*." She took Alex's hand and headed back into the restaurant.

"Yeah, we better hurry." Dee Dee checked the time on her cell phone as they pushed through the crowd. "We have just about an hour."

Alex shook his head. "We are *so* not gonna make it."

"Yes, we will!" Evie yelled over the music. "We gotta at least try."

❋ ❋ ❋

Evie, Dee Dee, and Alex sped north in Jumile on Pacific Coast Highway toward Isla del Mar.

"God, I hope we make it," Dee Dee said.

"We will, we will," Evie said.

"So," Dee Dee asked cautiously, "do you think that Cherry Bomb will be waiting for you when you get back to Duke's?"

"I have no idea," Evie said. "I haven't even been able to think. I mean, I just can't believe I still got my party."

"Why?" Dee Dee asked. "You worked your *nalgas* off. You did your work and you wrote, well, most of your essay, and by the deadline. That was the deal, right?"

"I dunno," Evie said. "Just everything has been crazy, and it was such a last-minute sprint to get this party. My parents were so stressed."

"Well, you could have turned in your work a bit earlier," Dee Dee said.

"I know, I know. But you know how plans can get rearranged at the last minute."

"Oh, yeah." Dee Dee raised her eyebrows in agreement. "I mean, I can't believe I didn't go back to D.F. with Rocio."

"You were gonna move back to Mexico?" Alex asked from the backseat.

"No." Dee Dee looked at Evie. "Not really. It was just a thought that I . . . thought through."

"And *I*"—Evie smiled—"like it when you think things through."

"So, Eves," Alex started, "did you get anything from Grandma Chablis?"

"What, am I gonna be, like, your sugar mama now?" Evie opened her macramé bag and ripped open the envelope. There was no check, but rather sixteen one-hundred-dollar bills.

"Wow, *pretty* nice!" She held up a fan of bills. "Sixteen hundred buckaroos."

"That's a lot of *lana*," Alex said. "What are you gonna do with it? Down payment for private driving lessons?"

"Lifetime bus pass?" Dee Dee teased.

"Ha, ha, very funny," Evie said. "Well, first I gotta pay Lindsay back, like right away, and then . . ." She paused. "I think I'm gonna donate the rest of the money to the reserve."

"*What?*" Alex exclaimed. "You gotta be kidding! The reserve? I thought you hated that place."

"No, not really," Evie answered slowly. "I mean, I hate that there *have* to be places like horse rescues and stuff because there are people who don't care about animals, but there is this one horse that I know, and four hundred dollars could really help him out."

"You are gonna give four hundred dollars to a *horse?*" Dee Dee asked. "But I overheard your grandma telling you to do something fun with it."

"I know." Evie looked at Dee Dee. "But it's not like Grandma Chablis is the only one giving me money. I saw a few envelopes on the gift table. I'll survive."

"Well, dang, that's a pretty generous gift," Dee Dee said.

"Yeah, I don't know . . . ," Alex started.

"You don't know what?" Evie asked.

"I'm not into the idea of you working at the reserve again with ol' what's his name."

"Who? You mean Chamuco?" Evie asked playfully.

"Huh?" Alex asked.

"If you're talking about Arturo"—Evie turned to look at him—"he most likely won't even be at the reserve by the time I start up again. He'll be starting UC Davis this spring. But Alex, you have nothing to worry about."

"Hmmm . . ."

"Alex . . ." Evie looked into his dark eyes. "Nothing."

"Oh, I can't believe I forgot to tell you!" Dee Dee suddenly exclaimed.

"What?" Evie asked.

"Alejandra de Los Santos tried to get into the party!"

"What?" Dee Dee was right. Evie could not believe it. "When? Where was I? Did someone get it on camera phone?"

"I don't know where you were," Dee Dee said. "Maybe dancing or eating more Huli Huli chicken or something. But she showed up with her three little *ah*-migas and of course she was denied access. Denied! In front of everyone, and she was so embarrassed!"

"Ha!" Evie laughed. "Okay, okay, birthday or no birthday, now *that's* the best gift ever!"

Dee Dee turned down RBD on her CD player. "I was just thinking. I have no idea what to expect at Isla. I hope I don't freak out."

"It's really not as bad as everyone makes it out to be," Alex said. "I know this guy through Gorby, and he actually went there. He said the staff was really cool and he got a lot of help. A lot."

"Well, that's a relief to hear," Evie said. She looked out the window at all the BEACH ACCESS signs lining Pacific Coast Highway.

"Alex," she asked, "do you think we can go surfing out here sometime? For, like, a change?"

"I dunno, Eves." He looked out toward the ocean. "It gets pretty territorial the farther south you get and—" He stopped himself. "No, you know what? If you wanna try another beach, why not?"

"Exactly," Evie said. "Why not?"

Evie read another sign on the highway. "Oh, hey, this is Leo Carrillo," she said as Dee Dee drove by the state beach. "Do you know I used to come here as a kid? My family used to go camping here."

"Oh, yeah." Dee Dee chuckled. "I remember that, but didn't you always come home to sleep?"

"Yeah." Evie laughed with her. "Hey, can you slow down just a bit, on the shoulder?"

"Evie, we don't have time for a little memory lane trip."

"Yeah, we're gonna be late," Alex agreed.

"It'll just take a second." Evie assured them.

Dee Dee slowed down, and Evie looked near Leo's main entrance kiosk. There were two wooden posts on opposite sides of the dirt road. Each post was about four feet high and had a row of yellow circular reflective lights attached to one side. One post had a gash on the side, and its bottom two lights were cracked.

The cracked lights and the gash had been courtesy of Sabrina years ago, when she and Evie were still kids. Evie remembered sneaking out with her when Sabrina was fifteen and she was eleven. Sabrina desperately wanted to take their parents' car for a little spin around the campground and had convinced Evie to go with her. They hadn't driven more than a few campsites away from their own before Sabrina hit the post. She was horrified. She had placed her head on the steering wheel and cried. It took Evie's urging to finally get her to wipe her tears, get the car in gear, and get it back to their own campsite before their parents found out. But they did find out. Their father was angry at Sabrina but then calmed down as she continued to cry. Evie remembered how her father had put his arm around Sabrina and told her that taking his car without permission was wrong, but that she had to get over the fact that she had made a mistake. It wasn't the end of the world.

"You have to forget about what's in the rearview window and just keep forging ahead," Evie remembered her father saying. *"Just focus on what's in front of you, what's ahead."*

"You know," Evie said, remembering her father's words, "I think I know what to say to Raquel when I see her."

"You think?" Dee Dee asked as she got back on PCH.

"Yeah." Evie nodded. "I think so." She looked at the time on her cell. "Oh, man, we're totally gonna be late getting back to my party, and I still gotta open presents. My mom is gonna be totally stressed."

"Not as stressed as she was trying to get those V-plates in time," Dee Dee remarked.

"Huh?" Evie's stomach flipped. "*What* V-plates?"

"Oh my God!" Dee Dee covered her mouth.

"Dee Dee!" Evie grabbed her arm. "*Tell* me."

"Dee Dee . . ." Alex shook his head.

"Evie, stop it." Dee Dee pulled her arm from Evie. "I'm driving. You're gonna bruise my arm!"

"*Tell* me, Dee Dee." Evie was not going to let up.

"I'm sorry, Evie!" Dee Dee exclaimed. "It was supposed to be a surprise. But your mother didn't even know if you were going to have your work done or not, and now, oh, she's going to kill me!"

"Are you serious?" Evie shrieked. "I'm getting my car? I'm getting Cherry Bomb!"

"I'm not saying anything else." Dee Dee ran her thumb and index finger across her closed mouth like she was zipping it closed.

"You don't have to." Evie's stomach continued to tingle with excitement. "If I'm supposed to be surprised, I will be. I won't flake on the fake."

"Well, you better start practicing now," Alex said.

Evie pulled down Jumile's sun visor and looked at herself in the small mirror. She raised her eyebrows, widened her eyes, and stretched her mouth as wide as she could. The expression on her face was a cross between sheer astonishment and pure shock.

Evie then looked deeper into her brown eyes. As of that morning, February 29, she was officially sixteen years old. But she didn't *feel* any older and, even considering what she had gone through in the last month and a half, she certainly didn't *look* any different. In just the last seven weeks, she'd had to confront the return of Sabrina, the tension between her and Arturo, the hearbreak over Alex, the anxiety with Dee Dee, the reunion with Alex and now the loss (temporarily) of Raquel. Maybe Lindsay should just forget *La Cueva Sucia* and set the TiVo on *her*! But those experiences—heartbreak, loss, and change—were what her mother had said everyone goes through in life, what made the difference between a girl and a woman.

Evie straightened her tiara. She really couldn't decide if she was still a girl, or now a woman, or if she felt more like a rock star or a princess. But she did know that she was a good friend, an ADA to the max, and when she really worked at it, she could be a good student and a good daughter.

But for today, her sixteenth birthday, she wasn't going to worry about definitions. If anything, she was going to do her best to carry herself like a queen.

Queen Evie. No problemo.